A DAUGHTER'S WAR

WAR

Emma Hornby

PENGUIN BOOKS

TRANSWORLD PUBLISHERS
Penguin Random House, One Embassy Gardens,
8 Viaduct Gardens, London SW11 7BW
www.penguin.co.uk

Transworld is part of the Penguin Random House group of companies
whose addresses can be found at global.penguinrandomhouse.com

First published in Great Britain in 2022 by Bantam Press
an imprint of Transworld Publishers
Penguin paperback edition published 2022

A CIP catalogue record for this book
is available from the British Library.

ISBN
9780552178112

Typeset in 12/14.5pt ITC New Baskerville Std by Jouve (UK), Milton Keynes.
Printed and bound in Great Britain by Clays Ltd, Elcograf S.p.A.

The authorized representative in the EEA is Penguin Random House Ireland,
Morrison Chambers, 32 Nassau Street, Dublin D02 YH68.

Penguin Random House is committed to a sustainable
future for our business, our readers and our planet. This book
is made from Forest Stewardship Council® certified paper.

For the real victims of the
Punch Street/Ardwick Street air raid,
12–13 October 1941.
God bless you all.

And my ABC, always x

He that loves not his wife and children feeds a lioness at home, and broods a nest of sorrows.

– *Bishop Jeremy Taylor*

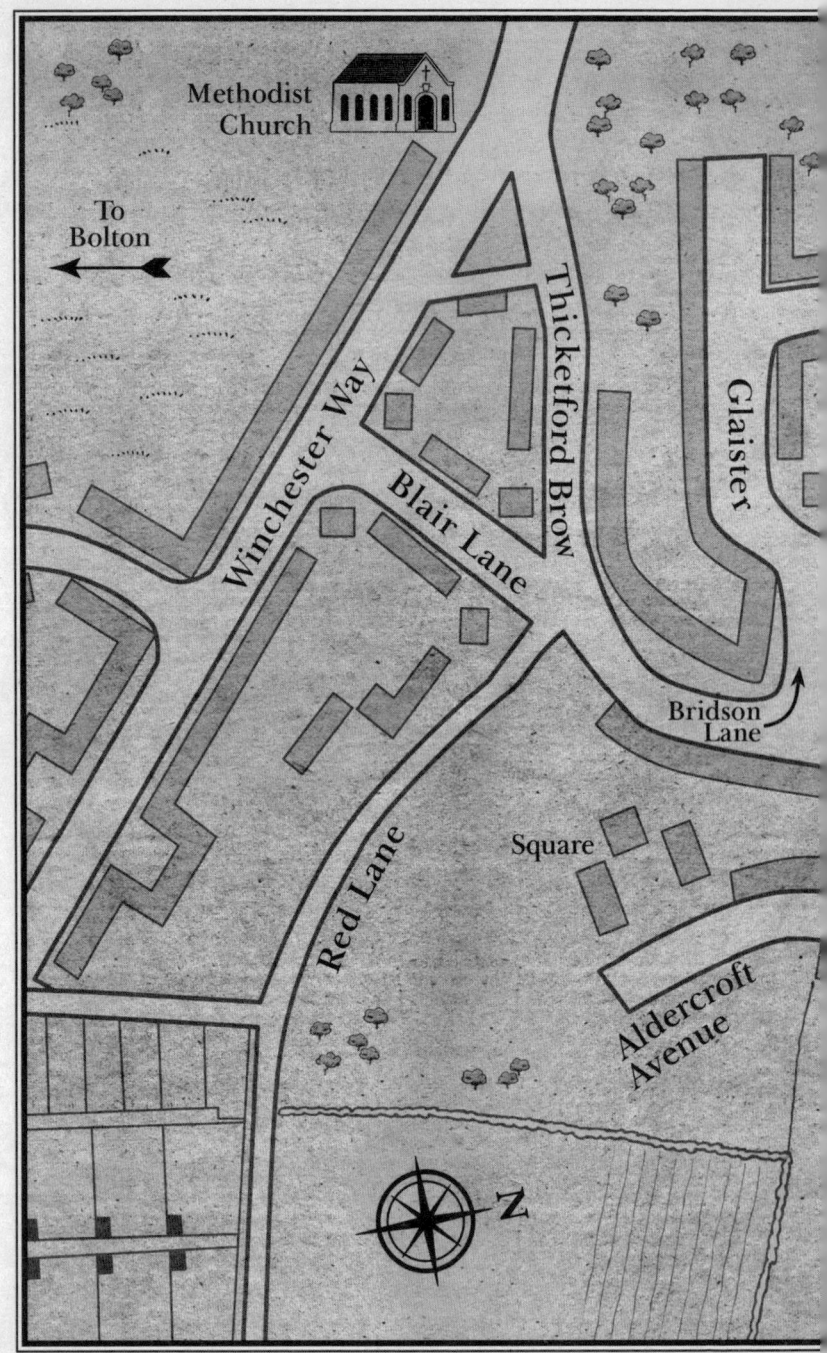

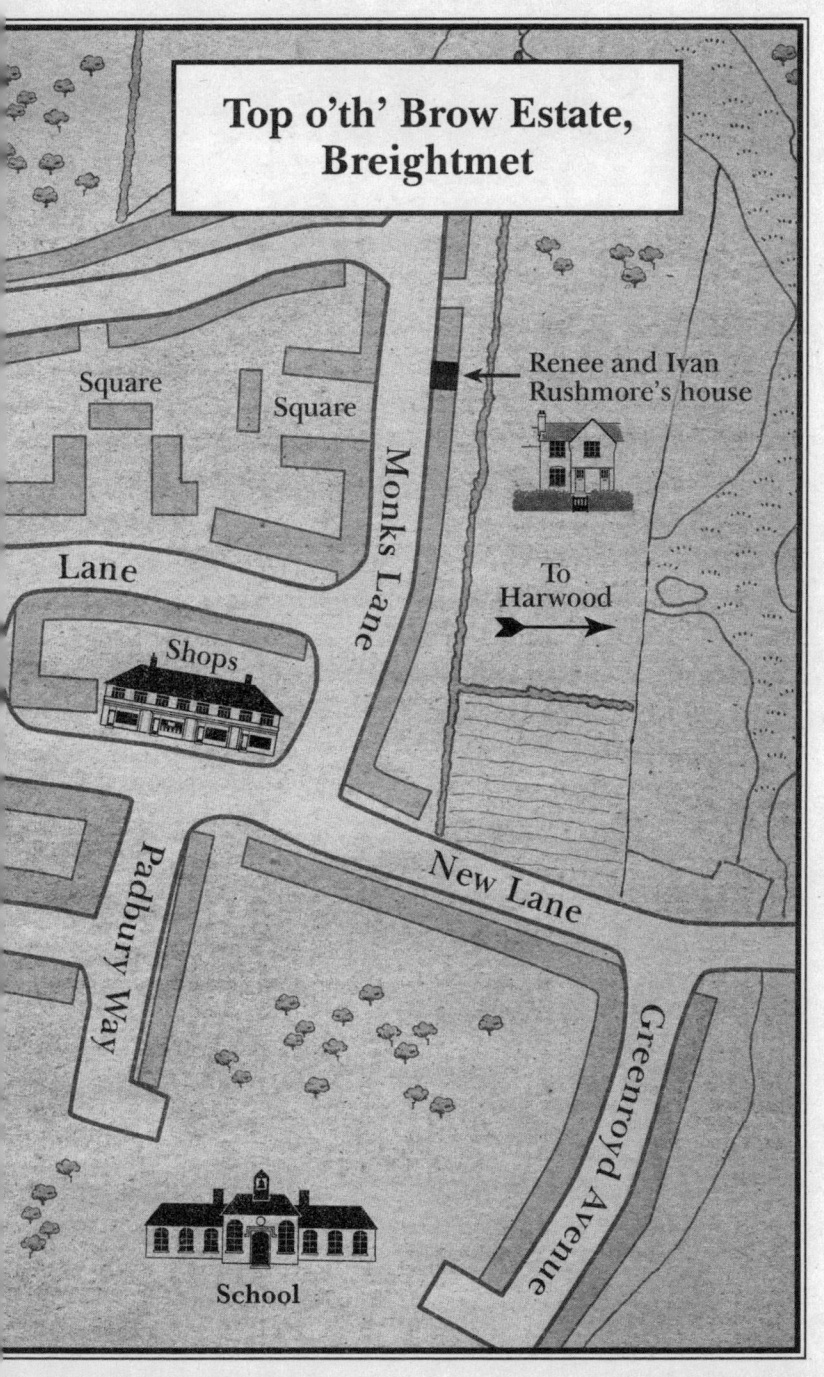

Top o'th' Brow Estate, Breightmet

Square

Square

Renee and Ivan Rushmore's house

Monks Lane

Lane

Shops

To Harwood

New Lane

Padbury Way

Greenroyd Avenue

School

Chapter 1

Bolton, Lancashire
1939

RENEE RUSHMORE HAD laid and lit the fire and was wiping down with a damp cloth the soot-smudged beige tiles of the fireplace when the heavy footfalls sounded on the stairs. Immediately, her stomach tightened in a ball of dread.

As though looking in on herself, she pictured her position: on her knees with her bottom in the air swaying from side to side as she worked, and a warning bell clanged shrilly inside her brain. Best not to give him any encouragement – certainly unintentional as it might be – if she could avoid it.

By the time the door was pushed open roughly, sending it banging against the wall, and Ivan entered the living room, his daughter had scrambled to her feet. The cloth she'd abandoned on the hearth, and her hands were folded together tightly in front of her lest he spied their trembling, which his presence never failed to produce.

1

Eyes downcast, she inclined her chin towards the kitchen and murmured, 'I'll see to your breakfast, Dad.'

'Wait.'

The single-word demand had the power to strip the colour from Renee's cheeks. Her every nerve jangled, and her heart knocked painfully several times against her breastbone. *Lord, no.*

'The tea ... it's mashed already. And your eggs, they're boiling as we speak – it'll not take me a minute,' she tried in a desperate attempt at escape. But as ever, it was useless; Ivan cut her off with a growl.

'Come here.'

'Please, Dad—'

'Here, damn it!' He clicked his fingers, then jutted his index towards the ground, as though calling to heel a dog. 'Don't make me come over there and collect you.'

She bit back a hopeless whimper. Then, with slumped shoulders, she edged across the worn oilcloth towards him.

The moment she was in reach, his hands were behind her to clamp on her buttocks. Ivan wrenched her body against his, and as always Renee sent her mind elsewhere. It was a place she'd been visiting now for over three years, ever since the night of her fourteenth birthday when this hell on earth first began.

Here, in the world she'd created for herself, pain and fear didn't exist. The dread and degradation that were part and parcel of her life were a million miles away and she was just like any other young

2

woman. Nothing, no one, could touch her once she lost herself in the safety of her imagination.

His depravity spent, Ivan released a last guttural grunt then lumbered to his feet. He peered for a moment at the girl he had forced down on to the sofa, and who still lay flat on her back unmoving, her gaze fastened on a spot on the ceiling. Then he nodded once.

'Reet, lass.' His tone was conversational now, friendly almost. 'Shift yourself, come on, else the breakfast will be spoiled. I'll not see good grub go to ruin.'

Mutely, Renee rose. Her expression and movements void of emotion, she straightened her skirt and headed out to the kitchen.

The silent tears came as she was spooning out the eggs from the saucepan. Her vision blurring brought fresh panic; she blinked rapidly. Dropping the breakfast and having to face his wrath on top of everything else was the last thing she needed. *Not much longer and he'll be gone*, she reminded herself as she placed the boiled eggs carefully in their blue cups and collected two spoons from the drawer. *Twenty minutes at best, then he'll be off to his work and you'll have the house and the whole of the day to yourself. Not much longer . . .*

'Done to a treat, that is,' Ivan remarked with satisfaction when he tapped, then lifted the top from his egg and was rewarded with the sight of a runny, golden yolk.

There was a marked difference in his appearance. Having got himself ready whilst his daughter was busy at her chore, he cut a very different figure. Gone were the off-white long johns and string vest. Now, he wore his dark train driver's uniform, shiny black shoes and snowy shirt with its stiff, starched collar. His greying hair, tousled and falling limply across his forehead earlier, had been brushed neatly back from his face, whilst atop it sat his smart peaked cap. Below, the stubble had disappeared; his trim salt-and-pepper moustache boasted not a hair out of place and his face was ruddy from the scrubbing it had received.

He seemed the epitome of respectability. Only Renee knew better. She, more than anyone, knew just how deceiving looks could be.

'Shall I be Mother?'

I wish you were my mam. I wish it were you what did a flit and not her. I'd do anything to have that be so, to have you gone from here for good and to have her back. I hate you, I hate you . . .

'Well? Are you even listening?'

Dragged unceremoniously back to the present by Ivan's barked questioning, Renee shook her head with a mumbled apology. 'Sorry, I were just . . .' Her words petered out and she directed her gaze to the chenille tablecloth as, with a black frown, her father reached for the pot and poured tea into two brown mugs. 'Ta,' she whispered, reaching for her brew when he'd resumed his meal, her own appetite flown and her food forgotten.

The minutes stole along agonisingly slowly. Finally, Ivan pushed back his chair and rose from the table – Renee had to fight the urge to sigh in blessed relief.

'Right, that's me. I'm away to the station.'

This was his self-same farewell every day, and in turn she repeated her usual response: 'Aye, Dad.'

'I'll see you this evening.'

'Aye.'

'Ta-ra.'

'Ta-ra.'

He nodded, turned on his heel and was gone. Not until the front door rattled shut at his back did Renee allow herself to breathe.

The very first thing she did was to make a dash for the stairs. These she took two at a time and headed straight for the bathroom. She made a grab for the striped flannel folded neatly by the sink and doused it with water. Then she rubbed the block of carbolic soap over the surface vigorously and carried the washcloth between her legs.

As she tried in vain to scour away her attacker's touch and smell, she asked herself for the millionth time why he did what he did. Surely, *surely*, he must know it was wrong, what it was doing to her? How much she loathed him for his actions – and herself for not possessing the courage to have attempted to put a stop to it by now. And yet, despite it all, he was her father and a part of her still loved him. She couldn't fathom that; however, the feeling was there, buried deep down inside her, all the same. If only he would stop. Just why did he choose to do it – and for how much longer would she stand it?

Renee made her way slowly back downstairs. She stood for a time in the centre of the living room and let the quietness calm her. A glance towards the table against the far wall reminded her that the breakfast things needed clearing away, but she made no move to see to it. Instead, she crossed to the teapot and refilled her cup. After adding two spoonfuls of sugar and a dash of milk, she headed for the kitchen and the back door.

The moment she stepped into the modest-sized rear garden, and her gaze came to rest on the pigeon loft by the wooden fence to her left, a smile crept over her face. Her friends always had the power to make her feel better, had never failed her yet.

'Morning, sweethearts.'

Her father had been a pigeon fancier and had kept them for as long as Renee could remember. Presently, there were eight in total, including two adorable squabs, and she loved them all. However, she did have to admit to having a favourite.

Ruby was different to the rest, and in Renee's opinion a beautiful specimen. Ivan had bought her from a man in a pub in town some eighteen months ago; Renee had been struck by her from the start. She was a speckled pigeon – or to give the correct term, according to Ivan, a Columba guinea. Indeed, she did possess similar colouring to a guineafowl. And with her red legs and deep patches of the same colour around each eye, naming her what she did had seemed the obvious choice for Renee.

However, it wasn't only Ruby's unusual appearance that she was drawn to. The bird was smaller than the rest and prone to being pushed around by her strutting, more dominant housemates. And to some degree, this reminded Renee of herself. Weak, vulnerable . . . She understood those qualities well enough, all right.

After wiggling a finger through the meshed roof to stroke Ruby's blue-grey head, Renee lifted the latch on the loft door. Gently, she cupped her hands around the bird and lifted her out.

Murmuring softly, she carried Ruby towards the doorstep and sat down. She held the bird against her chest with one hand, and with the other lifted her cup of tea from the space beside her, where she had placed it before approaching the loft. As she sipped the drink, she brushed the silky, white-streaked brown neck and rufous-hued back and wings, dotted with their white spots, with her thumb. For her part, Ruby sat and surveyed at ease with her small dark eyes the first September sunrays stroking the garden, as though she enjoyed this daily inter-action as much as her human companion did.

'Sometimes, I reckon you're the only one in the world who understands me, and I don't know what I'd do without you,' Renee told her. 'I'm tired of it all, I am. I don't know what to do any more.'

The bird seemed to consider the statement for a few moments, then opened its slim bill and gave a call – *doo, doo, doo* – in response.

Despite her misery, Renee couldn't help but chuckle. 'Eeh, if only I knew what you were saying. I bet you'd have some good advice for me, wouldn't you, girl? That's what I'm in need of more than owt, you know, Ruby: someone to talk with. But well, there ain't no one, is there? No – only you.'

After a quarter of an hour of pleasing silence and blissful calm, Renee's thoughts began drifting to the household duties that awaited her. Reluctantly, she drained the remainder of her brew and got to her feet. She dropped a butterfly kiss on to Ruby's head and with promises that she'd pop out and see her again later, returned her to the loft. Then, with her empty cup swinging in her hand, she headed indoors.

The breakfast things were cleared from the table and the cloth shaken out in the back garden within minutes. Next, she made back for the kitchen to tackle the dirty dishes piled on the wooden draining board. Finally, once satisfied that everywhere was neat and clean, she reached beneath the sink for the duster and polish and retraced her steps to the living room.

Mundane as her daily life was, Renee didn't mind unduly – it was all she'd known now for years. Since the night of her mother's disappearance, the running of the house – woman's work, as Ivan referred to it – had naturally fallen to her. Besides, what else would she have found with which to fill her hours? With no pals, and no family to speak of bar an aged great aunt living in Deane a few miles away, there was no one to help her while away the time. Nor had she ever known employment in the usual sense.

Her father preferred to have her here, where he could keep an eye to her. Unlike most young people, she'd never had a regular paying position since leaving school, and so there was no escaping the monotony through work, either. For her, the universe started and ended at home.

So far as she could predict, nothing would change that – at least not in the foreseeable future, at any rate. It was how it was, and there was no point dwelling on changes when they wouldn't come true. She had more chance of sprouting wings and flying to the moon than she had of escaping Monks Lane and this prison Ivan had created for his only child.

'Now to get a move on and nip to the shops,' she announced to the empty room when she'd polished the mahogany sideboard and table to a high sheen, given the upstairs rooms the once-over and made the beds. Best that she began preparing the evening meal in plenty of time of her father's return from Trinity Street Station and his job. 'Mind, I'd best change my cardigan first,' she added as she removed her pinny. 'That's right, and run the comb through my hair.'

Renee often talked to herself – there was nobody else to chat with throughout the long days alone, after all – and as she slipped her arms into her orange woollen cardigan, then collected the comb from the sideboard drawer, she kept up the one-sided conversation.

'I'll do liver and onions, I reckon,' she told her reflection as she brushed out her chin-length, chestnut-coloured hair. 'That's if the butcher's got any in – fingers crossed he ain't sold out because I just fancy it, aye, and liver always goes down well with Dad. We've got two onions in, so it's just the meat I need to get. Oh, and sugar – I'll do a nice rice pudding for afters. I'll keep some of the rice back, mind, for the pigeons – partial to a bit of that, they are.'

She felt within her chest a flutter of excitement as she lifted down the string shopping bag from the hook behind the kitchen door. This was her solitary opportunity each day of seeing the real world beyond these four walls. Not that the outing lasted anywhere near as long as she would have liked. Nonetheless, it was better than nothing, and Renee always looked forward to it.

Patting her pockets to check she had her purse and house key, she nodded. Then, with a quiet smile touching her lips, she exited the house and turned left in the direction of the small row of nearby shops.

Her home of Top o'th' Brow was a recently built estate in Breightmet and situated some two miles from the centre of Bolton. Away from the town's mills and factories and their smoke-spewing chimneys, surrounded by nearby woods and sprawling fields, it made for a pleasant place to live. The community of around a dozen streets was a close-knit one; everyone seemed to know everyone else. Everyone, that was, apart from Renee and her father.

They didn't count themselves part of this tight band of residents, thanks to Ivan's dogged insistence that they kept themselves to themselves. The Rushmores would have struggled to name even a handful of people from hereabouts. Even the folk living in their own street were virtual strangers to them; so much as a cursory 'hello' was unheard of.

Now, as Renee continued on towards New Lane, she saw neighbours passing the time of day over garden fences or nattering to each other in the streets, and she envied them. Yet the idea of attempting to strike up conversation with someone – and the consequences of such an action should her father find out – quashed the desire right away. Not that she'd have expected the people around here to want to chat with her even if she'd tried.

Their friendly nods and smiles had been ignored by Ivan and his daughter, now, for far too long – another of Ivan's orders, which Renee had had no choice but to follow. In the end, the neighbours had given up; there was only so much snubbing that a body could take, after all. Renee had no illusions that her family was thought of as queer at best. No – she'd be given the brush-off right away were she to try to speak to anyone, and nor would she have blamed them one bit.

The grocer's was half-full when she entered; head down, she stood silently to await her turn to be served. She felt one or two people crane their necks in her direction at her entrance, then discovering her identity they returned to their talk without a second glance. Keeping her eyes fixed firmly on the ground, Renee swallowed down her awkwardness and pretended not to have noticed.

'There we are,' said Seymour Briggs, the somewhat dour-looking owner, after fulfilling Renee's request. 'Anything else?'

Handing her money over, then placing the packet

11

of sugar in her bag, she cursed the shy blush creeping across her face. She shook her head without meeting his eye. 'No. That's all, ta.'

'Ta-ra, then.'

'Ta-ra,' she mumbled before scurrying for the door and into the street.

Here, she closed her eyes for a brief time and sighed inwardly. How did folk talk to one another naturally, laugh and gossip and exchange pleasantries, and all without a moment's thought? The concept was so alien to her she was at a loss to understand it. She was constantly fearful of saying the wrong thing, of looking foolish and having people believe she was even more of an oddity than they must do already, that she couldn't seem to get her brain and mouth to work in tandem without giving it considerable concentration.

I'm just so stupid and ugly and useless, fit for nothing . . .

'Stop it,' she whispered to herself, cutting short the destructive thoughts. 'That's Dad's words you're spouting there, not yours. Don't you go chucking them sort of insults at yourself – you've enough of it from him. You're not to heed his lies, remember? You're none of them things, Renee Rushmore, and don't you forget it.'

And yet the self-affirming speech failed to stem her moroseness; it always did. It was so very easy to believe such things – and equally as difficult to dismiss them – when you heard them every day of your life. With a weary shrug of her shoulders, she picked up her feet once more and headed next door to the butcher's.

'Half a pound of liver, please.'

With his round, red cheeks and wide mouth never short of a grin, Gordon Wallace was the polar opposite of the grocer and capable of dragging a smile from even the most miserable of customers, not to mention the highly bashful – Renee found it impossible to remain immune to his wiles. Her lips twitched at the corners at his broad wink of welcome and he responded with a hearty chuckle.

'That's the way, lass, that's the way! To hide that bonny smile of yourn would be nowt short of a travesty,' he boomed. 'Now then. Half a pound, you say?'

'That's right.'

Gordon took the metal tray from the window and carried it to the counter. He plucked out several slices of meat and slapped them on to the scales. 'Just right,' he announced before expertly wrapping the meat in brown paper and pushing it across to her. He wiped his hands down his navy and white striped apron, then eased back his straw hat to peer down at her. 'Will that do thee, lass? I've some tasty beef sausages in what might tickle your fancy. Melt in your mouth, they do.' He nodded to confirm his statement. 'Go nice with a bit of liver, they will.'

'Maybe tomorrow,' she stuttered, embarrassed by the fact she hadn't enough money on her for anything extra, yet not wanting to hurt his feelings. 'Just this for now, ta.'

'Right you are, lass, right you are. Ta-ra for now, then.'

'Ta-ra, Mr Wallace, and thanks.'

Despite her feelings of inadequacy with others, she knew a tug of regret at the sight of number forty-six as she turned back into Monks Lane. Back to the routine and loneliness once more; heaviness came to her chest at the prospect. Then her feathered friends came to mind and her sadness lifted slightly. Perhaps she could snatch a few minutes with Ruby and the others before preparing the meal . . .? Having made up her mind, she nodded. Yes, that's what she'd do.

Renee was abreast with her garden gate when pain shot through her big toe and the world seemed to tilt on its axis. She watched in a dreamlike state the grey concrete lurch up to meet her. In the next moment, she was sprawled across the pavement and something warm and wet was dripping down her face.

Dazed, she struggled to her knees and blinked down. Crimson droplets dotted the ground in front of her and lifting her fingers to her face, she realised that her nose was busted and was bleeding heavily. She positioned her hands either side of her and was about to push herself to her feet when a voice called out.

'Eeh, are you all right?'

Scrambling up, Renee turned to see a figure heading across the road towards her. She recognised her as Mrs Flynn, a woman in her middle years who had dwelled in the street longer than the Rushmores had. Cheeks blazing, and wanting only to flee indoors

14

and hide herself away with her crushing embarrassment, Renee scanned the ground for her shopping bag.

'I were making the beds and happened to glance outside and saw you take the tumble. You didn't half go with a bang, lass.'

'I must have tripped over the kerb . . . daft really. I'm all right, aye.' Having located her bag in the gutter, Renee held it to her chest and inched backwards towards her gate. 'Sorry, I, I have to go.'

Mrs Flynn's voice was concerned and kindly, her eyes likewise. 'You're sure you've not done no proper damage? Bleeding bad, your face is; it don't half look sore. Let me take a gander at it, eh, check nowt's broken—'

'No.' Shaking her head, Renee stepped back a few more paces. 'No, I'm fine. I must be going now.'

'Well, if you're sure, lass—'

'I am. Thanks anyway . . . Ta-ra.' Without another word, she turned and hurried for home.

Standing in the tiny hall, with the street shut out and trouble averted – her father would have a blue fit were he to discover she'd been speaking with the neighbours – Renee let her shoulders fall and the pretence melt away. By, but she was in a lot of pain despite her words to the contrary. Wincing, she made for the oval mirror above the fireplace to assess the damage.

'Stupid, stupid,' she muttered to herself. Mrs Flynn must think her a complete idiot. Praise be to God no one else had seen. And just how would she explain this away to Ivan? He'd give her a tongue-lashing of the highest order for being so clumsy and fetching attention upon herself.

A careful inspection of the injury once she'd wiped away the blood and grit with a damp cloth revealed a half-inch cut to her nose. Overall, it wasn't so bad as she'd feared. All she could do now was pray that her eyes didn't blacken.

Thankfully, after a sit-down and a cup of tea to soothe her shattered nerves, she felt moderately better and the pain had subsided. Mindful of the ticking clock and the tasks awaiting her attention, she rose from the table and headed for the kitchen.

By the time Ivan entered the room, home from his day's work, there was a healthy fire burning merrily in the grate and the tantalising aroma of good food permeating the air. Acknowledging his arrival with a small nod, Renee hurried to set the table.

'Summat smells good.'

Her heart lifted a little at the clear voice in which her father had spoken – no whisky slur coated the words this night, glory be. 'It's liver and onions, Dad, with rice pudding for afters.'

'Sounds gradely, I'm famished.'

They ate in silence for a few minutes and Renee was beginning to believe that her father wouldn't mention it. Then he lifted the piece of bread he'd been using to mop up the meat juices from his plate and pointed it in her direction: 'Well? Cat got your tongue?'

Her fingers fluttered to her nose. She swallowed hard. 'No, Dad.'

'In that case, you'd best start explaining yourself.'

'I . . . It were just . . .'

'Where did it occur?'

'The bathroom,' she stuttered, thinking on her feet. 'There were water on the floor, water I hadn't noticed, and—'

'You're lying.'

Renee shook her head quickly, sending her hair swinging. 'I'm not, Dad, honest, it was a slip I took upstairs, that's all. I bashed my face on the bathtub—'

'You did it outdoors, didn't you?' he cut in again, his voice low with menace.

'No—!'

'You gormless, brainless young bitch. You've been making a spectacle of yourself in front of the neighbours. Someone spotted you, didn't they, must have done? You've been spouting off to them bastards, ain't you? Spilling my business to strangers. Admit it. Admit it, damn it!'

Head beginning to spin with the terror of her situation, she attempted once more to have him believe her: 'Please, Dad, you're wrong. It was the bathroom . . .'

However, her words melted on the air like smoke as a sharp rap sounded at the front door.

Father and daughter gazed at one another, openmouthed.

Both knew what the other was thinking. Visitors? Here? That didn't happen, never had done. The incidents must be connected – there was no other explanation. Renee was done for.

17

'Oh aye?' Ivan eventually rasped. His eyes were bulging with fury. 'Then who the hell is this, eh?'

Oh, Mrs Flynn, why did you have to come? I told you I was all right. No, no . . .

'Answer me.'

'I don't know, I don't . . .!'

'No? Well, we soon will.'

She could only watch as he stalked across the room and into the hallway.

'Mr Rushmore?'

The voice was male – Renee's heart seemed to stop in its tracks and pure relief rushed through her. But who . . .? Biting her lip, she inched closer to snatch a peek of the newcomer.

'That's right,' Ivan was saying. 'What can I do for you?'

'My name's Ralph Robertson and I'm your new Air Raid Precautions warden.'

Air Raid Precautions . . .? What did that mean? Renee asked herself, taking in through the crack of the living room door the man. Dressed in a dark blue boiler suit, and black tin helmet emblazoned in bold white with the initials ARP, he wasn't someone she'd seen before and cut an authoritative figure.

'Right. Well, Mr Robertson, it were nice of you to stop by and introduce yourself but I'm a bit busy right now, so if you don't mind . . .'

'Hang about,' Ralph said in surprise as Ivan made to shut the door in his face, 'that's not the only reason I'm here the night.'

'Then what? Spit it out, man.'

The warden's face had stiffened at the unceremonious treatment – he stood up straight and lifted his chin. 'I'm doing the rounds of the estate to make sure the residents of Top o'th' Brow are aware of the news.'

'And what news would that be?'

'You didn't catch it on the wireless earlier?'

Ivan shook his head. 'We don't own one.'

'I see. Then it's my duty to inform you that, as of this evening, the government order for a full blackout is now in force.'

Renee glanced to her father for his response to this confusing piece of news, but he was staring back at the other man in silence. Finally, unable to bear the not knowing any longer, she plucked at his sleeve. 'Dad? What does it mean?'

Craning his neck, Ralph caught sight of her and nodded a greeting. 'To quote the message communicated from the Lord Privy Seal's office, it means, young miss, that until further notice, every night from sunset to sunrise all lights inside buildings must be obscured, and all lights outside buildings must be extinguished, subject to certain exceptions in the case of external lighting essential for the conduct of work of vital national importance, and these lights must be adequately shaded,' he revealed with a flourish and a curt nod.

'Oh.' It was all she could offer, hadn't a clue what he'd meant. 'Oh, right.'

'But surely . . .' Ivan's voice was shaky now and his complexion had taken on a sickly grey hue, much to

Renee's puzzlement. 'Surely it's not really going to happen?'

'Without a doubt, I'm afraid,' answered Ralph gravely.

'But it can't, it *can't*, it—'

'It can, Mr Rushmore, and it will. Make no mistake about it.'

'What can?' Renee whispered, mindless, in her desperation to understand, of incurring her father's wrath by speaking out. 'Please, sir. What's to happen?'

'Ain't it obvious? Why, this country will soon be at war, of course.'

Chapter 2

'WAR?' NOW, IT was Renee's turn to feel all colour drain from her face. She gazed across at Ivan in a stunned stupor. 'War, Dad?'

'Surely you must have heard—?'

'Yes, thank you, Mr Robertson,' Ivan interjected. 'If that's everything then don't let me keep you . . .'

'You've bought blackout material in readiness, then, I take it?' the warden pressed on regardless. 'You were warned to put such plans in place, after all. There's been a number of Civil Defence public information leaflets sent out over the past few months as well you'll know; I believe it was leaflet number two that covered the requirements for the blackout, along with details on taking care of your gas masks.'

'Gas masks?' Renee asked in a squeak.

'Aye, you know, to prevent against the possibility of attack from gas bombs . . .? By 'eck, lass,' he added with bemusement at her blank expression, 'where have you been living, under a rock? Oh aye,' he went on, turning back to Ivan, 'speaking of gas masks.' He

21

tapped his chin. 'They've now been delivered for this area and will be distributed house to house by me in due course, when you'll be fitted for size. This should really have been done long before now, but what with difficulties caused by delays . . . Anyroad, you'll hear from me again soon. Good evening to you, Mr Rushmore, Miss.'

Watching the warden turn on his heel and stride away up the street, Renee had to fight the urge to dart after him and demand further information. War? What war? Just what in the world was going on?

Ivan returned to his chair at the table; in a daze, she followed and dropped back into her own. Thick silence enveloped the room as her father stared into space for what seemed an age. Finally, he brought his stare to meet hers.

'So. There we have it.'

'Dad?' Doing her level best to keep the rising panic from her words, she took a deep breath. 'Will you tell me what that man meant? What war? *Who* will we be at war with? What's *happening*?'

'It's Germany. Their leader, Mr Hitler, is a mad swine what's after conquering the whole of Europe and beyond given half the chance.'

'Hitler . . . I think I remember his name from school. The Austrian Chancellor?' And at Ivan's nod: 'But . . . why? What's he doing it for? I don't understand.'

'I'm buggered if I know. He's deranged, that's what. Anyroad, don't fret on it. It'll blow over, you'll see.'

22

But although Renee would have liked to agree with him, for the alternative was too terrible to contemplate, she knew she couldn't, knew that what her father spoke was false. 'It doesn't sound as if it will from what Mr Robertson's just been saying, Dad. Blackout and gas masks . . .? We ain't had none of them information leaflets he mentioned, have we?' she added, remembering his words and trying desperately still to make sense of it all. 'I'd have seen them had they been delivered.'

'We did. I chucked them out.'

Her mouth fell open. 'Why?'

Shrugging, Ivan rose and crossed the space to settle into his fireside chair. He reached for his pipe on the mantel top before answering, 'I reckoned it would all come to nowt, so where was the point in dwelling on it.'

'What did the leaflets say? Dad, we might be in need of that information one day soon—'

'Oh, we'll not. Shurrup harking on about it, will yer?'

'But what about this blackout thing? Mr Robertson said we must have material—'

'I said shut up! I've had a bellyful of this all right. War, war, war – it's all you bloody well hear these days, 'specially at the station. Now enough of it, you listening?'

Enough of it? she wanted to scream into his face. Their country and its people – herself included – could very well be on the brink of entering a second world war and he was refusing to discuss it, help her understand? He, the only one who could do such a thing seeing as she had no one else who could answer her questions, ease her worries? And yet, had she really expected anything else from him? So far as Ivan Rushmore was concerned, it was a case of me, myself and I, it had always been that way. Even the most basic wants and needs of his daughter didn't come into it, never had.

How didn't I know about this? she questioned herself yet again as she lay in her bed that night, her mind all of a whirl. Then again, it didn't take much guess-work to find the solution to this: how *could* she have had an idea? As her father had himself pointed out to the ARP warden, they didn't own a wireless. Nor did Ivan read the newspaper – no such thing ever entered the house. As for outside communication . . . well. That was non-existent, wasn't it.

Turning on to her side, she bit her thumbnail and gazed into the darkness.

Just where would they be soon? What did the future have in store for her – for them all?

Not for the first time, she closed her eyes and prayed that her mother was here for all she was worth.

The following morning, Ivan acted as though nothing out of the ordinary had occurred the evening before. In turn, reluctant to spark his temper, Renee followed suit. Yet long after he'd left for the train station, she sat on, staring at nothing, couldn't seem to put her mind to anything.

Would this war be announced today? How would she even know? Bombs could begin raining on their heads at any moment and she'd be powerless to do a thing to help herself escape them – she was done for, she was. One terrifying thought preceded another on a loop, allowing her brain no let-up. Her nerves in tatters, she spent the remainder of the morning with a continual fist of dread in her guts and her heart doing somersaults.

She went about her domestic duties as though in a trance: table cleared and the chenille cloth shaken outside, breakfast dishes washed and dried and put away, fire raked out and relaid, furniture dusted, beds made. All the while, but one thought predominated – the overhanging threat of war – until she thought she might go mad with the worry of it all and she knew she had to get out of the house for a while.

Donning her cardigan, she made to cross to the back door, figuring a visit to her feathered friends and Ruby in particular would help soothe her. Then she halted and her eyes flitted to the window and the front garden instead. She bit her lip. Then, making up her mind, she nodded once and headed for the hallway.

Letting herself out, she pulled the front door to and walked slowly down the path. Pausing by the gate, she leaned her elbows on it and glanced up and down the street.

Besides one or two housewives out scrubbing their doorsteps further up, the lane was deserted.

Wondering just what she'd hoped to achieve anyway, Renee heaved a long breath.

Even if she had spotted a neighbour near by, what could she have done? Struck up conversation with them? The prospect was laughable and she knew it. Desperate to speak with someone about this whole war business she might be, but with whom, and how would she have gone about it? It had been a stupid idea – not to mention a dangerous one should her father catch wind of her intentions; she'd been foolish to even consider it. With a shrug and a sigh, she turned and retraced her steps indoors.

Planning what to prepare for the evening meal was normally something she enjoyed; it broke up the monotony for a while and gave her something to do. Today, however, her heart wasn't in it. She collected the string bag sometime later and once more left the house without a single thought of what her purchases might be. Nor was she any closer to making up her mind when she reached the shops. On impulse alone, she turned her feet in the direction of the grocer's.

She was met with a myriad of voices the moment she pushed open the door – the shop was packed out. At least a dozen women huddled in small groups speaking in grave tones, and Renee was made aware immediately as to their topic of conversation: war. Heart fluttering in relieved excitement, she edged her way inside.

'They'll not get my lad, I'll tell you that for nowt,'

an overweight customer announced to her associates in a steely voice. 'That shower what'll be making all the decisions down in that London can go and eat shit if they think they're using my Kenny as cannon fodder!'

'But Freda, wench, you'll not get a say in it, none of us will,' pointed out another woman miserably. 'You know the score: the nobs click their fingers and we obey; ain't it always been the way? We shan't have a choice.'

'Aye?' the indomitable Freda responded. 'Well just let the bleeders try it, that's all I'll say. I'll tear them limb from limb, the lot, with my two hands, I will. Just you watch and see.'

'I'll be right behind you, love,' piped up another, equally formidable-looking member of the group. Her scarf-covered head bobbed sharply in a firm nod. 'All three of my lads are of age to go into battle but I'll tell you this much, it'll not be happening, no friggin' way.' She hitched up her generous bosom to reaffirm her point. 'Them plummy-gobbed politicians want a war, do they, well they can just go and fight the bugger themselves, can't they? And why not, eh? What's it to do with us, that's what I'd like to know. Nay, they're getting norra single one of *my* sons.'

Her eyes on the display of tinned goods, on the pretext of deciding what to choose, Renee kept her ears cocked, hungry for more detail.

'He's gorra screw loose that Hitler bloke, must have,' someone else stated darkly. 'Fancy his soldiers

27

marching into Poland like that yesterday, the hard-faced blighters.'

'Will they surrender, d'you reckon, the Poles?' someone else wanted to know.

'Makes no odds, does it? According to my fella, it's sealed our fate regardless. Poland, well she's one of our allies, ain't she? Britain shall have no option but to enter the war, now, aye.'

So, it definitely was true. Renee felt the hairs on her arms spring to attention. May God help them!

'Is anyone actually wanting to be served?' The grocer's exasperated voice rang out above the medley. 'This is a business, you know, not a meeting hall. What about you?' he called across to Renee, seeing her standing on her own. 'Do you know what you want yet?'

Though she'd have preferred to remain where she was and listen in some more, several pairs of eyes had now swivelled in her direction and she felt unable to disagree. Inclining her head, she squeezed her way to the counter.

'Carrots, please,' she blurted for want of something to say. 'And half a pound of spuds.'

'That'll be thruppence.'

Nodding, she placed the vegetables in her bag, then slipped her hand into her cardigan pocket for her money, but her fingers brushed empty wool. Immediately, her cheeks bloomed in a deep blush; she shook her head. 'I . . . I think I've left my purse at home.'

Seymour Briggs released a sigh. 'Well, I'm sorry

but I'm not running a charity here. Either go back and collect it or I'll have to have the items back.'

Renee was wishing the ground would swallow her up and had made to remove the vegetables from her bag when a hand on her arm stopped her. Glancing up, she found herself looking into the smiling face of Mrs Flynn.

'I'll lend you the brass, lass.'

'Oh! Oh, but I couldn't—'

'Course you can. You can pay me back when we get home.'

For a long moment, Renee hesitated. Then, seeing that her neighbour wasn't to be dissuaded, she conceded. 'Aye. All right. Ta very much, Mrs Flynn.'

'Your fall weren't too serious, then, after all?' she asked as they waited for her to be served, motioning to Renee's nose.

'Oh no, I'm fine now.'

After paying for her own purchases as well as Renee's, the woman took Renee's elbow and led the way through the throng and into the mild late morning. Shy now and mumbling that she'd drop the threepence into Mrs Flynn's house later, Renee attempted to make a sharp exit, but Mrs Flynn was having none of it.

''Ere, not so fast, lass. Surely you ain't for serving up just carrot and tatties this evening? Come on, come with me to the butcher's. I'll pay again for what it is you're wanting.'

'But—'

'But nowt. And I'll not take no for an answer.'

29

At the clear twinkle in the woman's eye, a smile crept across Renee's mouth. She nodded. 'Ta, thanks.'

'Well hello to you both!' Gordon's florid face split in a welcoming grin. 'You're a sight for sore eyes, I must say – aye, my two favourite customers.'

'Enough of your blarney. I bet you say that to everyone what walks through yon door,' Mrs Flynn retorted good-naturedly.

Throwing back his head, the butcher roared with laughter. 'Mebbe I does, mebbe I don't. I'll tell you what, though, Iris, you're looking lovelier than ever today. And that's summat I wouldn't jest about, nay. Bloomin' glowing, you are.'

'Tsk! Go on with you, you smooth-tongued charmer, yer!'

Chuckling, he spread his enormous hands to encompass the prime cuts on display. 'And what can I tempt youse with today, then, ladies? I've some nice, thick lamb chops here. A bit of mint sauce drizzled over them and you'll think you've died and gone to heaven. What d'you reckon?'

Eyeing the tray, Mrs Flynn licked her lips. 'Aye, go on, then. You've twisted my arm. I'm partial to a bit of lamb, I am – give us four, will you, Gordon.'

'And how about you, lass?' He wiggled his bushy brows at Renee. 'Have I to wrap you up the same?'

'Yes please. I'll have four as well.'

'Good, good! Aye, you've made a sound choice.'

'I'll be paying for both orders, lad,' Mrs Flynn informed him when the chops were safely inside their string bags. 'What do I owe you?'

'Call it a tanner, my lovely.' He threw the silver coin into the till, then lifted his straw hat and his beaming grin lit his face once more. 'Until Monday, then. Ta-ra to you both.'

'Ta-ra, Gordon.'

'Thanks, Mr Wallace, ta-ra,' Renee added quietly, throwing him a small smile before hurrying after her neighbour.

'D'you need owt else, lass?' Mrs Flynn asked when they were outside once more.

Renee shook her head.

'You're sure?'

'Aye, Mrs Flynn.'

'Right, well. Let's set off for home.'

They walked the short distance along New Lane before turning into their street, their shopping bags swinging between them. All the while, Renee was acutely aware of the novelty of this experience. It was as though they were just two friends out for a stroll – for once in her life, she almost felt normal. Altogether new for sure, but nonetheless pleasurable. What a pity it wasn't a reality and never could be – not with Mrs Flynn nor anyone else.

Ivan would sooner kill her than allow the possibility of such a thing, she was certain. He could never afford her to get too close to people for fear of them discovering their terrible secret and warped family set-up, this she knew. Nor would she have wanted anyone else to know, either. The prospect was unfathomable. She'd surely die from shame, she would.

'Here we are, then,' Mrs Flynn said suddenly,

coming to a halt outside her house, shattering Renee's brooding – and bringing a sadness to her young heart that the short excursion was at an end, despite her recent ruminations.

'Just give me half a minute, Mrs Flynn, whilst I run and fetch from home what I owe you—'

'Oh, there's no rush, lass. Call in with it later if you like.'

But Ivan would be back shortly, worked only a half-day on Saturday, and then he'd know . . . 'No. Really, I'd rather you had it now. I'll not be long.'

The woman shrugged and, flashing an awkward smile, Renee flew across the road to number forty-six. She was back in a trice; murmuring her thanks, she held out the correct amount of money.

'Ta, lass. You know, if you've got half an hour going spare, you're welcome to come inside for a cup of tea?'

This was completely unexpected; for a minute, Renee was thrown. Not only was she incredibly grateful for the kind offer but also sorely tempted. *Agree*, a part of her brain insisted, whilst at the same time another part reminded her it would be unwise. In the end, common sense prevailed – reluctantly, she shook her head.

'I've got a lot on, so I'll not if you don't mind.'

'All right, lass. Another time mebbe.'

'Aye, maybe. Sorry.'

Brushing aside Renee's apology with an easy smile, the woman turned for home. 'Don't be daft; you can't help being busy, eh? Well, ta-ra for now.'

'Ta-ra, Mrs Flynn.' She could barely speak past the lump of regret and disappointment that had lodged in her throat. 'Thanks again.'

Once indoors, Renee made straight for the back garden and the pigeon loft.

'Hello, girl.'

She lifted out Ruby and cradled her gently. And, as the bird's soft coos wrapped around her like an embrace, Renee finally let the tears fall.

That night, Ivan came to her bed.

Her feeble attempts to push him away as her blankets were wrenched from her earned her a hefty slap to her mouth and, in the end, she submitted to his will.

Turning her face away on the pillow from his whisky-fumed breath and switching her brain from the reality of his hot, hairy body and disgusting clammy hands, she prayed it would soon be over.

Renee found that tonight, however, differed in one aspect. This time, the safe and happy place she normally took her thoughts to when this was going on remained out of reach. Instead, it was the ever-growing issue of war that held captive her mind.

She relived the day's scenes, heard again the conversations in the grocer's shop. And a wholly impossible yet tantalising notion overtook her.

She pictured her father receiving his call-up papers to join the armed forces – out of the question, of course, given his age, but she nonetheless experienced a surge of pure joy pretending he'd soon be gone. She saw him dressed in khaki leave the house, watched him walk away up Monks Lane, away from her life, please God, for good. Then, reminding herself that this was her dream and that she could make anything happen if she chose to, she did just that: she had Ivan blown to bits on the battlefield. She watched herself opening the door to the telegram boy, read slowly the words, savouring every one, printed on the slip of paper – her ticket to liberty. Ivan Rushmore had been killed. Renee Rushmore was at long last free.

No palpable fear on *her* part at the prospect, as had been the case with those mothers she'd overheard. None, never. If only it could be true, but of course it couldn't be. Nevertheless, Renee knew that simply the imagining of it would help see her through, bring her just a modicum of peace when she found herself in need to call upon it. The thought of a bloody and violent end to the man who had caused her unfathomable pain proved a great comfort.

Even after her father had stumbled off back to his own bedroom, and his loud snores had long since been pushing through the adjoining wall, Renee kept the visions inside her head in play.

That night, the first she could ever recall, she went to sleep with a smile on her face.

Chapter 3

SUNDAYS WERE THE worst. A full day in Ivan's company was nothing short of hell.

Usually, Renee would spend the day on housework – not a day for rest so far as she was concerned. Anything she could think of, from scrubbing the floors and cleaning the windows to breaking the recognised national tradition of Monday washday and tackling the weekly laundry a day early, was preferrable to sitting in the same room as her father for extended lengths of time. She would fall into bed at the evening's end exhausted to the marrow, but by God it was worth it.

This first Sabbath of the month had begun like any other. Breakfast came and went, then Renee had seen to her usual duties before stripping both beds and putting the sheets in to steep in the dolly tub. After brewing a fresh pot of tea, she was crossing to the small door set into the corner of the kitchen which gave access to the coal shed, when muffled voices reached her ears. Pausing for a moment, she listened with a frown. Then she took the small shovel from the hook behind the door, filled it with coal and carried it through to the living room.

In here, the voices were louder and more pronounced. She threw the fuel on to the fire then stood with her back towards the flames, head cocked. A quick look to the wooden clock atop the mantel revealed the time to be just shy of quarter past eleven. A further glance to the armchair near by showed her father slumbering still, enjoying his usual late-morning nap.

Folding her arms, Renee trained her gaze on the far wall separating them from their neighbours and the source of the noise.

The family next door, normally a quiet lot, were conversing loudly in what were obviously agitated tones. Then a hush fell and suddenly a solitary voice, clear and refined, leaked through the plaster to suffuse the Rushmores' living room:

'This is London. You will now hear a statement by the Prime Minister.'

The breath caught in Renee's chest as she realised that what she was hearing was a news bulletin on the wireless. Slowly, her heart beginning to drum, she made her way across the room and pressed her ear to the wall.

Seconds later, another voice sounded. This was as cultured as the last, although slightly tremulous with evident emotion:

'I am speaking to you from the Cabinet Room at Ten Downing Street. This morning, the British Ambassador in Berlin handed the German government a final note, stating that unless we heard from them by eleven o'clock that they were prepared at once to withdraw their troops from Poland, a state of war would exist between us.'

In the charged pause that followed, Renee bit down on the fist she'd crushed to her mouth. *Dear God, let the Germans have agreed. Please, please . . .*

'I have to tell you now that no such undertaking has been received and that, consequently, this country is at war with Germany.'

The words seemed to hold the very air by the throat, shattering not only Renee's desperate hopes but, she was certain, those of an entire nation. Her body slumped. She closed her eyes in despair.

'You can imagine what a bitter blow it is to me that all my long struggle to win peace has failed . . .'

Neville Chamberlain's speech droned on, though Renee barely registered it, could take in nothing more besides the devastating truth already lodged like a cancer in her spinning brain.

'We're at war.' She whispered the words to the sideboard. 'We all might die and I'm scared. I want my mam. I want my mam!'

'Renee?'

Her gaze swivelled round. Ivan was sat forward in the chair knuckling his eyes. 'Dad . . .'

'What's to do with you? You favour you've seen a ghost.'

'It's been announced, Dad.' She pointed a finger in the direction of next door. 'Our country . . . it's at war.'

Stare wide, he blinked at her mutely for several seconds. Then he reached for his pipe and held a lighted match to the bowl with shaking hands. He sucked deeply on the stem and released a plume of smoke slowly.

Finally, he murmured, 'That's that.'

Renee nodded.

Nothing happened. No planes filled the skies, no bombs fell, no clomp of enemy boots sounded in the streets. Everything continued as it always had.

Renee had expected destruction and death at any moment, but as yet it hadn't come. The constant state of limbo was both hopeful and unnerving, and she knew the rest of Top o'th' Brow felt it, too. The residents went about their business subdued and tense-faced and the streets and stores were quieter than usual. It was a queer time for them all with uncertainty a constant companion.

From the snippets she'd heard whilst out buying provisions, Renee learned that children all over the country were being sent away from the towns and cities to live with strangers in the safety of the countryside. Evacuation, they were calling it. If only she was younger and had the excuse to join them, she thought to herself. Not that Bolton's youngsters were being relocated elsewhere, mind you, theirs being a neutral town with little military importance – the Germans surely wouldn't deem it necessary enough to waste their bombs on them. Still, a lass could dream after all, and it didn't stop her from imagining starting a fresh life in a new, kind and loving household.

True to his word, the ARP warden had returned to deliver the family's promised gas masks. Posters had already begun appearing on walls and in shops instructing people on how to put them on and what to do if you were attacked by vapour, liquid or blister gas. There were also reminders of the importance of carrying your mask at all times or risk being slapped with a hefty fine. And yet, life-saving though the apparatuses might prove to be should the worst come to pass, by God, what monstrous contraptions they were! The black rubber grew hot very quickly and made it difficult to breathe. And the smell! Within seconds of trying it for size for Ralph Robertson's approval, Renee had been bent double with nausea.

The subject of blackout material, or the lack thereof in the Rushmores' case – Ivan had upheld his steadfast opinion that it was a waste of time and had refused to adhere to the government order – had got him a stern ticking off from the warden. Albeit reluctantly, in the end he'd agreed to address the issue. However, there was one thing he refused to be swayed upon and that was the unnecessary, as he deemed it, frittering of money. Instead, he'd brought home from the station one evening a quantity of sheets of cardboard and a small tin of black paint, which he'd insisted would serve the job just as well as curtains or blinds.

The task had fallen to Renee to carefully measure and cut the card and paint the pieces, which she would painstakingly tape to every single windowpane in the house each day at nightfall. And Lord help them all on the estate should they accidentally be showing a chink of light from within when the warden passed by on his patrol!

Now, as September gave way to October and the weather turned cooler, Renee began to grow restless. She still passed the time of day with Mrs Flynn across the road, but it just didn't seem enough any more, and she'd taken to going on short strolls around the open woodland stretching off at the bottom of her street, desperate for a change of scenery.

It was during one of these walks that she first caught the attention of a young mother out enjoying the fresh air with her twin sons. Lynn Ball was funny, smart and beautiful – all the qualities that Renee had ever wished to have. Five-month-old Brian and Bobby were their mother's pride and joy, it was clear to see, and Renee had been struck by their heart-gladdening family scene when first encountering the trio some weeks previously.

The woman had been sitting in the warm grasses with a baby tucked under each arm, and she was singing. The lads gurgled and giggled along, making Lynn laugh, and Renee had watched on from afar with a thickness in her throat and a smile in her heart. For that was how it was meant to be, wasn't it, between mother and child. Safe and easy, secure in the knowledge that togetherness was all you needed, that such a love was unquestionable, unbreakable, and all was well with the world. Only it never quite worked out like that all of the time, did it? Just look at her own mother, wherever she was. Gone, lost to Renee forever, never to return . . .

'Morning!' Lynn had called out suddenly, glimpsing Renee and lifting her arm in cheery acknowledgement. 'Or is it afternoon by now . . .? Anyroad, hello.'

'Oh, er, hello.' Tongue-tied as ever when conversing with the outside world, Renee had flushed scarlet and scuttled off in the direction of home.

The following day, however, she'd crossed paths with Lynn and the children again. This time, when the young woman had extended a greeting once more, Renee had not only returned it but was bold enough to wave back, too. Now, names had been exchanged and the merry passing of pleasantries was a daily occurrence.

Today, Renee had her housework done with record speed and, eager not to miss the Balls, had combed her hair and was out of the house well ahead of time. She'd been perambulating along the bank of the brook for a handful of minutes when a flash of colour in the distance caught her attention, and to her delight she saw it was Lynn and her sons passing through a cluster of trees up ahead. As nonchalant as she could manage, she headed as though by chance towards them.

'Morning! How're you keeping, all right?'

'Morning, Lynn. Morning, Bobby, Brian,' Renee added, grinning down at the boys in turn. 'It's a bit on the nippy side today, ain't it?'

'You're right, aye.' Lynn shot the murky sky a bright

smile. 'But well, it's nice to catch the air, eh? You been here long, lass?'

'Not really, ten minutes or thereabouts.'

'Renee, are you working?'

The unexpected question brought her eyebrows up in surprise. She shook her head. 'I look after the home for Dad.'

'Would you like to be?' Lynn went on with shining eyes.

'Would I like to be in employment?'

'That's right.'

'Well . . . aye, I would, yes.'

'Well, it's like this, you see, lass. Duncan, that's my husband, joined up right at the start of things. His army pay don't stretch all that far, you know, and I've been thinking I might be better off looking for a little part-time position somewhere. Only, what with the lads here . . .' She jiggled the twins in her arms, making them chuckle. 'That's where you could come in.'

'You'd like me to watch Bobby and Brian for you, you mean, whilst you go out to work?'

'Aye. So, what d'you reckon?'

Renee was breathless with excitement. 'You'd trust me with your sons, Lynn?'

The woman's tinkling laugh rang out across the treetops. 'Course I would! You're a sensible sort, and I've seen for myself how much you like them. Am I right?'

'Oh, yes. They're a bonny pair and sunny natured with it. Eeh, Lynn, I'd love to.'

'Hold your horses, lass, I ain't secured myself a place yet! Aye, but you have my promise that when I do, you'll be the first to know. All right?'

Nodding, Renee clapped her hands, her cup of joy fit to overflow. 'Ta very much. You don't know what this means to me.'

''Ere, your dad'll not mind us agreeing to this without his say-so, will he?'

'No,' she was quick to assure Lynn. 'He won't.'

Indeed, Ivan wouldn't mind; that much was true. For Renee had no intention whatsoever of telling him.

The days crawled along agonisingly slowly. Each afternoon Renee would greet Lynn in the fields and they would chat for a few minutes before parting ways, yet still there had been no development – each time, the woman had no fresh information on the job front.

Renee was getting close to giving up hope when, towards the end of the month, she arrived at the brook to find Lynn and the boys waiting for her. Her stomach flipped over in dizzy anticipation; it was clear by the expression on Lynn's face that good news awaited her.

'I know you said you dwell on Monks Lane, and I'd have come to see you at home, only I don't think you've ever mentioned what number house it is.'

And for good reason. It was a risk she hadn't been prepared to take. 'You've found summat?' she asked.

The woman laughed heartily. 'I have indeed, lass. Eeh, and guess where?'

43

Beaming, Renee shrugged her shoulders.

'Only the grocer's on New Lane!'

'Eeh, that'll be ideal!'

'It will that. I couldn't believe it when owd Seymour Briggs agreed to taking me on on a trial basis, him being a right misery arse, an' all. But well, he did, and I start tomorrow morning.'

Renee felt delirious with happiness. She closed her eyes and breathed deeply.

This was going to be the start of something wonderful, she just knew it. Not only would it fill the lonely hours, but for the first time in her life she'd be earning a wage. Money of her own . . . it was a lovely thought. It would give her a sense of purpose, pride, and afford her some independence. After all, who knew what the future had in store? Better still, Ivan would never find out, not with his long working hours. She'd be away to Lynn's house after he'd left for Trinity Street and would easily be back home and have her chores completed before he returned. It was all proving so simple.

This time tomorrow, she'd have begun her life anew. And nothing, *no one*, was going to stand in her way.

Chapter 4

JITTERY AS A squirrel, Renee followed the routine of old the next morning as she'd always done. Despite her best efforts, she could manage no more than a few morsels of her breakfast, but thankfully her father didn't seem to notice. Finally, after what felt like an eternity, he rose from the table and donned his peaked cap.

'Right, that's me. I'm away to the station.'

'Aye, Dad.'

'I'll see you this evening.'

'Aye.'

'Ta-ra.'

'Ta-ra.'

He nodded, then was gone. Her face breaking into a smile, Renee hugged herself and sighed.

Within minutes, she was standing outside number fifteen Padbury Way, and Lynn was inviting her inside.

'Now, you're sure you know what to do, lass, should they grow fractious?' the anxious mother asked some time afterwards, hovering by the door as though she might be having second thoughts.

Renee hastened to put her concerns to rest. 'I'm to put them both down for a nap in their cot and check on them once.'

'And their dinner . . .?'

'You've made up a pan of vegetable soup and it just needs warming through on the stove. I'm to test it myself first, to make sure it's not too hot for them.' She smiled. 'Please don't worry, Lynn. I'll not forget everything you've told me.'

'I know, lass. Take no notice – it's just me being overprotective. I ain't never left them with anyone else before. Even so, I know they'll be all right; they're in capable hands.'

Renee's chest swelled with pride. No one had ever deemed her capable before, or at least they hadn't voiced it. 'We'll see you later. Ta-ra for now.'

'Ta-ra. Ta-ra you two little monsters,' Lynn added to the twins, 'now you be good lads for your Aunty Renee, d'you hear?'

When she'd gone, Renee breathed happily and gazed around. The living room was spick and span, the fireplace brasses highly polished and gleaming. Her eyes travelled up to the mantel and came to rest on a photograph in a silver frame engraved with roses. Curious, she crossed the floor and picked it up.

A tall man dressed in full army uniform stared back. He had honey-coloured hair and laughing eyes – Duncan, Lynn's husband. Renee reckoned he was very handsome, and she couldn't stop the pang of envy; Lynn Ball really did have it all.

Would she ever get to experience the love of a

good man, have a family of her own one day? Mind you, who in their right mind would look twice at her once they knew? Damaged goods, that's what she was. Soiled. Used. Disgusting . . .

'Stop it,' she murmured to herself firmly. 'From this day forth, things are going to be different, remember?'

Smiling now, she placed the picture back carefully and went to sit on the floor, where lay her charges on a soft blanket, punching and kicking the air.

'We're going to have a lot of fun together, lads, ain't we, eh?' she told them, tickling their tummies and making them shriek with laughter. 'I'll be the best minder in the whole wide world, you'll see.'

The hours seemed to fly by. She played with the children for a while, then tidied around whilst they had their nap. She fed them their lunch, which they gobbled up without a problem – not surprising, she thought, after tasting the food herself; Lynn was a marvellous cook. Before Renee knew it, Lynn was back, and it was time for her to return to Monks Lane. She was more than a little sad to leave.

'It went great today, and the grocer was happy with my work. So, same time tomorrow, lass?'

'Oh yes, I've really enjoyed myself,' she replied truthfully.

'I'm glad to hear it, aye. I just knew you'd do well.'

After bidding her employer goodbye and kissing the children's podgy cheeks in turn, Renee swallowed a sigh and made reluctantly for home.

She'd bought in provisions in preparation for

today's evening meal the previous day; now, she hurried to light the gas ring on the stove. They were having fried egg, chips and tomatoes. Nice and easy but tasty with it – it wouldn't take too long.

Whilst she waited for the food to cook, she cleared away the breakfast dishes from earlier and had the pots washed in no time. Next, she raced upstairs and made the beds before speeding down to the living room once more to sweep out and build up the fire. The dusting, she decided, could wait for one day; it wouldn't do any harm. With a nod to seal her decision, she headed back to the kitchen to begin dishing out the meal.

She'd just relaid the table and placed a pot of tea in the centre when the front door rattled, heralding her father's return. Proud of herself that she'd managed to complete all that needed doing and he wouldn't be any the wiser, she allowed herself a discreet smile and went to fetch the plates in.

'You seem different.'

With her thoughts consumed by the lovely day she'd just spent, her father's quiet words, breaking the lengthy silence midway through the meal, failed to register fully – Renee blinked. 'Sorry, Dad?'

'I said you seem different.'

Praying a blush didn't surface, she licked her lips. 'Do I?'

'Aye.'

'Well, I don't know why that could be—'

'What have you been up to while I've been out?'

'Nowt, Dad.'

Ivan narrowed his gaze. 'If you say so. Oh, by the way,' he added after some moments, his tone lower still, 'I've come to a decision about the pigeons.'

Renee's head shot up, the chip speared on her fork pausing halfway to her mouth. 'What d'you mean?'

'They'll have to go, won't they? It's the kindest thing all round.'

'The kindest . . . Go? Dad, I don't understand. *Why?*'

'Because of the war, of course. Think about it – should the enemy decide to start dropping explosives on our heads, them birds'll not stand a chance, will they? It's happening in zoos all across the country, you know. They're destroying animals left, right and centre.'

Destroying . . . *Ruby*. No. This couldn't be happening. He didn't mean it. He didn't!

'I mean to say,' her father went on as though oblivious to his daughter's building distress, 'imagine their enclosures being damaged in a raid and them ending up free to roam the streets. The authorities can't risk that. Full grown lions and tigers, wolves and hyenas, gorillas and bears, running amok amongst the general public . . .? Eeh no, no.'

'The pigeons ain't dangerous animals. They'd do no one no harm, Dad!'

'Mebbe not, but you never can tell, can you?'

'But . . . well, happen if it really does come to it, and the Germans do one day darken our skies, perhaps we could set them free instead?' *Rather that, than kill the poor innocent souls. Anything but that.* 'It's

49

only right to give them the chance of saving their-selves, in't it? They'd fare far better finding safety out in the open than they would locked in that loft.'

'Set them ... They're bloody homing pigeons, yer daft sow. They'd be back before the day was through!'

'Please, Dad.' Renee was becoming desperate. 'Don't do it. They're ... well, they're my friends.'

To her relief, Ivan seemed to consider this for a while. Then, to her great dismay, he shattered her hopes to dust by shaking his head. 'No. I've made up my mind.'

He was doing this to spite her, she realised suddenly, spying the deviousness glinting in his eyes. He was well aware how fond she was of them. All this, it was nothing but a ploy.

He suspected she was hiding something from him – which, truth be told, she was, but that was neither here nor there! – and this was his way of punishing her until she cracked.

Why did he derive such pleasure from causing her pain? Just what went on in the workings of that mind of his at all? Cruel, that's what he was. Plain *cruel*. Well, he wouldn't beat her, not this time. She'd sooner die herself than admit to him her secret.

'I'll wring their necks tomorrow, get it over with. Best to be well prepared, after all. We'll not be wast-ing them, mind; no, you can use their meat for pies.'

Drawing on all the strength and fortitude she could conjure up, Renee took a risk: she nodded.

'All right, Dad. If you really think it ought to be done . . . then do it.'

Ivan's face contorted into several expressions as he attempted to process her words. 'You're calling my bluff? Is that what you're doing, girl?' he growled.

'No, Dad. As you said, your mind's made up. Nothing I can do or say will make a difference, will it?'

He glared at her for an age as she calmly continued eating her meal. Then he was speaking, and Renee knew that this night, a breakthrough had been made: 'I suppose we could leave it awhile, wait and see what happens with the war, if it's what you really want.'

Lifting her head, she held his stare steadily. Then she nodded and turned her attention back to her food. Without another word, her father did likewise.

For the first time in her life, she'd won one of their battles. Something had shifted, they both felt it, and somehow she knew things wouldn't be quite the same again.

'Hello. What's all this then?'

Bringing the large and cumbersome pram to a stop, Renee pushed the hair out of her eyes and flashed her neighbour a smile. 'Hello, Mrs Flynn.'

'All reet, lass? And who do these babbies belong to?'

Renee fell into step with the older woman. 'I'm all right, ta, aye. This is Bobby and Brian Ball. I took on the job as their minder yesterday.'

51

Venturing outside with the boys for a bit of air didn't concern Renee. It wasn't as though it could heighten the chance of Ivan discovering what she was up to these days if she was seen. He spoke not a word to a soul hereabouts after all, and vice versa.

'Well, good on you, lass. Liking it, are you?'

'Oh aye.' Casting her gaze over the twins, snuggled up together and well wrapped against the mild wind, she sighed happily. 'They're a smashing pair.'

'I bet your father's pleased you've found summat you enjoy to occupy your time, eh?'

The remark, innocent as it might be, momentarily robbed the smile from her face. Renee was about to spin her a lie, that yes, her dad was agreeable to the arrangement, when the prospect of her neighbour making mention of it to Ivan – remote as it may be but possible nonetheless – flitted into her mind. She couldn't risk that.

'Actually, Mrs Flynn . . . he doesn't know. And I'd prefer to keep it that way.'

Though the woman's forehead creased in a small frown, she didn't pass comment on this. Instead, she asked, 'Are you in any big rush to get back?'

'Not really, no. I fed the lads before we came out, and though they're due their nap, it won't harm them none to sleep in their pram. Why d'you ask, Mrs Flynn?'

'Fancy taking me up on my earlier offer of that brew?'

She opened and closed her mouth but couldn't think of a single excuse to offer her.

'I've some boiled ham in t' larder; reet tasty, it is. I'll make us up a nice butty to go with our tea, eh?'

Out of nowhere, and much to her bewilderment, tears sprang to Renee's eyes and before she could stop them they spilled over to pour down her cheeks. 'Oh, Mrs Flynn . . .'

'Eeh, what's to do?'

'It's just . . . you're all just . . .'

'What, lass?'

'Kind. That's what. You're all so very kind. You, Lynn Ball, even Mr Wallace the butcher . . . And I don't deserve it, I don't!'

'Tsk, tsk.' The woman brushed aside her words with a flap of her hand. 'Course you deserve it, everyone does. And you such a likeable lass. Besides, it costs nowt, does it, to show a kindness? Come on. A nice, sweet cup of tea will sort you out. You'll be feeling right as rain in no time.'

Now, Renee made no attempt at refusal. Just why the hell shouldn't she, after all? This is what normal folk did. They spoke to each other, spent time with friends, enjoyed a natter and a cup of tea in each other's company . . . and she did so want to be normal, more than anything else. So why shouldn't she?

'All right, Mrs Flynn, aye,' she heard herself say. 'I'd love to.'

Ten minutes later, with the twins sleeping peacefully in their pram outside, which Renee had parked beneath the window where she could keep an eye to it, the two women were sitting facing one another in the warmth of Mrs Flynn's living room.

53

A snow-white cloth, its edges hand-embroidered with pretty sprigs of flowers, covered the oval table and in the centre there stood a brown pot holding freshly brewed tea, a plate of sandwiches cut into rectangles alongside it. Renee was in her element.

'It all looks lovely, Mrs Flynn.'

'Well, tuck in. There's no standing on ceremony here.'

They chatted about this and that whilst they ate, and after a while, Renee was brave enough to say, 'Can I ask you summat, Mrs Flynn?'

'Go ahead.'

'Why do you choose to speak to me now, after all these years?'

The woman's eyes turned thoughtful. 'There's not been no opportunity to before. Whenever I've seen you out and about, you skittered around with your head down like the devil were on your heels. That day, when I saw you take the fall outside . . . well. I had to check you were all right, didn't I? And aye, it broke the ice.'

'People round here don't like us. They think us rude and a bit queer.' She shrugged. 'I suppose they're right.'

'You're what your father's made you into, lass. He's the queer 'un, not you.'

Renee's brows rose slowly in astonishment. When finally she found her voice, it was little above a whisper: 'You mean . . . you *know*?'

'That Ivan Rushmore's a bad bugger? Aye, I do. You only had to look at his wife for proof of it.'

'You knew my mam?' Renee asked. And at the woman's nod: 'But Dad, he didn't . . . he wouldn't allow . . .'

'Wouldn't allow Sylvia to speak a word to nobody outside his home, same as he don't with you? Is that what you mean?'

'Well . . . yes.'

Mrs Flynn took a sip of her drink before returning her stare to Renee's. 'Aye, well. What his eye didn't see, his heart didn't grieve over.'

'You and Mam were friends?'

'We weren't what you might call bosom friends, I grant you, but aye, we were pally so far as Sylvia deemed it safe to allow. You're a lot like her, you know.'

'Am I?' It had been so long; Renee couldn't really remember.

'She led a dog's life under his rule. She'd not say boo to a goose, poor lamb.'

It sounded as if they were indeed alike, then, after all. 'The thing is, Mrs Flynn, if she knew that Dad was so bad . . .'

'Why did she leave you behind to face it alone?'

'Exactly that. I'll never understand it, never.'

'It were desperation what drove her thinking, I reckon. She loved you very much, did Sylvia, and if she could've taken you with her, she would have done, make no mistake about that.'

'And you don't know where she went to, where she might be now?'

'I don't, love, no. Sorry.'

They lapsed into silence for a few minutes and drank their tea. Then, in a tone deep with meaning, Mrs Flynn said, 'You know, lass, don't you, that if you're ever in need of help, you know where to find me?'

It was on the tip of her tongue: to spill her guts, to tell this woman everything that went on in that house of horrors across the way. What her father made her do, the terrible depravity . . . But she couldn't do it. She just couldn't.

Instead, taking even herself by surprise at her unaccustomed display of familiarity, she reached across the table and placed her hand on top of her neighbour's. 'Thank you, Mrs Flynn,' she told her sincerely. 'Thank you.'

'So, what d'you make of this war, then, eh?' the older woman asked a short while later, after making a fresh pot of tea. 'I can't hardly believe we're in t' grip of another. It don't seem two minutes since the last one – mind you, you'll not remember nowt about that, will you, young as you are. Aye, it's a damn shame. All our poor, brave boys being shipped off to God knows where; and aye, how many will be fortunate enough to ever put feet back on English soil? A bleedin' travesty, it is.'

'I never even knew there was a war brewing. Dad didn't bother to tell me. It didn't half come as a shock when the warden turned up at our door.'

'Eeh, the rotten beggar.' Mrs Flynn shook her head in disgust. 'Fancy him not preparing you! D'you know, I don't know why you don't take this opportunity to get yourself away from here and him,' she declared with a decisive sniff.

'What do you mean?'

'Well, there's places of war work opening up all over the place, so I've heard. Factories and the like are being requisitioned for making items vital to us winning the war – you know, things like munitions and that. And aye, the hours might be long, but the pay's good. I've a cousin what dwells in Daubhill whose daughter works at a textiles – Tootal, Broadhurst and Lee – and they've gone the same road. You know them cases what gas masks come in? Well, it's been her job to sew and examine them for the company. There's rumour they'll be working on parachute cloth next, what they use to make barrage balloons. I could ask her to put a word in for you if you'd like?'

Renee was biting her lip. The idea *was* an exciting one. 'But I've just got myself a job minding the twins. Besides, Dad would never allow it. He fetches in a decent wage from the trains, has been with them for many years. He says I don't have to go out and toil, says I should be thankful of the fact.'

'Never mind whether you *have* to or not; what if you *want* to? The choice should be yours alone to make, not his. I reckon you ought to go for it, find yourself a position and fresh digs away from Top o'th' Brow. Get yourself as far from him as you can, lass, and never look back.'

'I'm not of age. He'd have the law on me.'

'I can't see Ivan Rushmore running to them, can

you? I don't believe someone like him, with all his failings, would be likely to regard the police as friends.'

'But he'd kill me.'

'He'd have to find you first – and who's to say he will if you go about it clever enough?' With a nod and a wink, Mrs Flynn added, 'Just think on it, lass. For you at least, this war could well prove to be a blessing in disguise.'

Her neighbour's words were still ringing in Renee's ears later as she whizzed round the house completing her chores.

Could it really be done? she mused for the dozenth time. But how, and where would she live? On *what* would she live until she received her first week's pay?

She could save her wages from looking after the Ball lads . . . Aye, she'd save it all up, every farthing, and should she ever decide to take Mrs Flynn's advice, she'd be in a better position to support herself, wouldn't she?

However, words and thoughts were all well and good – the real question remained: could it really be done?

If her father ever got so much as a sniff of what she was contemplating . . . God above, the consequences didn't bear thinking about. He'd never set her free, never.

He needed her here to see to the running of the house. To clean and scrub, launder his clothes and cook his meals. And there was the other thing . . . Screwing up her face in disgust, she sighed deeply. She was his plaything, on hand to use as and when he desired. Lord, how she loathed him and what he'd become.

Though Ivan made no mention this night of his suspicions from the previous evening as to her hiding something from him, still there hung over them a tangible air of unease as they ate their meal. Renee was glad when it was over and she could escape to the kitchen to wash the dishes.

'Don't sit down.'

Pausing midway as she eased herself into the fireside chair facing her father's, her duties for the day done, she frowned. 'Was there summat else you wanted, Dad? Another pot of tea making?'

Puffing on his pipe and staring into the fire, he shook his head. 'No, not that.'

'Then what? Why can't I sit down?'

'You can. Over here.'

Watching him pat his knee, her stomach lurched.

'Come on, hop to it. Then I can show you what it is I'm really after.'

'No.'

The room seemed to hold its breath. From where she'd found the strength to defy him, she hadn't a single clue, would never have believed it possible. As shocked as each other, they gazed at one another in numb silence.

'I'll not tell you again, Renee. Here. Now.'

'Dad . . .'

'*Now.*'

'No, damn it. I said no. No, no, no!'

Ivan was on his feet in a trice. Shoulders back and head down, like a bull preparing to charge, he drew his top lip back from his teeth in a menacing snarl. 'You young upstart. You bloody young slut—!'

'Lay a hand on me, Dad, and I swear to God, I'll scream blue murder. I'll have the neighbours round here quicker than that.' She gave a sharp click of her fingers. 'And d'you know what else? I'll tell them everything, I will. I'll leave *nowt* out. Then everyone on the whole of this estate and beyond will know exactly what you are!'

Breathing heavily, they stared each other out. Then:

'Get to bed.' Ivan's tone was tight with unadulterated rage. 'Go on, get out of my sight.'

Renee didn't need telling twice. She flew past him out of the room and sprinted up the stairs.

Only when his snores had steadied, and she was adamant he was asleep, did she slip from beneath her blankets and tiptoe towards the door.

Whilst lying in bed over the past few hours, the tears rolling down her cheeks, she'd slowly come to the conclusion that this wasn't the end of things. Her show of bravado tonight would carry no substance in the long run. All she'd done was made matters a thousand times worse for herself – she should have known better.

Ivan's control over her was slipping and he knew

it. Renee also knew that it would only make him desperate to regain it. Why, how, she couldn't be sure, but he'd make her suffer for what she'd done and the things she'd said. He would that, all right.

Standing stock-still on the landing, she listened out for an age. When at last she was confident that he hadn't been disturbed and she wouldn't be detected, she continued on, down the stairs towards the front door.

The latch lifted noiselessly, much to her gratitude, and seconds later she was dashing across the moonlit road.

'Lass?'

'Aye, Mrs Flynn, it's me,' Renee hissed up at the tousled head that had appeared at the bedroom window at her frantic knocking. 'I'm sorry, I am . . . Please, I must speak to you.'

The woman was opening the door to her in moments: 'Eeh, what's afoot? Come on in—'

'No, I'd best not.' Shooting her house a fearful look over her shoulder, Renee bit her lip. 'I had to come, had to ask you . . .'

'What, lass?'

'Your offer earlier. Well, my answer's yes. Yes, please. Ask your cousin's daughter if she can help get me fixed up. As soon as possible, Mrs Flynn, for I have to get away. I must, 'cause if I have to spend very much longer beneath that roof, I'll finish up stark raving mad.'

Chapter 5

'Morning, lass.'

As she always did, Renee felt the tension rise from her the moment she stepped into Lynn's home. Smiling, she took the boys from their mother and kissed their cheeks in turn. 'Eeh, I've missed these two.'

Lynn laughed. 'It's not even twenty-four hours since you saw them last!'

'I know but I've taken to them. And you,' she said shyly, her cheeks pinkening.

'And the feeling's mutual, lass, aye. Now, I'd best be on my way else owd Briggs will have my guts for garters. You'll be all right?'

She nodded. 'Have a good day, Lynn. Ta-ra.'

'Ta-ra for now. Ta-ra, lads!'

When she'd gone, Renee looked from one baby to the other. 'Right then, you two. How d'you fancy a trip to Daubhill?'

Mrs Flynn had been watching for Ivan leaving for work this morning and had nipped across to number forty-six soon after he'd gone. Renee had been horrified to find her on the doorstep – what if her father should return home for whatever reason, had forgotten something for example – but when she'd heard her neighbour's reason for calling, her anxiety had been quick to switch to excitement.

The woman planned to visit her cousin today, wanted for Renee's sake to put the wheels in motion right away, and she'd asked if Renee fancied joining her on the outing. She'd figured it would be better if she heard whatever details they could glean about the textile works herself, and that although her cousin's daughter would be away at her work, her mother might well be able to throw up some information on the matter.

Renee had readily agreed. Her fear of strangers and their possible negative opinion of her had gradually waned somewhat over the passing weeks. Now, she was more inclined to believe that more good people existed in this world than bad – you only had to look at the new friendships she'd forged of late as proof. Mrs Flynn had assured her that they would be back in Breightmet before Lynn finished her shift at the grocer's with more than enough time to spare. Now, all Renee had to contend with was her nervousness at riding on the tram!

Whether she'd accompanied her parents on public transport in the past, she couldn't recall. Her family had moved to this estate shortly after it was built, when she was a small child, and in her living memory her life had revolved around it ever since. Home, shops, and until a few years ago, school. All were situated within a few minutes' walk of each other – she'd never had a reason to leave Top o'th' Brow at all, and she hadn't done. She just hoped the trams didn't go too fast and make her sick; she'd hate to make an exhibition of herself.

After wrapping Bobby and Brian up well, Renee left the house and, making sure the door was firmly shut behind them, she turned out of the modest garden and headed right in the direction of Monks Lane.

Mrs Flynn had her long grey coat and navy blue headscarf on in readiness when she answered the door to the knock. 'All set, lass?'

'Aye.'

To Renee's relief, the journey was a pleasant one. With a twin on each knee, she watched the passing scenery with interest, realising, not for the first time, just how much she was missing out on in life – there really was a big wide world out here beyond her four walls. And, what's more, if today went well and Mrs Flynn's family could indeed help her – fingers firmly crossed on that – she intended to grasp the opportunity to experience more of it with both hands.

'Here we are, lass,' Mrs Flynn announced some half an hour later when they turned down yet another street of two-up, two-down terraced houses. Nonetheless, despite the drab uniformity, every doorstep they had passed shone from diligent scrubbing and donkey stoning, and the windowsills were free from grime – these people may be poor in money but they were rich in pride. 'This is the one.'

Renee nodded. Then, her insides in knots, she

stood back whilst the woman rapped on the black door and prayed for a positive outcome for all she was worth.

'Hello, Iris! Eeh, this is a nice surprise.' The short, plump woman who answered then broadened her grin to encompass Renee and the children. 'And who're your friends, then?'

'Nice to see you, Maureen. This is Renee, a neighbour of mine, and the babbies belong to another neighbour – Renee here minds them whilst their mother goes out to work. Anyroad, love, are you for letting us over the step or what? My bunions ain't half giving me gyp, and I could murder a brew.'

Chuckling, Maureen waved them inside. 'Come on through and take the weight off your trotters, I'll stick the kettle on.'

Once the three of them had a piping hot cup of tea in their hands and the cousins had enquired over one another's health and exchanged news, Mrs Flynn got down to business.

'Right then, Maureen love, my reason for being here. Young Renee here is interested in war work, and we wondered if your Linda might be able to put in a word to get her taken on at her place.'

Her cousin nodded, then pulled a less-than-hopeful face. 'I can ask her, Iris, by all means. But from what I've heard, there's a queue of girls a mile long wanting employment there. The company's a good one to work for, 'specially now, what with the war, and the pay's not to be sniffed at.'

The bubble of enthusiasm that Renee had carried

with her all morning slowly evaporated and her heart plummeted to her toes. And she'd bet all she owned that those other girls Maureen mentioned would have the advantage of experience over her, too. She didn't stand an earthly. She could have cried.

'Well, if you could ask Linda anyway, love, we'd be grateful,' said Mrs Flynn. 'Her recommendation might just carry that bit more weight, eh, her being a trusted employee. Nowt ventured, nowt gained, and all that.'

Outside, she faced Renee and let her shoulders rise and fall with a small sigh. 'Chin up, lass. No point in looking for bad news before it meets you. Like Maureen said, our Linda will do her best. Let's just wait and see what happens.'

Though not holding out much hope and bitterly disappointed, Renee smiled and nodded nonetheless. To allow her true feelings to show would seem ungrateful, and that was the last thing she wanted to appear. Mrs Flynn had gone out of her way today to do her a good turn and had tried her very best, after all. Renee was loath to throw her generosity back in her face.

They parted company on New Lane after alighting from the tram – Mrs Flynn heading one way for Monks Lane and home, and Renee and the children in the opposite direction towards Padbury Way.

For the first time, this day Renee could garner no pleasure from her work. But one thought dominated her mind and refused to be swayed: her chance of escape was once again next to none. She really was destined to be stuck with her jailor for eternity, wasn't she? Why, *why*, must life be so hard? Some people appeared to sail through it on a golden cloud whilst others were scratching at survival, day in, day out, without a moment's let-up to catch their breath. It just didn't seem fair to her.

Lynn returned home just as Renee was washing the last of the dishes from the twins' meal. As usual, she clicked her tongue softly: 'I've told you, lass, there's no need to do all that. Your job's to mind these two terrors; I'd have seen to the clearing up myself.'

'I don't mind,' she told her, though it was an effort to fetch a smile to her lips. 'Besides, the lads were quiet after their grub – there were nowt else to do, and I like to keep myself busy.'

'Well, you take yourself off home now and put your feet up forra bit, you deserve it. Aye, and I'm for doing the same, I reckon. It's been all go in that grocer's today.'

Though she nodded, Renee knew there would be little chance of her sitting idle when she got home. What with her time taken up by her duties here, she'd been lax on her own housework for days now, and before getting started on the evening meal she intended giving the furniture a good seeing to when she got in.

She had the sideboard and small table beneath the window, which held the old aspidistra, gleaming in no time and, after returning the cloths and polish to their rightful place under the sink, Renee pottered about seeing that everything else was just so.

She straightened the burgundy runner on the mantel, paying attention to the tassels and making sure they were falling neatly, and tweaked the few cheap ornaments and clock back into their rightful places. Next, she plumped up the cushions on the sofa and repositioned the dark wooden chairs at the table. Finally, after nudging the rag rug in front of the hearth a little to the left with the toe of her shoe, she was satisfied that all was as it should be. Nodding, she headed for the kitchen to begin peeling the potatoes.

The meal had been dished up, and the plates placed on top of pans of hot water to prevent the food from drying out, for some time when she noticed her father was later than usual arriving home. Her stomach did an uncomfortable flip at the realisation. *Pray God he's been kept on at the station for longer and that he hasn't got waylaid by the pubs.*

With the way things were between them at present, it would be a sure-fire recipe for disaster. Ivan was insufferable when stone-cold sober; in his cups, he was utterly intolerable . . .

The minutes ticked on, Renee's anxiety growing with them. When the time was nearing ten thirty, she was contemplating taking the front door off the latch and going up to bed when a crashing at the window that nearly put the pane through had her leaping almost clean from her skin. Holding a hand to her racing chest, she rose slowly from the sofa. Then, with her heart in her mouth, she made with trepidation for the hallway.

As she opened the door, her father stumbled forward into the house, catching her off guard and almost knocking her off her feet. Clinging on to the door frame to steady herself, she hazarded a glance at his face. Yet she didn't need to take in the slack-jawed grin or glassy stare to know he was drunk – the stench of strong spirits that emanated from him put her in no doubt whatever. Swallowing a sigh, she closed her eyes.

'Dad.' Taking pains not to evoke his anger, she spoke softly. 'What have you done to yourself?'

'Eh?'

'Just look at you. It's a wonder you managed to find your way home . . .' Her words petered out as her gaze came to rest on what he was holding. *What the . . . ?*

Seeing she'd noticed, Ivan's tongue shot out to lick the spittle from his lips as though he was mightily pleased with himself. Tapping the side of his nose clumsily, he gave a slow wink. 'Ah-ha. I bet you're wondering what I've got here, ain't yer? Shall I tell you?'

'I can see what you've got.' A terrible foreboding was washing over her. 'A bottle of whisky and an axe.'

'Ah no, that's where you're wrong, you see. This is a present for me,' he said, lifting up the bottle. 'And *this* . . .' He swiped the tool through the air between them, making her flinch. 'This is a present for you.'

'I, I don't want it,' she stammered in her fear and confusion, backing away into the living room. 'Dad, please . . . You're scaring me.'

He answered with a guttural laugh. Then, without another word, he spun on his heel and stumbled at speed back into the hallway.

Struck dumb and trembling from head to toe, Renee gazed upwards as bangs and thumps seeped through the ceiling. What he was doing up there, she hadn't the slightest idea, and one thing was clear: she certainly had no intention of venturing up to find out! Her father, mad with drink and wielding a dangerous and deadly weapon . . .? Wild horses wouldn't have dragged her up those stairs.

Minutes later, his footfalls sounded on the landing, then there he was.

Forcing her stare up to meet him as he staggered into the living room, her eyes widened to saucers and a cry left her lips. 'Dad, no! What are you doing!'

Swaying on the spot, he jerked his chin to the mound of broken and splintered wood – that had shortly before been her bed – piled in his arms. 'Why waste it, eh? Make sound firewood, this will.'

With that, and before Renee had a chance to move, Ivan dashed to the fire and launched the lot on top. He made for the stairs again and returned this time with handfuls of her bedding, which were quick to follow the same route as the furniture.

Locked in shock, watching the orange flames lick over her possessions, she had tears coursing down her cheeks.

'You're a slut.'

Feeling her soul wither to nothing, Renee dipped her head.

'What are you? Say it.'

'A slut,' she rasped.

'But not just any slut, no. You're *my* slut. Ain't that right?'

She bobbed her head.

'Nowt can change that, nowt. So don't you ever even think to defy me – deny me – again. Well? Are you hearing me?'

Again, she nodded.

'Now then. I think I'm ready for my meal.'

She tore her eyes, raw with misery, from the smouldering, devastating scene. Then, as if in a trance, she turned and headed for the kitchen.

Some time later, Ivan pushed his empty plate away and burped loudly. 'I enjoyed that,' he announced. Then he hooked his finger towards where Renee sat, perched on the arm of the sofa gazing into space, and beckoned her across. And, with nothing left inside of her any more to fight, she obeyed.

Having led her up the stairs by the hand, he pushed her on ahead of him into his bedroom. Renee offered no resistance, nor did she give her own door even half of a glance. That room was gone from her. They would share a room now, and they would share a bed. Father and daughter – husband and wife? Just what did it matter any more? What did *any* of it matter?

She'd been stupid to think she could stand up to

him, stop him, should have known better than to try.
Stupid.

*I'm stupid, stupid, stupid, stupid. A slut, a slut. Foul,
rancid, worthless. Dead inside.*

'Please, God. Let me die.'

'Please, God,' Renee repeated into the darkness several hours later, when the ordeal was finally over and
Ivan was snoring beside her, his arm flung across her
stomach, his sour breath fanning her neck. 'Please.
Please . . .'

Chapter 6

'Brrr! Eeh, it's perishing!'

Smiling, Lynn let Renee inside. Rubbing her arms as she led the way into the living room, the woman shook her head. 'I've got goosepimples on me the size of gobstoppers and I were only at that door then a few seconds! We're in forra bad 'un, I reckon, this year.'

Blowing into her cupped hands to tease some life into her frozen fingers, Renee nodded in agreement. Over the past weeks, the temperature had plummeted alarmingly. She couldn't recall a winter this intense before. Even Mrs Flynn had said she'd never known cold like it in all her born days. This first Christmas of the war was set to prove a harsh and difficult time, in more ways than one, for everyone.

'Now, there's plenty of coal in t' coal shed, so don't be shy with the shovel, lass. Keep them flames fed and the lads and yourself toasty warm. All right?'

'Aye, Lynn.'

'There's a pan of broth on t' stove for your dinners and it's got plenty of barley in it; will fill youse up nicely. Now, I'd best be on my way.'

Renee relieved her of the children and watched as she donned her coat, wrapped a thick, red woollen scarf around her head and pulled on matching gloves. Then, telling Bobby and Brian to wave to their mother, and smiling when they wagged their podgy hands, she bade Lynn goodbye before settling down in the comfortable chair by the blazing fire.

'So, then, you two,' she said to the boys, sitting them in her lap and hugging them close. 'Who's coming to visit youse tomorrow when you're all tucked up fast asleep? That's right, Father Christmas.' The purity and innocence shining from their perfect little faces made her heart melt. This was how it should be always, with all children. 'I wonder what he'll fetch you, eh? A toy each perhaps?' Grinning, she nodded. 'How about . . . a doll and a drum and a kick up the bum!'

Bouncing up and down, the boys shrieked with laughter, and Renee had to turn her face away to hide the tears that had sprung to her eyes.

Her mam used to say that same line to her each year, when Renee had been attempting to wheedle a clue out of her as to what gift she might receive. The memory had come from nowhere, catching her unawares, and the renewed sear of loss was breath-snatching. Sylvia Rushmore had been on her daughter's mind a lot more of late.

In sharp contrast, home life was something she dwelled upon as little as was humanly possible. Not that she had the energy for it, even if the inclination had been there – which of course it wasn't; she didn't want to think.

She felt hollowed out these days, her life force sucked dry. Her will to go forward, battle on for a new start, had deserted her. The dream had been but a fantasy that would never be hers, she knew that now. Why torture herself with possibilities, when for her, they were as distant as the sun? And so, she didn't. This was her lot, and this she accepted. Nothing would save her now.

Lynn was working a longer shift. Christmas Eve would dawn tomorrow on a Sunday, and so the last opportunity to buy for the festivities was today – the shops would be busier than usual. Thankfully, however, Ivan was working later, too, and so Renee wouldn't miss his return and be caught out, glory be to God.

With her own shopping in mind and thoughts of the stack of work awaiting her the following day with preparations for the meal, Renee sighed. Then seconds later as realisation came – she would be lucky to get to bed before midnight, and a blessing that would be despite her exhaustion – she found herself brightening.

She could, she supposed, stretch out the inevitable tomorrow even longer. If she took her time, she might not be finished with her duties until one, perhaps two . . . and Ivan would surely be asleep by then? She could bed down on the sofa, and if he questioned her the next morning, she'd say she must have been so worn out she'd fallen asleep. One night away from that bedroom would be heaven; it was certainly worth trying? Oh, it was – that is what she'd do.

With the plan cemented, she knew a modicum of happiness and she went about the rest of her morning with a smile at her mouth and a lightness in her heart. When the afternoon rolled around and she and the twins had finished their dinner, it was time to head to the shops to collect the provisions she'd ordered in readiness the day before, and her spirits lifted further still.

Swept along with the yuletide atmosphere, the housewives and store owners of the estate would be more jovial and livelier than normal this day, Renee knew, which was always nice to witness. And, with any luck, she might bump into Mrs Flynn on her travels, and they could enjoy a quick natter on the walk to Monks Lane before Renee dropped off the shopping at home.

Soon, the children were wrapped up in their pram, and Renee was directing it through the garden gate. Peering ahead towards the shops a short distance away and spying the steady stream of customers that were coming and going, their breath glowing white in the cold air and fanning their faces as they laughed and joked and called out best wishes for the season to one another, put a spring in her step. Smiling, she hurried on.

Her first port of call was the grocer's. There were several people in front of her, but Seymour and Lynn's speed and efficiency made short work of the queue, and in no time, it was Renee's turn to be served.

Seeing her approaching the counter, the grocer

held up a finger to indicate that he wouldn't be a moment, before disappearing out back. He returned with a small wooden crate pre-packed with her potatoes, carrots, turnip and sprouts.

Renee brought out her purse, paid him, and returned it to her pocket. She lifted the crate and, after carrying it outside to where she'd left the pram by the door, she stooped and balanced it carefully in the metal basket between the wheels. Then she straightened, popped her head back inside the shop and thanked Seymour and shyly wished him a merry Christmas, which he returned with uncharacteristic cheerfulness. A quick wave to Lynn, and a thumbs up to let her know that the boys were all right, and Renee was ready to tackle the butcher's.

Here, it was much busier and the medley of voices vying for Gordon's attention reached Renee's ears before she'd opened the door: 'Come on, lad, shake a leg. I've much to be getting on with back home; ain't got time to waste hanging around here.'

'That's right!' called out another woman. 'If you go any slower, you, you'll stop. Ay, there's no danger of you meeting yourself coming back, nay!'

Pausing in his task of weighing out an order, the butcher pointed a pork sausage at the customers in turn. 'One more remark like that out of you, Maud and Alice, and I'll take my foot to your backsides. You'll be out there in the cold without an ounce of meat between youse. See what your owd men will have to say when you're forced to serve them up for their dinner on Monday egg and chips, and all because you're too ruddy impatient to wait a few minutes like everyone else.'

'Here, hold your horses, Gordon lad, we were only pulling your leg. Weren't we, Alice?' Maud was quick to respond. The butcher was good for a laugh, it was true, but you never could tell how far you could push your luck with some folk, and it wasn't worth risking depriving her husband of his Christmas turkey. 'You're doing a gradely job, lad, under the circumstances and don't let no one tell you no different!'

'Oh aye, I'll second that.' Alice nodded vigorously, sending her ample chins swaying in all directions. 'Sound as a pound is Gordon, and I'll flatten anyone what says otherwise!'

'All right, ladies, all right.' The mountain of a man held up his hands in defeat with a wink. 'Bloomin' 'eck, my head's big enough as it is. Any more from you two and, come the end of the day, I'll not be able to get through the door.'

Relieved that their words had done the trick, the customers smiled back sweetly, then wisely fell silent. As for Renee, she'd found the exchange hilarious. Thankful the women had their backs to her and couldn't see her shaking shoulders, she banked down a chuckle and awaited her turn to be served.

'Eeh, I'm fagged!' Gordon announced minutes later, after greeting Renee at the counter. He whipped out a snowy handkerchief from his trouser pocket, dabbed at his glistening brow, then bestowed upon her a dazzling grin. 'All right, lass?'

'I am, ta, Mr Wallace. I'm here to collect the turkey I ordered.'

'Right you are, lass, right you are. It's a small bird you asked for, weren't it?' he confirmed, reaching to the poultry hanging by their necks on silver hooks suspended from the ceiling.

'Aye, that's right.'

'Owt else? You'll no doubt get a few meals out of this to see you through the next couple of days – aye, and the same goes for the rest of the nation – myself included! Turkey pie on Boxing Day, turkey casserole on the twenty-seventh . . . and not forgetting the cold turkey butties in between! It's a good job we only eat it once a year, eh, else we'd soon grow sick of it. Anyroad, where was I . . .?' He scratched his bewhiskered face in thought, then clicked his fingers. 'Oh aye, that were it. Is there owt else you're wanting? Summat for tonight and tomorrow's evening meal, like?'

'Well, I've stuff in for tonight's meal, so I'll just have half a pound of sausages for tomorrow, please.'

Gordon nodded and moved to collect the tray in the window.

Whilst he prepared her parcel, Renee asked, 'Mr Wallace, has Mrs Flynn been in today?'

He passed her purchase across, and after taking her money shook his head. 'Iris? No, lass, not yet. She'll be in soon enough, no doubt.'

'Aye. Well thanks, Mr Wallace, and a very merry Christmas to you.'

'And to you, lass! Take care, now, ta-ra.'

Returning outside to the twins, Renee smiled to see they had dropped off to sleep snuggled up together, then placed the meat beside the vegetables. She'd turned the pram around and was making for home to drop her shopping off when she spotted a familiar figure turning out of Monks Lane and heading in her direction. Lifting a hand in greeting, she hastened to catch Mrs Flynn up.

'By, it's bloody Baltic!' the woman declared, stamping her feet to get the circulation moving. Nodding down at the children, she smiled. 'They look cosy enough all right, at any rate, lucky devils.'

'I thought I might catch you in the shops, but Mr Wallace said you hadn't been in.'

'Aye, I'm a bit behind today getting my bits in; the tree was delivered, and I've been busy putting it up.' She grinned. 'It's daft, I know, at my age. But eeh, I do love having a nice tree up at this time of year. It don't feel like a proper Christmas without one, does it, lass?'

Though Renee murmured agreement, she knew a pang of loss for Christmases past. Truth was, since her mother left, aside from their meal the Rushmore household barely acknowledged the festive period with more than a passing glance.

Ivan refused to fritter his hard-earned brass on what he considered 'the trimmings and trappings of just another day'. No brightly dressed tree or colourful decorations adorned their home any more on Christmas Day. The living room remained as bleak as it always did – to go hand in hand with the atmosphere in general.

''Ere, and speaking of trees, that Gordon Wallace had better have put a decent-sized turkey aside for me, that's all I can say, or I'll have his you-know-whats for baubles,' Iris added, then sighed with pleasure. 'I've our Maureen and Linda coming to mine this year for dinner, you see – I'm not letting nowt spoil it. It'll be a belter, aye. Mind you, I'll likely not be mithered about owt if our Maureen's on her usual good form.' She winked. 'My cousin fetches enough milk stout along to sink a battleship and I'll be too squiffy to care about anything once I've a couple of bottles down my neck.'

Renee had a vision of the threesome sat in the woman's warm and cosy living room, and it made her chest ache with longing. It all sounded so lovely. A day surrounded by family and love, laughter and merriment. Happy. Normal. Exactly as it should be. What she wouldn't give to be part of something like that herself.

'It'll be magical, Mrs Flynn, I'm sure,' she told her whilst praying she hadn't let her envy show. 'I'd best be getting on now; don't like to keep the babies out too long in this cold. Ta-ra for now.'

'Lass?'

Having already begun to walk away, Renee turned her head to glance over her shoulder. 'Aye, Mrs Flynn?'

'You know I'd have you over to mine on Monday in a heartbeat if it were possible, don't you?' she said earnestly. 'There's nowt I'd like better, aye. But well . . .'

'I know,' Renee replied softly. She smiled. 'You're a very kind woman, and my life's all the better for having you as a friend. Don't be worrying over me, I'll be all right.'

Fifteen minutes later, with her shopping deposited in her own house and she and the boys back in the warmth at Padbury Way, Renee took a sip of her tea and flicked her eyes around the room, trying to visualise what it would look like when Lynn had finished with it. Her employer had had a tree delivered, too – she'd seen it earlier standing propped against the wall in the back garden. Lynn would have the place looking wonderful and festive, she'd bet. Bobby and Brian were truly fortunate to be part of such a loving family.

It was several hours later, when Lynn's shift was over and she'd relieved Renee of her duties and sent her on her way with a hug and a kiss and her best wishes for the season, that Renee came up with an idea.

Passing through New Lane and on down Monks Lane, she couldn't fail to wonder over the activities going on behind the black-covered windows of the houses and just how very different it would be in her own home. Everywhere she looked, people would be busy preparing for a brilliant Christmas – everyone bar her, it seemed. And really, by rights, shouldn't they all be doing their utmost, this year in particular, to do all in their power to make this Christmas even better than any that had gone before? Show the enemy that despite it all, Britain and her people wouldn't be cowed, *wouldn't* be brought down?

She had more to be thankful for than most. So many families up and down the land would be spending the festive period pining for folk they loved. She was lucky in that respect. Of course, Renee would be missing her mother, but she didn't have the heartache of her children being evacuated, of brothers or uncles or cousins or a loving father off fighting, risking life and limb for King and country, to fret over. She was spared that at least, glory be, and she ought to be more grateful, ought to be making the most of what others would give their eye teeth for.

She should do something about it, aye. What's more, she ruddy well would.

If Ivan wasn't willing to put in an ounce of effort, then she would make sure she did instead. There was nothing stopping her, after all.

Upon entering number forty-six, Renee made straight for the stairs and her old room.

As she knew she would, she found what she was looking for right away: the axe Ivan had used to wreak destruction on her bed, still lying in the middle of the floor where he'd discarded it weeks before. She nodded firmly. Then she snatched it up and ran with it down to the living room.

Here, she made for the sideboard and pulled open the deep bottom drawer. A quick rummage around and she emerged triumphant with her father's torch. She checked to see if the batteries still held life and was gladdened to see that they did. Drawing in a determined breath, she crossed the room and left the house.

Renee turned right and, walking at a sensible pace lest she lost her footing in the blackout, set off for the nearby woodland. She kept the jaundice glow from the torch directed at the ground, as the populace had been instructed they must by the government when venturing out at night, until she was safely in the fields, then shone the light up and around.

One after the other, each tree that her eyes came to rest upon proved unsuitable: all were either full-grown and too large or very young and weak-looking saplings. Then her gaze alighted on a shrub-like plant a short walk away – full and thick and just the right height. True, it wasn't the tree she'd envisaged, and just what type it was she hadn't a clue, but it nonetheless looked perfect. Her mind made up, she strode towards it.

Positioning the torch on the grass, so that it shone on the main woody stem where she needed to strike, she held the axe in both hands and took aim. The first swing made good contact. A few more, and with a creak and a snap, the bush swayed, then fell to the ground.

With a soft whoop, Renee tucked the axe under her arm and picked up the torch. With her free hand, she clasped the severed stem and, dragging the makeshift Christmas tree behind her, made her slow and steady way back the way she had come.

'Excuse me— Oh, I'm sorry, I didn't mean to startle you.'

The voice had come from nowhere, within moments of her emerging into the street – Renee's squeak of fear still clung to the frost-stroked air between them. Dropping the shrub, she held a hand to her thumping heart and brought the torch up to shine it in the stranger's face: 'Who goes there?'

A lad around her own age came into focus – blinded by the glare, he put up his arm to shield his eyes. 'I'm looking for Tarzan, my dog. When I saw you coming off the field, well, I wondered if you might have seen him at all down there.'

Renee brought the torch down to chest level and, when the lad lowered his arm, scrutinised him discreetly. She recognised that voice somehow, she was certain of it . . .

'So, did you see him?'

Embarrassed that she'd been staring at him for so long without a word – he must surely think her a complete simpleton – she blushed furiously. 'Sorry, I . . . no. No, I didn't notice no dog.'

The lad closed his eyes and released a deep sigh. 'Well, that's me freezing to death 'til all hours until he's found. He's a terror, that one, is always up to these tricks,' he said. Then a grin spread across his face, revealing strong white teeth and bringing a twinkle to his dark green eyes. 'That's why he's called Tarzan. Ever since being a pup he's been drawn like a magnet to them woods, would live in them trees if we let him.'

Remembering her mother telling her when she was younger the strange story of the boy raised by animals, a nostalgic smile lifted the corners of her mouth. 'The jungle prince.'

'Aye, that's right. Well, we have our very own *forest* prince – though you'd think he were more of a ruddy king the way he has us running about after him!'

His laughter was infectious – Renee giggled. 'Well, I hope you find him soon. I'd better be going, now.'

'Oh. Aye, course.' He motioned down at the shrub by her feet but didn't question it, asking instead, 'Do you need a hand with that?'

'No, ta. I can manage.'

He nodded, smiled. 'Ta-ra, then.'

'Ta-ra,' she echoed, flashing him a shy smile in return and continuing for her house.

'I'm Jimmy, by the way.'

She'd reached the other side of the road when the words rang out, taking her by surprise; she thought he would have gone by now. But no – turning, she discovered he was still standing where she'd left him, watching her. Her lips parted to tell him her name, then clamped shut again. *God above, if her father was ever to catch wind of this.* Then from nowhere, something deep within her stirred, and her chin lifted without her say-so in unfamiliar yet burning defiance. *To hell with Ivan Rushmore.* Where was the harm in it? Besides, he would never know . . .

'I'm Renee,' she called back.

'Well, it was nice meeting you, Renee. Goodnight. And Merry Christmas.'

'You too, Jimmy.'

His smile saw her on her way, and for the first time

in many a long year Renee noticed she was inexplicably happy. If it hadn't been for her weighty cargo, she reckoned she might have floated home.

'Eeh, what a godawful bloody shift that was—'

'D'you like it, Dad?'

Ivan had juddered to a halt on the threshold of the living room. His eyes wide, he took in every inch slowly.

'I got the tree off the field. And I found the Christmas ornaments in that box on top of your wardrobe.' Reaching out, Renee fingered gently the colourful glass baubles hanging from the stubby branches that were twinkling like stars in the glow of the gas lamp. She'd even nipped across to Mrs Flynn's house earlier and begged from her an old newspaper, and this she'd cut into strips, hooping the pieces together to create a few paper chains, which she'd draped around the sideboard and mantel top.

'And look at these, Dad,' she went on, her pleasure in her work bringing forth a childlike exuberance. 'Don't they look nice?'

Coming to stand beside her, Ivan surveyed the greenery adorning the mirror and the pictures on the walls.

'It's holly from that bush what grows wild behind the back garden. I pulled some through the slats in the fence and snipped a few sprigs off.'

He stabbed at one of the leaves with his finger. 'They're all sparkly.'

'Aye. You dip them in a strong solution of Epsom

salts, leave them to dry, and they turn out all frosted. Clever, eh?'

'How've you learned to do that?'

'Oh, I overheard some women talking about it in the shop,' she lied. Mrs Flynn had been the one to give her the tip along with the newspaper. 'Anyroad, all this . . . I just thought it'd be nice to make an effort this Christmas forra change.'

In the silence that followed as Renee awaited his response, Ivan gave the room a last sweeping look. Then he nodded once and crossed to the table.

'I'm clemmed – what have we got to eat?'

Though disappointed by his lack of praise or even enthusiasm, Renee wasn't surprised. He hadn't gone mad or disagreed with what she'd done, which was something to be thankful for, she supposed. This she would have to be content with.

As they ate, she made mention as subtly as she could of all the work she had to do tomorrow night: 'There's the pudding to see to first – I want to get that out of the way as it'll mean one less thing to do on Christmas Day. And I'll prepare the bird ready, an' all, then I'll only have to put it in the oven on the morning. I think I'll peel all the veg as well while I'm at it and leave it in pans of cold water. Then there's the cleaning. I want everything to be spick and span, aye.' She paused to shoot him a glance and gauge his reaction before adding, 'I'll be on t' go for hours, I reckon.'

Ivan shoved a piece of bread into his mouth, chewed and swallowed, then lifted his head to look at her. Then he shrugged and resumed his meal. 'It's no skin off my nose. I'm fagged anyroad, could do with a few nights of sound sleep. I'll no doubt be akip the minute my head hits the pillow.'

Thank God. Masking a relieved smile, she returned her attention to her own food.

That night, with her chores completed and her father sleeping the sleep of the exhausted, Renee settled down in his bed and heaved a long and contented sigh. How lovely it would be tomorrow not to have to lie beside him – for one glorious night at least. She intended to enjoy it for all she was worth, she determined.

Though she'd have liked to have enjoyed her dreaming a bit longer, she found that her eyelids were flickering within seconds, leaving her precious little time to relish the situation to come.

'Today has been one of the best of my life,' she murmured drowsily, snuggling into the blankets and smiling in the darkness.

Just before sleep claimed her, the image of a handsome lad with brown hair and dancing eyes floated welcomingly into her mind to cement the fact.

Chapter 7

THE AROMA OF roasting turkey and potatoes was heavenly; Renee breathed it in with quiet satisfaction. All that was left to do now was to light the gas under the pans of vegetables and then, later on, make the gravy. Everything was running smoothly and on schedule. Even last night had, as she'd hoped, gone without a hitch – Ivan had made no mention of her bedding down on the sofa as per her plan. Perhaps this Christmas might not be as bad as the couple that had gone before it after all.

'Well, I have to say, lass, you've surpassed yourself this year,' Ivan stated later, putting down his knife and fork. He loosened the button on his trousers and breathed in relief. 'That's better. By, I'm stuffed.'

'Will I fetch the pudding in now, Dad, or wait a bit?' She was already half-rising from her chair as she spoke, and her father put a hand on her wrist and stopped her:

'Wait a bit. I wanted to . . . well, I've got summat for you.'

'A present?' Dropping back into her seat, she stared

at him in surprise. Along with everything else, gifts at Christmas had become a thing of the past when her mother left. 'What is it?'

He fiddled in his waistcoat pocket and pulled something out. Then he motioned for Renee to hold out her hand and dropped the object into her palm.

'Dad?' She glanced up at him, then back down. 'A key?'

'Aye. It's to your mam's wardrobe. I thought, well, mebbe you might like the things of hers what she left behind.'

Renee released a small gasp. 'Oh aye, Dad, I would. *Course* I would. But why now?'

'Well, you've been a good girl again lately, ain't given me no bother. I reckon you've earned yourself a treat.'

The implication was clear: he was rewarding his daughter for moving into his bed, as he'd insisted, without kicking up a fuss. The truth of it made her skin prickle with familiar shame and disgust; however, she dampened it down and told herself it didn't matter – gaining possession of the key overrode everything. Gripping it tightly, she held her bunched fist to her chest and made herself meet Ivan's gaze. Then she brought a smile to her lips and murmured, 'Ta.'

'Merry Christmas, Renee.'

'Merry Christmas, Dad.'

'Go on,' he relented, watching her staring longingly at the door. 'You're excused.'

Bursting with expectation, giddy with impatience,

Renee had bolted from the room and was taking the stairs two at a time in seconds.

As she entered the bedroom and made for the dark brown wardrobe by the window, her mind conjured up all sorts of possibilities she might find inside. Photographs were her main desire – as time had rolled on, she'd struggled to remember her mother's face properly. And she did recall there being at least one framed image of her and Ivan downstairs when Renee was younger – a picture taken on their wedding day stuck in her memory particularly, aye. By, it would be great to discover that, please God.

Her hands shook slightly as she inserted the key, and when she heard the lock spring back her heart did a merry dance against her breastbone. Licking her lips, she closed her fingers around the door handle and eased it open.

Several items of clothing hung still on the rail. Smiling, Renee fingered them one after another. Then she stood on tiptoe and felt along the built-in shelf above. She put each thing she lifted down into a neat pile on the floor. Finally, after brushing her hand across the surface one last time, and satisfied there was nothing on the shelf she'd missed, she lowered herself to her knees and studied the items one by one.

With a soft cry, Renee lifted a hairbrush and mirror set backed in tortoiseshell and held it to her cheek. She remembered these so well, recalled vividly sitting on the edge of her parents' bed after her bath each week and her mother teasing out the knots in her hair with gentle strokes, whilst Renee distracted herself from the discomfort by studying her reflection in the hand-held looking glass.

There were a few old hair slides, each missing a full set of teeth, a compact of cracked face powder and a small white puff, a tube of lipstick in soft pink, several lengths of ribbon in various shades . . . Two crumpled pieces of paper revealed, when Renee smoothed them open, drawings of animals in a young child's shaky hand, which had her shedding a few tears to think her mother had deemed her daughter's artwork special enough to keep for all those years. Yet it was the last item she came to that had her weeping harder and wishing more than she ever had before for answers: her mother's wedding band.

Imagining Sylvia removing the ring that had bound her to Ivan – and shedding the invisible shackles in the process – was like a knife in Renee's heart. Her mother was *so* lucky. If only it was in her power to do the same . . .

'Why, Mam?' she whispered to the cold and dreary room. 'Why didn't you take me with you? How could you leave me here with him? Didn't you love me enough, was that it?'

Of course, as usual, no answers were forthcoming. There likely never would be.

A few minutes later, feeling more composed, she scrubbed the emotion from her face and carefully placed everything back inside the wardrobe. She locked the door, dropped the key into the pocket of her pinny and headed for the stairs.

Though disappointed that there had been no photographs after all, it was nonetheless lovely to now have what items she did. Her dad had likely destroyed the pictures, either torn them up or fed them to the fire long ago. Why he hadn't discarded the remainder of his wife's possessions that she'd either chosen to leave behind, or had been in too much of a hurry to pack, she didn't know. Nor did it matter really. They were here, and they were now hers, and that was the main thing.

Ivan made no mention of it when she re-entered the living room, simply continued smoking his pipe by the good fire, and Renee likewise said nothing. For once, he'd done the right thing; they both knew it. Years too late, maybe – those items could have helped to make her feel closer to her mother, fetched her a modicum of comfort over the last few years – but better now than never, she supposed.

'Are you ready for afters, now, Dad? Another cup of tea, perhaps, to go with it?'

He winked, nodded. 'Aye, go on, lass.'

Renee collected the small bottle of brandy from the pantry and, after pouring a little on top of the dark brown pudding, she struck a match and set the top alight. Poking out her tongue in concentration, her gaze never leaving the shimmering blue flames, she carried it through. The sight induced a round of applause from Ivan. She'd just placed the glass dish on the table and stepped back to survey her handiwork properly when a knock sounded at the door.

'Who the bloody hell can that be?' her father said

in astonishment. Then his eyes turned suspicious, and he pointed a finger in Renee's direction. 'Do you know owt about this?'

'Course not.' She was as flummoxed as him. 'I'll go and see, Dad. It's likely just the warden on his ARP duties – I bet we've a bit of light showing somewhere.'

Yet it wasn't Ralph Robertson at all.

'Mrs Flynn?' Renee's involuntary delight at seeing her friend swiftly turned to horror as common sense hit. 'What are you doing here?' she hissed.

'Fret not, lass, I'll not stop long.' She spoke in a loud, theatrical whisper, and Renee could tell by her bright eyes and cherry cheeks that the milk stout she'd mentioned, which their Maureen normally supplied, had indeed put in an appearance again this year. It was clear she was more than a tad merry and that with her inhibitions dulled, she'd seen no harm in taking the risk coming here, blast it. 'I just came to say that our Linda has some news. You know, about you gaining employment at her place?'

'Aye?' Renee barely registered the words, was too busy shooting glances over her own shoulder in case Ivan suddenly appeared. 'And what news is it?'

'You'll not believe it, lass.'

'Please, I must get back inside . . . Just tell me.'

'They've agreed to interview you.'

'Wha . . .?' Now, her neighbour had her full attention. She slapped a hand to her mouth in all-consuming excitement. 'I never dreamed . . . When is it, Mrs Flynn?'

'Three days' time, lass. You've to be there at half past eleven on t' dot.'

'I will. I'll be there. Oh, Mrs Flynn . . .!'

'Eeh, don't take on so. You go on inside now and enjoy the rest of your Christmas. I just had to come across and tell you, lass, knew you'd be over t' moon to hear it.'

'Thank you. Truly. And please thank Linda for me, won't you?'

'That I will, lass. Goodnight, God bless.'

'Goodnight, God bless. Ta-ra.'

After she'd closed the front door, Renee sucked in several deep breaths before attempting to return to the living room. Her heart was threatening to smash through her chest and she felt light-headed. It was happening. It actually was! Right from the very start she'd convinced herself she didn't stand a chance, and with the passing weeks had accepted that she'd been correct in her assumption all along. Now this! She could barely comprehend it.

'Well?' Ivan barked when she re-entered.

Thinking on her feet, and worried he might have overheard the visitor's tone to be that of a woman, Renee decided that honesty was the best policy – in part at least. 'It weren't the warden, Dad, but a neighbour from over the road. She came to ask if we could change a two bob bit for her for the gas meter, what with the shops being shut. I told her we only had enough coppers for our own.'

Her father gave a satisfied nod. 'You did right, an' all. Nosey bloody mob, they are, on this estate. Give them an inch and they'll take a mile, aye; will be in our business before you can say Jack Robinson.'

And that would never do, would it, Dad, with the secrets you have to hide, she retorted inwardly, turning her attention back to the pudding. *Well, I've got one over on you this time, oh, have I. And the best part about it? You haven't the slightest clue. See, Ivan Rushmore, you're not as wily as you think you are, are you? Not by a long chalk.*

Iris was full of apologies on Wednesday when Renee met her in the street on their way to the shops: 'Eeh, I'm that sorry for turning up as I did, lass, don't know what I were thinking . . . I'd supped one too many, I'm embarrassed to say. Your dad didn't cotton on, didn't overhear me, did he?'

'It's all right, really. I'm glad you came to tell me. It's all what's kept me going these past days. And no, Dad doesn't know, thank the Lord.'

The woman nodded, relieved. 'So, you're all ready for tomorrow then?'

'As I'll ever be. Oh, Mrs Flynn, I'm that nervous.'

'Never mind all that – chin up, chest out, lass. Pretend you feel confident and before too long, you'll start to believe it, aye. It's a case of mind over matter. You'll likely not get another opportunity, so you make the most of it, do your best. All right?'

Renee nodded determinedly. 'I'll do whatever it takes, I swear it. Too much depends on this going well.'

'I know. Fret not, you'll be just fine.'

Everything had fallen into place beautifully.

Tomorrow was Lynn's day off at the grocer's which meant Renee wasn't needed to mind the twins. The time of the interview wasn't too early that she'd have been unable to slip away before her father left for work, and wasn't late enough that she wouldn't be back home before his shift ended. She even had a nice new outfit to wear to make a good impression. Well, not new exactly, but it was better than anything she owned.

Having gone through her mother's leftover clothing again, this time more thoroughly, she'd come across a white nylon blouse and a granite-coloured, calf-length skirt that to her sheer delight had fitted her like a glove. She'd looked so grown up, hardly recognised herself, and took satisfaction in the fact that she'd inherited her mother's height and build entirely. It made her feel part of her again in a way she couldn't describe.

Add to these the pale green voile scarf, which she'd found crumpled up in the foot of the wardrobe, and Renee knew she had the perfect outfit. It would be a pity about her feet, mind you. The plain, walnut-coloured court shoes – the only pair she possessed – were old-fashioned and down at heel, had definitely seen better days. But well, you couldn't have everything, could you, and she was sure she'd still pass muster.

That evening, the minutes appeared to crawl along, and hours seemed an eternity. Not even the prospect of sharing a bed with her father could dampen her desire to see the back of today, not this night. For she knew that the sooner she went to sleep, the sooner the morning would be here and, oh please Lord, the start of what may well be a brand-new life could begin.

It was well into the early hours when Renee did eventually drop off, despite her best intentions. Fizzing excitement had kept her staring wide-eyed through the darkness, whilst an oblivious Ivan snored a bad chorus beside her.

'Wherever you are, hear my prayers, Mam, and send me strength tomorrow,' she murmured in her mind.

On that note, she finally drifted off to sleep.

Chapter 8

THE FOLLOWING DAY, Ivan awoke with a raging cold.

Taking one look at his streaming eyes and bright red nose as he coughed and wheezed his way into the living room, all Renee's hopes and dreams came crashing down around her ears. She couldn't believe this. It was almost as if, subconsciously, he somehow knew . . .

'Christ, I feel rotten.'

'You'll be going to the station, though, won't you, Dad?' she asked with barely suppressed horror.

Before he had a chance to answer, he was forced to whip out his hanky from his dressing-gown pocket and release a series of explosive sneezes. Gasping for breath, he peered up at her witheringly. 'Does it look like I'm fit for work? It's back to bed I'm bound for and nowt else.'

'Happen a Beecham's powder will put you right.' She was dangerously close to tears by now. 'I'll mix you one, eh, shall I?'

To her great relief, he nodded. Unprepared to waste a second, and afraid he might change his mind, she left him standing looking like death warmed up and dashed off to the kitchen. All fingers and thumbs in her desperation, she emptied a packet of the white powder into a cup of water and carried it through.

'I hate that stuff.'

'I know, but it'll make you feel better. Go on, drink it all, and I'll brew a pot of tea to take the taste away.'

Renee waited, watching him like a hawk, as he gulped it down amidst groans of dissatisfaction. He handed the empty cup back to her and she made for the other room once again, saying over her shoulder with more confidence than she felt, 'You wait and see, Dad. You'll feel right as rain in no time.'

In the seclusion of the kitchen, she gripped the sink with both hands and closed her eyes. Why now? *Why*, of all the days it could happen, did it have to be this one? How come fate had it in for her so much – just when would she ever catch a break at all? What was she going to do?

'How you feeling?' Placing the teapot on the table, Renee hazarded a look at him. 'Any better?'

'No.'

She hated to admit it, but she could see that he meant it. His pallor was that of dirty putty and his breathing was laboured.

'I feel worse if owt,' Ivan added in a pained voice. 'If I don't lie down soon, I'll fall down. I'm off back to bed.'

'But . . .'

'Fetch my tea up, will you, lass?'

No. *No*. God damn it!

What now?

Was this it? Had he snatched her only chance of escaping here from under her nose without him even realising it? Was it really all lost to her? Or could she still see this through, sneak out to the interview, after all? Surely if he felt as bad as he claimed and looked to be, he'd be asleep soon? And if he should waken and find her gone . . .? Well, she could say she'd been to the shops. Aye, that could work. Couldn't it? Would she get away with it?

The agonising questions swam dizzyingly through her brain as she poured out the tea, added milk and sugar, then carried a cup up the stairs.

She entered the bedroom and placed the drink on the bedside chest. Now, when she addressed him, her tone was soothing, gentle, her mind made up: 'Happen you are better off in bed, Dad; you look terrible. Take a sip of your tea then lie down and get a good sleep, eh?' she told him, doing her utmost to act as natural as she could. 'A nice long kip will do you the power of good.'

Ivan grunted agreement and began to lament again how awful he felt, but Renee had stopped listening. Her gaze had suddenly lighted on the wardrobe, and now she was filled once more with devastation as her dream of landing the job and the possibilities that would bring began to slip from her grasp once more. The clothes! She'd never manage to smuggle them out of here with her father present. Why hadn't she put her mother's things in her own bedroom the moment she had that key in her hand? Why had she left everything in that damned wardrobe? God, she could kick herself. She could really!

'Are you even listening to me?'

'What? Oh aye. Course I am. But mebbe you should rest, now, eh?' Trying her hardest not to glance back to the wardrobe – she would only be torturing herself, and Ivan might wonder that she was up to something – Renee backed towards the bedroom door. 'Try and get some sleep.'

Downstairs, she bit back tears and paced the living room for several minutes. Then, finally pulling herself together, she sat down and took some deep breaths. 'I'll just have to go in what I'm wearing,' she told the fireplace. 'There's nowt else for it. Anyroad, it's how I conduct myself in the interview that'll matter, not what I've got on. I'll say all the right things, tell them everything they want to hear, aye. They'll find me satisfactory so long as I'm polite and be myself, surely?'

Feeling a smidgen more positive, she allowed herself a wobbly smile.

A quick look to the clock showed her she had a little over an hour before she must think about making tracks. What with the wait for the tram, then the journey to Tootal, Broadhurst and Lee – not to mention the several minutes she'd require to compose herself and stem her nerves before she went in – she didn't want to leave herself running late. What impression would that make? No, she must make sure to arrive in plenty of time.

'Renee? Renee?'

Pulled back to the present, she swivelled her eyes

towards the stairs. Lord, what now? *Just go to ruddy sleep, won't you?*

'Oi, d'you hear me?'

'Aye, Dad?' she called back.

'Come here.'

Heaving a sigh, she pulled herself up and went to answer his command.

Ivan squinted at her through one eye as she approached the bed. 'What took you so long?'

'Sorry. Do you need me to get you summat?'

He shook his head. Then, to her sheer horror, he patted the space beside him. 'Lie with me awhile, keep me company.'

'Dad—'

'Come on. Slip your shoes off and get in.'

But then she'd never get away . . . *Think*, her mind screamed. *Think!*

'Now, Renee.'

'But Dad, I've jobs to do downstairs, and—'

'They can wait. Do as you're told, damn it!'

She had no choice, none, couldn't deny him. Her shoulders sagged in defeat. In a world of devastation, she climbed on to the bed and curled into a ball.

'There, that's better. Snuggle up close, lass, keep me warm.'

With the dead feeling back in both mind and body, she did as he bid.

It was finished. It was all finished.

'So, lass, how did it go earlier?'

'It didn't.'

104

'Eh? What d'you mean?'

Renee didn't slow her pace, and Mrs Flynn was forced to break into a trot to keep up with her. 'I never went to the interview.' Voice flat, she shrugged. 'It don't matter. They probably wouldn't have took me on anyroad, so nowt's been lost.'

'Nowt's been . . .? Renee, what's going on? Renee, will you talk to me? *Stop*, lass.' Iris pulled her to a halt. 'Just what in the world—?'

'Oh, Mrs Flynn!' she burst out, dissolving into tears and falling, shaking with sobs, into her arms. 'He ruined it, just like he ruins everything. I hate him, I hate him!'

'Eeh, you poor young thing . . . Come on.' Guiding Renee around, she led her back down the street. 'The shops can wait. It's a cup of tea you need – aye, and me, an' all, for that matter.'

'I'll not get another look-in with them now, will I?' Renee said miserably when they were sat at her neighbour's table with a cup of tea in their hands.

'No, lass, I'm sorry to say,' the woman was forced to confirm. 'As our Maureen said when we visited her in Daubhill, there's a queue of girls looking to be took on a mile long . . .'

'Aye. And after your Linda going to the trouble of securing me an interview as well. Pass on my apologies to her, won't you, when next you see her?'

'Eeh, Renee . . .' Watching sadly the fresh tears spill over to pour down her cheeks, Iris reached for her hand and squeezed. 'What's to be done, eh?'

'I don't know, Mrs Flynn. I just do not know.'

'You could take a ride into town one day, try your luck at a few factories and the like? Happen you'd get snapped up some place else?'

'Maybe,' Renee replied, but her heart just wasn't in it any more.

'It's worth a try, lass.'

Her nod was non-committal. 'We'll see.'

'Have we to collect our bits, then, lass?' Iris asked some twenty minutes later when Renee was sufficiently composed.

Renee nodded. She'd filled her in on the story of this morning's disastrous turnout and it was clear the woman was concerned about her leaving Ivan home alone for too long, lest he started asking awkward questions. The last thing the friends wanted was for him to get wind of their new acquaintanceship and put the mockers on it. 'Aye, we'd best had.'

Having called at the grocer's first, their next stop was the butcher's. As usual, the proprietor greeted them with much jollity.

'Here they are: Top o'th' Brow's answer to Bette Davis and Myrna Loy!'

Iris threw back her head and hooted with laughter. 'Pull the other one, it's got bells on! Eeh, the drivel you do talk.'

He held a hand to his heart in mock offence. 'I meant every word!'

'Aye,' she retorted, 'and I'm a monkey's aunty! Now young Renee here, she could pass as Myrna Loy any day, she's bonny enough – even more so, I'd say, if truth be told. But me, Bette Davis? Huh! Tessie

O'Shea would be nearer the mark.' She smoothed her hands down her plentiful hips with a decisive sniff. 'So don't you try charming me with your tall tales, Gordon Wallace, for it won't wash.'

Despite herself, Renee couldn't help but giggle. Not that she had a clue who these people they referred to were. Celebrities, she would have hazarded a guess at. She'd never been to the pictures in her life, hadn't the first idea who the popular singers and film stars of the day were. Nonetheless, she was enjoying the entertainment playing out in the shop. And Mrs Flynn's compliment about her had been appreciated.

The butcher held up his hands in surrender. 'Just trying to brighten up a frosty winter's day, wench, that's all. Aye, and I could ruddy well do with it, an' all, after the night I had, let me tell you!'

Her curiosity piqued, Iris raised her brows. 'Why, lad, what occurred?'

'Tarzan, as per usual, that's what.'

Renee's lips parted in surprise. 'Tarzan?' she piped in before her neighbour had the chance to respond. 'Did you say Tarzan, Mr Wallace?'

'It's a daft name forra dog, lass, I grant you. But well, it were our Jimmy what came up with it, and I hadn't the heart to say no.'

Jimmy. Renee's stomach flipped, and she felt her cheeks grow hot.

'So, what's the blighter been up to this time, then?' Mrs Flynn went on, oblivious to Renee's discomfiture.

'Oh, the same old story! Escaped from the back garden and went off careering around the ruddy forest, didn't it? Out 'til gone two in the morn, I was, searching for the mutt. The swine will finish up on a tray in that window there the next time it tries it, aye, for I've had a bellyful and that's a fact!'

There was laughter in Iris's tone. 'Eeh, it'll be the death of you will that hound.'

'Too ruddy true, wench. I'm powfagged with it, I am.'

'You should have got the lad to go and look for it. After all, it is his dog, in't it?'

'Aye, I know, but what with the hours Jimmy's working lately at Oak Valley . . . I don't like to disturb him once he's away to his bed. He were dead to the world when Tarzan got out, and so it were left to me to find the frigger.'

The woman nodded understandingly. 'Maisie still bad, is she?'

'Aye. She's a good little worker – or was, anyroad. This last stroke looks to have been too much for her. She got stuck into the work in the fields when needed, on top of her duties in the farmhouse, and course now she's not able to, it means they're a pair of hands down and the farm is suffering for it. Least it would be if not for Jimmy. Been toiling like a Trojan for them, he has, and for barely any extra brass. They can only just afford to pay a daily to come in to cook and clean whilst Maisie's out of action, you see. Not that Jimmy complains, you know him; if he was any more laid-back he'd be horizontal. And Jack and Maisie are more than grateful to him for it.'

A look had appeared on Mrs Flynn's face that Renee couldn't identify, and when her neighbour turned her head to look at her fully, there was a gleam of interest in her gaze – though for the life of her, Renee couldn't grasp why.

'Aye, well, I hope things turn around for them soon,' the woman told Gordon before adding brusquely in the next breath, 'now, are you for serving us, lad, or what? We can't stand around here gassing all day, you know. We've things to be getting on with.'

The moment they were outside, she grasped Renee's arm and pulled her to a halt. 'Well, lass? Are you thinking what I'm thinking?'

'Sorry?' Still preoccupied processing the information she'd just learned – namely that the lad Jimmy she'd met the night before Christmas Eve was the butcher's son – Renee was flummoxed. She stared back at her blankly. 'What d'you mean, Mrs Flynn?'

'Saints preserve us . . . Don't you know an opportunity when you see one?' She rolled her eyes, then took hold of Renee's arm once more. 'Come on, let's walk and talk – there's too many people here. I'll explain on t' way.'

'So, what is it you're thinking?' Renee asked when they had turned the corner into Monks Lane.

'It's like this, lass. Jack and Maisie Crawley sound to be having a tough time of it right now. Well, you heard yourself, didn't you, what Gordon had to say? I'm just wondering whether . . .'

'Whether what, Mrs Flynn?'

Iris tapped her chin thoughtfully. 'Whether you ought to try your luck at gaining employment with them at Oak Valley Farm. As a domestic help, like. Cooking and cleaning and the like, you know.'

'Mr Wallace said himself that they already have someone who comes in every day for all that.'

'He also said they're barely able to scratch a wage together for her. What I were thinking is this: happen they might consider taking *you* on instead, as a live-in maid. Say, perhaps, for half of what they're paying the other woman now? They'll jump at it, surely. In return, you'd get free board and lodgings.'

'And the chance to get away from Dad . . .'

'Exactly. This could be just the thing you're looking for to get you out of this estate and away from Ivan Rushmore for good.'

'But where is it? The farm, I mean. Not Harwood . . .?' She flicked her stare to the green hills and fields stretching off in the distance to her right. Then, at the woman's nod: 'But it's not far away enough, surely?'

'What does that matter?'

'Well, Dad might get wind of where I am—'

'How?'

Renee shrugged, then bit her lip. 'I don't know, but . . .'

'But what? How will he find out? I for one ain't going to tell him, am I? And if you don't neither,

110

he'll not have the foggiest idea where you are, will he? For all he knew, you could have scarpered to the other end of the country.'

'I suppose . . . Eeh, but Mrs Flynn, it's taking a mighty big risk . . .'

'Nowt that's worth having ever comes easy to us. Besides, what's the alternative? Stop here, without even giving this a try, and put up with him for many more years to come? Come on, lass, think about it. This opportunity could be just what you've been waiting for.'

'All right.' Renee nodded, and a confidence that was quite new to her began first to trickle, then seep through her veins, lending her a rush of strength. 'You're right. I can't – won't – live like this any longer. I must get away. I'll do it, aye.'

'Good girl! Now, I think your best bet would be getting Jimmy to put in a word for you. The Crawleys trust him, you see, and it'll stand you in better stead, I reckon. I could nip round to the Wallaces this evening and talk to him on your behalf. I've known him since he was a nipper in short trousers – he's a nice, dependable lad. He'll help if he can, I'm certain.

'Actually,' Iris continued after some thought, 'I'll wait on t' corner for him coming home from work and speak to him on his own. The butcher will want to know the reason if I go knocking at his door for his son, and though Gordon's a sound enough fella and would likely not repeat your business, I think it wiser that he doesn't know owt to begin with. The fewer folk who know what you're about, the least chance there is of it somehow getting back to Ivan. It's for the best, and I'll swear Jimmy to secrecy, aye.'

Renee's heart was thumping so loudly she was surprised her neighbour couldn't hear it. This was really happening. After the turbulent day she'd had, from dizzying excitement this morning at the prospect of the interview, quickly followed by soul-crushing devastation at missing it, and now back to fizzing hope again . . . she could barely keep up – struggled to believe it more so. Just what would she do without this golden-hearted woman she was lucky enough to call a friend, at all?

Her voice was a thick whisper. 'I don't know how to thank you, Mrs Flynn.'

'Tsk, no need for that. I'll let you know tomorrow how I got on with Jimmy, all right?'

'Aye.'

'It's a pity you don't know him yourself, lass. He'd find it harder to turn away a pretty face than this craggy owd thing I'm stuck with,' she said on a chuckle. Then her brow furrowed and she cocked her head. 'The Wallaces live on t' other side of the estate on the edge of Blair Lane, so it's unlikely your paths would have crossed what with you only ever venturing out to go to the shops. Even so, he's about your age, aye, would have gone to Top o'th' Brow School the same time as you.'

She'd told herself she recognised his voice that night in the darkness . . . Now she came to think of it, Mrs Flynn must be right: that was probably where she recalled him from. He hadn't been in her class

112

though, that much she did know – was likely in the one above.

'Don't you remember him, then?'

'Well truth be told, I have met him,' Renee admitted, which brought back her blush, much to her chagrin. 'A few nights since, it was. He was out searching for Tarzan, and we got talking.'

'There you are, then! Have a word with him about speaking to the Crawleys on your behalf, see what he says.'

'Oh, I don't know if I could . . .'

'Course you can. He'll not refuse you, lass, will Jimmy.'

Renee felt a stirring of something she couldn't put her finger on at the prospect of seeing him again. It was like a warm rush in her stomach that smouldered and spread to encompass every inch of her – it was a sensation she'd never known before but was one she didn't find unpleasurable all the same. She'd thought about him often since that night, would go over their encounter in the seclusion and safety of her mind in bed. She would recall each word that had passed between them, hear again the friendly way he'd spoken to her, see his kindly eyes, his handsome smile . . . She'd wished for the opportunity to meet him again. Now was her chance.

'So, lass? Will you seek him out yourself?'

Quashing the toxic voice of anxiety before it could influence her decision, Renee stretched to her full height and lifted her chin resolutely. 'Aye, Mrs Flynn. Aye, I will.'

113

Chapter 9

'I'LL NOT BE long, Dad.'

'Aye, and make sure you ain't. There and straight back, d'you hear?'

Nodding, not daring to catch his eye lest he saw the deception that would surely be written in her own, Renee turned from the bed and headed downstairs. She threw on her coat, grabbed the string bag and torch and hurried from the house.

In the front garden, she paused for a brief moment and sucked in a few lungfuls of the icy night air hoping it would lend her strength. Then she allowed herself a shaky smile of anticipation and made as quickly as the blackout would allow towards the shops.

Now, as she awaited a sighting of Jimmy returning from work – he'd have to pass along New Lane to get home, she knew – Renee prayed he wouldn't be too long.

Her father hadn't been best pleased with the lie she'd spun him about forgetting to buy sugar earlier, had blasted her forgetfulness and stupidity. He'd initially refused her suggestion that she pop back to buy a packet, had told her it could wait until tomorrow, that no daughter of his was going gallivanting about the streets at this time of the evening. Yet her mention of him having to go without his sweet cup of tea in the morning had soon changed his tune – much to her relief, he'd relented. Now, she was determined not to waste this opportunity, *must* get to speak with Jimmy, whatever it took.

The thick darkness made it impossible to see who was passing, and so each time she heard footsteps approaching, she gave the torch a quick flick upwards to scan the face. The minutes ticked on and still, of the lad there was no sign. Then suddenly, as she was about to give up hope, she saw him.

With his cap pulled low against winter's cruel bite and his hands in his pockets, he walked by at a brisk pace; Renee had to run to catch up with his long stride.

'Jimmy.'

'Hello?'

In contrast to their first meeting, this time she brought up the glow to illuminate her own features. 'It's me, Renee.'

'Renee. Oh aye.' His teeth flashed in clear pleasure, making her heart soar. 'How're you?'

'Gradely. Ta.' She'd become terribly tongue-twisted, had to force the words out. 'And you, Jimmy?'

'Aye, same.'

An awkward silence hung over them for several seconds, then both started talking at once, making them laugh.

'You go,' said Renee.

'No, you, please,' Jimmy insisted.

'The thing is . . .' She related all that she and Mrs Flynn had discussed, adding, 'I know it's a lot to ask of you – we barely know each other, after all. But I'm desperate, you see, and so if there is a chance you could help . . .'

'Well, that answers the question I were about to put to you: I reckoned there had to be summat important going on for you to be hanging about out here in the pitch black and freezing cold.' He blew out air slowly. 'Are things really so bad at home?'

'They are,' she murmured, dipping her head.

'I've a good mind to pay this father of yours a visit—'

'No, don't do that!' Renee was horrified. 'Please, Jimmy. He'd kill me. Dad,' she went on in a stutter, keen now to make the lad believe he wasn't really as bad as he was, so as not to cause ructions, 'he's overly strict, that's all it is. I . . . I'm feeling trapped at home and need to spread my wings.'

'Aye?'

Oh, if only he knew the real truth of things . . . She nodded. 'Aye. I just want my freedom.'

'It's been this way for you forra long time, ain't it?' he stated quietly, his eyes creasing. 'You were always the kid what stood in the corner of the playground on their own, weren't you? I thought I recognised you when we met near the woods, and it weren't 'til later on that I realised who you were. Everyone at school thought you a bit odd because you hardly spoke to anyone and never joined in any games, but

116

I see the way of things different now I'm older. It's not that you didn't want pals, was it? You kept yourself to yourself on purpose, didn't you?'

Tears wobbled on Renee's lashes. She swiped them away with the back of her hand. 'I couldn't take friends back to my house to play, not with how Dad is. I thought it best not to get too close to the others in case they found out. Truth be told, I've been doing it all my life and still am. Well, besides Mrs Flynn.' The shadow of a smile stroked her lips. 'I did let my guard down with her, and now she's my very best friend. And Lynn Ball's lovely, too. She's who I work for at the moment.'

'And me.' Jimmy's eyes creased at the corners. 'I hope you deem me a friend now, an' all, Renee?'

Her chest expanded with overwhelming happiness, and fresh tears pricked her eyes. 'Aye.' Her tone was soft. 'Aye, I do.'

'Right then.' He nodded purposefully. 'Here's what we'll do—'

'You mean you'll help me, Jimmy?' she cut in in wonder. 'You really will?'

'Of course. What are friends for?'

At his slow smile, she couldn't hold back her emotion; a single tear escaped to splash to her cheek. 'Ta,' she mouthed.

'I'll speak to Jack and Maisie in t' morning. You have my promise that I'll do my utmost to convince them it would be a good idea taking you on. All right?'

'Aye.'

'They shouldn't turn the suggestion down, but

either way, I'll let you know their answer when I finish work. Can we meet here tomorrow night at the same time?'

'No, I don't think so,' she was forced to say. 'I were lucky to hoodwink Dad into letting me out tonight – there's no way he'd fall for it a second time.'

Jimmy's expression had saddened. He broke their gaze with a small shake of his head and muttered, 'The controlling old . . . It's bloody ridiculous.'

'Aye, and that's exactly why I need to get away.'

'So, how will we get to talk?'

Chewing on her bottom lip, Renee thought for a minute, then her face smoothed out and she raised an eyebrow. 'I could always come to you – at the farm, I mean. You're allowed a break for your midday meal, ain't you?'

'Aye. All right, that sounds good to me. You know where Oak Valley is?'

She shook her head. 'But don't worry, I'll find it. What time shall we meet and where?'

'One o'clock by the cowshed. I'll be waiting for you outside.'

'Right. Well, I'd better be getting back.' Again, Renee was lost for adequate words to express her gratitude. 'I don't really know what to say, Jimmy,' she admitted. 'Other than . . . Thank you. You'll never know just what this means to me. You've saved my life.'

He seemed deeply affected by her statement. With a large, calloused hand, he cupped her shoulder and squeezed gently. 'See you tomorrow. Good night, Renee.'

Following the beam of the torch when they had parted company, she ran along New Lane and on down Monks Lane and was home in thirty seconds flat. Panting in the hall, she took off her coat and called upstairs, 'I'm back, Dad.'

'What in hell took you so long? I were debating whether to come and look for you.'

Thank God he hadn't! The prospect of him catching her with Jimmy was one that was too terrible to even contemplate. 'Sorry. The shop was full; I had to wait to be served.'

'It's a name you'll be getting for yourself if you're not careful – and woe betide you if you do. There's but one type of female what walks about in the dark of a night, and they does that for a single reason only: whoring. You want to finish up like that one in the next street, do you? You want folk talking, want them saying you're a doxy like her? Well, it's coming, my lass, oh aye. It's coming, you mark my words.'

The comparison stung. Livvy Bryant, who resided in the square on Glaister Lane, was a prostitute. More to the point, everyone knew it. It was difficult not to. She could be regularly seen arriving home at dawn, her hair and clothing askew and her bright red lipstick smudged, after a heavy night on the tiles and entertaining her 'gentlemen friends' in the back entries behind the town-centre pubs. Nor did the woman attempt to hide or deny it. Brazen to the point of reckless, she seemed to flaunt her profession as though she was proud of it, and decent folk hereabouts avoided her like the plague.

119

And to think her disgusting father had the gall to say she'd end up like that . . . Renee clenched her fists in anger. He ranked fouler than Livvy any day of the week, hands down! At least the men who she messed about with were grown adults – and consenting at that. What Ivan Rushmore got up to behind closed doors . . . It would curl the hair of the devil himself, and that was the truth.

'Aye, well, I've said my piece so let's leave it at that,' Ivan's voice floated down now. 'Finish up what needs doing down there and come up to bed. 'T'ain't the same without you beside me.'

Renee's flesh crawled with repulsion. She squeezed shut her eyes.

'Hurry up, then.'

'Coming,' she replied dully.

And as she dragged herself up the stairs shortly afterwards, but one thought beat a consolatory reminder inside her brain: *Have strength, Renee. Not long, now. Soon, God willing, you'll never have to suffer this again. Please, Jimmy . . .*

Mrs Flynn held out her arms and chuckled when Bobby and Brian went to her willingly with matching grins. 'Eeh, you're a bonny pair, youse are. Come on to your Aunty Iris, my lovelies.'

'Ta for offering to mind the twins for me,' Renee said, turning back for the door. 'Only it's much too cold to have them out for long, and besides, it would be a nightmare trekking along the fields with that pram.'

'The pleasure's all mine, lass. We'll have a jolly owd time here playing games in the warmth.' She leaned forward and planted a swift kiss on Renee's cheek. 'Now, go on and see what information Jimmy Wallace has for you. I'll be keeping everything crossed – fingers, toes and at a push even my ruddy eyes – that it's good news.'

With a wave to the boys and a last, strength-drawing nod to her neighbour, Renee forced herself forward and exited the house. When she reached the top of her street, she turned left and set forth for Harwood.

Some thirty minutes later and despite following Mrs Flynn's directions, Renee found she was hope-lessly lost. Spying a farmer tending to his sheep on a nearby strip of land, she crossed to the boundary wall and flapped her arms. 'Excuse me, mister! Can you point me in the direction of Oak Valley Farm, please?'

'Just keep on the way you're going, lass,' he called back. 'You'll find yourself there in a handful of minutes.'

Thanking him, Renee did as he'd instructed. Sure enough, the rutted track gradually petered out, and a cobblestoned clearing appeared in the distance. Catching sight of a white-painted structure, which she took to be the cowshed, she took a deep breath in an attempt to calm herself. Then, with a belly full of nerves, she pushed herself on and slipped through the thick metal gate.

Jimmy appeared around the corner of the shed as

she was nearing its doors. 'Renee – hello! I worried you might not come.'

'Hello, Jimmy. I'm sorry if I'm late. I got a bit lost.'

He flopped down on to a nearby straw bale and patted the space beside him. 'Take the weight off.'

She sat down, then turned to search his face, her own full of expectancy. 'So, Jimmy? Did you manage to ask the Crawleys?'

'I did.'

'And?' she whispered, hardly daring to breathe.

He laughed. 'Don't look so scared: they were over the moon with the idea.'

'Aye?'

'Aye.'

'Oh!' In her euphoria, she forgot herself and threw her arms around his neck. Then, returning to her senses, she sprang back, flushing scarlet. 'I'm sorry, I am, I—'

'It's all right, Renee.' His voice was soft, his pleasure in her joy clear. 'Don't ever apologise for being happy.'

'Eeh, Jimmy.'

They stared at one another for a long moment. Then Jimmy grinned, Renee followed suit, and they jumped to their feet.

'Shall I take you to meet Jack and Maisie?'

She nodded eagerly. 'Yes please.'

'Well, I don't need to ask how it went, lass. Your face tells its own tale.'

Following her neighbour through the hallway and

into the living room, Renee was smiling from ear to ear. 'Aye, I got the job, Mrs Flynn.'

'Well, the babbies have been fed and are fast akip upstairs in my bed, so sit yourself down. I'll brew us a pot of tea, and you can tell me all about it.'

'The Crawleys are very nice,' Renee revealed minutes later when they were facing one another at the table. 'Mr Crawley's a bit quiet, didn't say much, but he was kind to me all the same. His wife is really lovely, though. She's paralysed down one side from the stroke and can't speak all that clever, but she was happy to see me. She held my hand all the time I were there, and she told me I was the answer to her and Jack's prayers. Fair brought a tear to my eye, it did. If only they knew it was *them* what's turned out to be *my* saviours.'

'Jimmy didn't mention to them your circumstances, then, lass?'

'I asked him not to and he didn't. They mightn't have wanted to risk taking me on if they thought Dad might track me down and go storming round there on the rampage, and I can't say I'd blame them. It's the last thing they need with how ill Maisie is.'

The woman nodded. 'And he shan't say nowt to his dad Gordon nor anyone else?'

'No, he gave me his word. No one knows owt bar Jimmy and us in this room.'

'That's good then. You see, I told you yer could rely on him, didn't I? He's a sound lad, is Jimmy.'

Though she lowered her gaze, Renee couldn't stem the smile that crept to her mouth. 'Aye. He is.'

Mrs Flynn chuckled knowingly, much to Renee's embarrassment, but mercifully refrained from speaking her mind. Instead, she asked, 'So, when will you be away, then?'

'Aye, I was getting around to that . . .'

'What is it, what's wrong?'

A little of the spark had left Renee's eyes. 'The daily they employ now is paid up 'til the middle of next month. So, it'll be a few weeks before I can start.'

'Eeh, lass.'

She shrugged. 'It's a disappointment, aye. I'd hoped to be gone from here as soon as possible – I'd leave this very day if I could – but well, it can't be helped. I'll have to be patient. Just knowing I've secured a position, have someplace to go to, is reason enough to be grateful.'

'It'll fly by, you'll see. Ay, but I will miss you, Renee,' Iris added quietly with a sniff.

'And I you, Mrs Flynn. More than you'll know.'

The evening meal of steak and kidney pie had just come out of the oven and Renee was busy straining off the cabbage when Ivan arrived home from work. She crossed to the kitchen door to pop her head around. 'I'm just dishing up, now, Dad.'

Ivan flopped into his fireside chair and tossed his peaked hat on to the mantel. 'I knew I shouldn't have gone in today, knew I weren't up to it, that it were too soon. I'm fagged.'

'You'll feel better when you've got some grub

inside you,' she hastened to say, hoping it would convince him – the last thing she needed was for him to decide he was too ill to go to the station tomorrow. The prospect of another full day in his company like the one before was more than she could bear. 'You relax, I'll pour you out a cup of tea.'

'So, what did you get up to today?' he asked as they were eating.

Please don't blush, please don't blush, she begged of herself. 'Oh, you know. The usual.'

'And what might that be?'

She looked to see whether he was testing her or knew something, but his expression gave nothing away. He must just be making conversation, she reasoned with blessed relief. 'I cleaned the house, spent some time with the pigeons, shopped and cooked—'

'And?'

Puzzled, she shook her head. 'Nowt, Dad.'

'You're lying.'

'I'm not, I—'

The noise as he banged the tabletop with his fist had her almost leaping from her skin. She shrank back, both afraid and baffled in equal measure. *He can't know, surely . . . ?* But how – it was impossible!

'I want to know what's been going on, damn it.' His voice was a growl. He leaned in, teeth bared. 'I want to know *now.*'

Renee was quailing and tears were dangerously close by. 'Dad, please . . .' She licked her dry lips, praying for a miracle. 'I've not done nowt.'

'No? Then why have I just spotted your shoes

125

caked in grass and mud? Go on, you answer me that, eh?'

She'd kicked them off in the hallway upon arriving home earlier, had forgotten to move them ... Stupid, stupid! 'That's come from the back garden,' she told him, blurting the first thing that came to mind, and hoping beyond hope it would wash. 'It was when I were seeing to the birds, aye. Next door's cat jumped over the fence trying to get at them, and I chased it off across the lawn. Honest, Dad.'

Eyes like slits, Ivan glared at her for what felt like an age. Finally, and to his daughter's sheer relief, he picked up his fork to resume his meal. Yet he had one final threat to throw her way before he was done: 'You can't pull the wool over my eyes. You're up to summat you are, my girl. What's more, I intend to find out what.'

Renee didn't respond, simply kept her head lowered and returned her attention to her own food. However, her heart was thumping painfully, and she knew it would be for some time to come.

That had been a close one, all right. It was vital that she tread even more carefully from now on. She couldn't afford to be remiss, wouldn't ruin all she'd built up at this late stage, never. Not long now ...

Lord, help me endure these next few weeks!

Chapter 10

THE ARRIVAL OF the new year fetched with it ferocious blizzards, the like of which some had never known and which brought the nation to a shuddering halt. Not only did the snows cause major disruption to industry and everyday life in general but it also put out of action all main modes of transport – trains included.

Days drifted by and with each that went, Renee grew more jittery. The sheer irony of the situation would have been laughable if not so tragic. Her first opportunity of escape from here had been scuppered by a common cold. Now, it may be that her next chance was ruined by something as simple as the weather. Why did this keep happening to her? It wasn't fair, blast it!

Ivan was sent home from work yet again on the morning before Renee was set to leave Monks Lane for Oak Valley Farm. Spotting him trudging up the garden path, her heart sank to her guts, and she released a small moan of desperation. She'd planned to use today to sort through her possessions and tie up loose ends with her friends, namely saying a proper goodbye to Mrs Flynn and explaining the situation to Lynn Ball – now, with her father here and watching her like a hawk, that wasn't going to happen.

'Make some tea, I'm frozzen through to the marrow,' he announced as he entered, shaking the flakes from his heavy coat and hurrying to the fire to warm himself.

Nodding resignedly, Renee did as he bid her.

'It'll be a few weeks more before everything gets back to normal, or so they're reckoning up at the station,' he called through to her as she was setting the cups and saucers on the tray.

Her hands stilled and she closed her eyes. God above, surely not . . .

'So, it looks like you'll have to put up with having me under your feet for the foreseeable, lass.'

'Oh no I won't, for I shan't be here,' she whispered to the teapot. 'Whatever it takes, I'll be gone from this house come the morning. And there won't be a thing you can do to stop me.'

The statement instilled in her fresh strength, and she squared her shoulders, her determination renewed. Nothing would spoil this for her. She must get away.

'I'll have to brave the shops in a minute,' she told him when she'd returned to the living room and poured them out a drink. 'I have to get summat in for the evening meal.'

'Aye, well, you make sure you're quick about it. I want you in here with me in this cowd weather.'

Doing her level best not to throw his way a look of contempt as she passed him, she made for the glass bowl on the sideboard in which lay for safekeeping the new coupon books they had been issued with.

The government had introduced food rationing for every man, woman and child four days earlier. Overseen by the Ministry of Food, the scheme was to ensure fair shares for everyone at a time of national shortage. Bacon, butter and sugar were first to go on the list, and rumour had it that other staples would soon follow suit.

Mrs Flynn must have been keeping an eye out for Renee leaving number forty-six, for she was calling her name and hurrying to catch up with her before Renee was halfway up the street.

'Careful, Mrs Flynn,' Renee urged as her neighbour almost lost her footing in the thick drifts of snow. She held out her arm for the woman to link. 'Eeh, it's treacherous, ain't it? Someone will finish up breaking their skull before this winter's through.'

'Aye, I'm that weary with it, I am. So,' she added, squeezing Renee's arm, 'tomorrow, eh, lass?'

'Tomorrow,' Renee repeated with little enthusiasm. 'Thing is, Dad's been sent home again, and it'll likely be the same news tomorrow. I just don't know how I'll manage to leave. I ain't even packed yet! I could have that done today, I suppose, whilst he's busy enjoying his pipe after our meal. He'll assume I'm tidying up or some such and won't suspect nowt different so long as I'm quick about it – I'll hide my things under the bed. It's how I'm to sneak from home and be safely away in

129

the morning what's worrying me. If he *is* there . . . he's bound to notice for sure. I can't risk him putting a halt to my gallop, I can't.'

'Then we'll have to come up with a diversion, won't we?'

She turned to look at her neighbour's face fully and saw there a cunning gleam in the faded blue eyes. 'Diversion? What have you in mind?'

The woman tapped the side of her nose with a wink. 'You just leave it to me, lass. We'll have you out of that house and on your way to Oak Valley as planned, or my name's not Iris Elizabeth Flynn. Fret not, I shan't let you down.'

That evening, desperate not to make a sound and with her tongue poking out of the side of her mouth in concentration, Renee dragged out the small mustard-coloured case and placed it on top of the counterpane. Now came the dangerous part – praying with everything she had that Ivan wouldn't hear, she took a deep breath and pressed the double brass catches with her thumbs. The lid snapped open with a sharp clink, sounding as loud as a gunshot to her heightened senses. She paused to listen for movement on the stairs, and hearing none, heaved a sigh and hastily got to work.

First, she darted to the wardrobe and pulled open its doors. Everything belonging to her mother she lifted out and bundled inside the case. Then she rushed to the room next door and gathered together her meagre personal possessions and packed these too. A last quick scan of the bedroom to make sure she'd forgotten nothing, then she closed the case and pushed it back under the bed. Finally, satisfied that nothing looked out of place and all was as it should be, she nodded and returned downstairs to the living room.

Her heart was beating heavily as she crossed the floor and made for the kitchen to make a calming pot of tea. Throughout it all, her father raised not a single hair, hadn't the slightest notion that anything was amiss.

That night in bed, Renee's thoughts remained locked on second-guessing what the following morning would bring.

Could it really be that in a few short hours all of this would be over with, and she'd be free of this place and the man she'd come to loathe?

Time would shortly tell.

'Breakfast is on t' table, Dad.'

To say Renee was anxious would be the understatement of the century. She'd barely snatched a wink of sleep and her stretched nerves were on a blade's edge – may God lend her the strength to get through this!

Still, she hadn't an idea what Mrs Flynn had planned to enable her to slip from the house undetected. What she did know, however, was that her neighbour would come through for her. This she trusted implicitly. She'd have depended on her with her life.

Ivan lumbered into the living room, where a good fire was burning, and sighed in appreciation after the cold of the bedroom. Yawning and rubbing his eyes, he took his seat. And with her heart in her mouth and her legs like jelly, his daughter joined him.

They made small talk as they ate – at least her father chatted and put food into his mouth; she could hardly manage either – and all was going as it normally did this time of the day. Then suddenly, there came the knock Renee had been waiting for, and which would change everything.

She was only just fast enough to press a hand to her mouth to stop a cry from escaping. Without a word or glance to her father, she rose and crossed to the door.

'Oh, Mrs Flynn . . .'

'Now then, none of that,' the woman insisted, though there was a definite quaver to her tone. 'We don't have the time for it. Besides, we've already said our goodbyes.'

Remembering their emotional farewell before they parted company yesterday, Renee gulped back her tears.

'Good lass. Eeh, God speed to you, Renee.' Iris grasped her hand and squeezed. Then she straightened up and jerked her head in a decisive nod. 'Now then. Go and tell that father of yours I want a word with him. Go on,' she pressed when Renee made to question this, 'and don't worry. Once he's heard what I have to say, he'll be out of this house like a bat out of hell. And the second he's gone, you snatch your chance and do the same. D'you hear me, lass? You run just as quick as you can, and don't look back.'

They shared a shaky smile. Then Renee was turning and heading back for the living room. 'Dad?'

'What's up? Who was it calling here at this time of the morning?'

'Mrs Flynn from across the way . . . she's at the door still. She said I'm to fetch you.'

'What the devil does she want?'

'I . . . I don't . . .'

With a low growl of irritation, he pushed back his chair and wearing a face like thunder marched to the hallway.

Sick to the stomach with fright, Renee stood and listened to Mrs Flynn's muffled words, wondering what on earth she was saying to him. Then Ivan's voice followed, this one loud and clear – 'Christ sake!' – and in the next instant, she heard the duo's footsteps hurrying down the garden path and across the road.

For a split second, she was struck dumb with shock that her friend's scheme had actually worked. Then she was bolting for the stairs and the bedroom.

Throwing herself to her knees, Renee scrambled beneath the bed and snatched up the case. Moments later, shaking like a leaf, she was standing once more in the hallway.

A glance to the street showed there to be no sign of either her friend or her father – they must be in Mrs Flynn's house. But Renee hadn't the time to reason why. Gripping the case's leather handle, she stepped outside.

She was about to make a run for it when a familiar noise reached her ears, and of their own accord her feet juddered to a halt. *Ruby*. It was her coo – she'd recognise it anywhere. The bird knew she was leaving, was calling to her . . .

'I must go, I must,' Renee whimpered, telling herself she had to ignore it. However, the pull was too strong – on a groan, she whipped back around and re-entered the house.

She flew across the living room, through the kitchen and into the back garden. She found Ruby gazing at her through the chicken wire and her heart broke in two. On impulse, she opened the pigeon loft and lifted her out. A quick goodbye and an apology to the other birds and Renee was once more running back for the front door, her favourite feathered friend snuggled safely inside her coat.

Again, she checked the street to make sure the coast was clear before leaving the house.

Now, there was no pausing, no hesitation. Keeping a tight hold of her belongings, Renee picked up her feet and ran for all she was worth.

She expected a hand to clamp down on her shoulder at every step, yet it never came. Nevertheless, she wasn't taking any chances and didn't break pace the length of Monks Lane. Upon reaching New Lane, she found her gaze drifting towards Padbury Way. Then, as guilt stabbed, she tore her eyes away and, keeping her stare straight ahead, continued on for Harwood.

Leaving without a word to the woman who had treated her only with kindness was a terrible thing to do, she knew this. She'd already let Lynn down enough, hadn't been able to watch Bobby and Brian since the snows had started in earnest and her father had been stuck at home. Not wanting to admit to her she'd lied about Ivan being aware of his daughter's job, Renee had told her he was poorly and that she had to be there to care for him. Consequently, her employer had been forced to take time off work from the grocer's.

And now this.

Lynn had been so good to her and here was she, repaying her by leaving her in the lurch good and proper. Renee *had* been tempted to reveal to her her plans more than once but had coward out each time at the last second, loath to disappoint her, and Mrs Flynn had offered to set Lynn straight instead once she was safely at the Crawleys' farm.

By, but she felt wretched, she did really, and would miss her and the twins something awful. As for dear Iris . . . However, there was no time to dwell on all that at this moment, Renee told herself firmly, mentally shaking herself back to the present. Right now, her main concern must be getting away from Top o'th' Brow.

'Goodbye,' she whispered to those she was leaving behind who mattered. Pushing all thoughts of them to the back of her mind, she sprinted on.

A figure in a thick overcoat and oilskin trousers waved to Renee from across the snow-smothered field as she reached the gate of Oak Valley Farm.

135

Though their face was obscured by a woollen muffler, she knew instinctively it was Jimmy. Only now, seeing him, did the true impact of what she'd managed to do hit her. The fierce yearning to succeed, which had kept her going through the terror of detection and the hard trek here, seemed to drain from her suddenly and her legs went weak. Tears sprang to her eyes. On a heavy gasp, she burst out crying and sank to her knees.

Jimmy was at her side in seconds. He dropped to his haunches and, as though sensing what this meant to her, wrapped her in his arms without speaking.

'I did it, Jimmy,' she sobbed against his chest.

'Aye, Renee.'

'I'm free.'

'That you are.'

Finally, when her emotions had subsided, she drew back and flashed him a bashful smile. 'I'm sorry. I just . . . It's overwhelming, the relief, you know?'

'Come on.' He straightened up and held out a hand to help her to her feet. 'Let's get you to the house and out of this cold.'

They walked in silence. When they reached the front door, she brought him to a stop.

'What is it?'

Biting her lip, she lifted aside her coat and watched the surprise on his face as he took in the pigeon nestled there. 'I had to fetch her, Jimmy . . . Will the Crawleys mind, d'you think?'

He was smiling. He shook his head. 'Not a bit, no. Come with me to the barn, and I'll find her a crate to

136

sleep in. Lined with a bit of straw, she'll be as snug as a bug in a rug.'

The air inside the modest-sized structure was thick and warm and smelled sweetly of hay. Renee watched him collect a small wooden box from the back and carry it across. After pressing inside it a few handfuls of straw from a nearby bale, he held it out to her and she gently put Ruby inside.

'Ta, thanks.'

'She'll be safe here,' he told her, taking the crate from her grasp and placing it against the far wall. Then he made his way back to where Renee was standing by the door and stopped in front of her. Ever so slowly, he reached for her hands and held them in his. 'So will you, Renee.'

Though she blushed to the roots of her hair, she found that her heart was singing. Never in the whole of her life could she remember being as complete and happy as she was in this moment. She glanced up and met his eye shyly. 'I'm glad I'm here, Jimmy.'

'Aye. So am I.'

Chapter 11

WHAT HER FATHER was thinking, Renee tried not to dwell upon. His shock and fearsome fury must be a terrible sight to behold, she was sure.

Just what had he done when he returned home yesterday to find her gone? Turned the place upside down in his rage? Scoured the area looking for her? Did he suspect Mrs Flynn was involved, give her a hard time to reveal to him where his daughter had fled to? Not that her friend would ever tell him her whereabouts, Renee was certain of this. Yet still, she was riddled with guilt at the prospect of Iris being on the receiving end of Ivan's wrath due to her.

The worries were a constant companion, and yet in the midst of it all but one truth overrode everything: she'd done it. At long last, she was finally free. For how long it would last, whether her father would manage to track her down somehow, she couldn't say. But she intended to enjoy this period of happiness and calm and normality, for however long it may last, for all she was worth.

Snow continued to fall steadily with the days, and

matters of the farm were starting to become a concern. Once Renee had seen to the needs of the house and those of Maisie, and when the invalid was sleeping, she would change into a thick woollen jumper, waterproof trousers and rubber boots and join the men to assist them in the fields.

Jimmy had explained that caring for cattle was a skilled task and called for a hardy constitution at the best of times. In the frigid months, it could prove infinitely more difficult for herdsmen and their workhands. Though the usual trials that came with the hotter weather, such as insects and water shortage, no longer posed a problem, wintertime brought with it an even greater level of danger that could prove devastating, if mishandled, to man and beast alike. Renee therefore made it her mission to help the exhausted men in whatever ways she could.

The main priority was the prevention of disease. Viral and bacterial pneumonia along with winter dysentery were common enough, and ensuring a close watch on possible symptoms which could lead to outbreaks was of paramount importance. So far, keeping the cattle protected from the elements in the dry and well-ventilated byre looked to be doing the trick in staving off ailments. None appeared to be off their feed or suffering respiratory problems. Nor were they depressed or listless – tell-tale warnings of the onset of pneumonia.

Additionally, there were no signs of greenish-black diarrhoea that came with dysentery – which Renee had been assigned the unenviable yet necessary job of spotting. More importantly still, the dairy cows were producing milk at a normal rate, and that was always a good omen.

'You've been a godsend, Renee,' said Jimmy one late-January morning as she aided him in bringing the first group of animals to the milking shed, whilst Mr Crawley cleaned out the cows' stalls next door. 'Really, I don't know how me and Jack would have coped without you.'

Her chest swelled with pride at the compliment, though she did her best to play it down: 'Oh, I'm sure I ain't done much. Anyroad, I'm just happy to be of help.'

'No, no.' Jimmy was emphatic in his praise. 'Credit where it's due. You ain't turned your nose up once at anything we've asked of you, took to the farming life like you were born to it, you have. And besides, the dinners you knock up have more about them than owt what that daily maid could rustle together. Talking of which . . .' He swivelled his eyes to her and flashed a wink. 'What's on the menu today?'

'Leg of lamb with roast spuds,' she told him, grinning when he closed his eyes in rapture. 'But that's a long way off, so, have we to get to work here before I'm needed back at the house?'

'Slave driver,' he muttered, and chuckling, they turned their attentions back to the cows.

'I'll say one thing: I'll be damned glad to see the back of this weather,' Jimmy stated afterwards as they were sitting on a straw bale, taking a short break. 'It's a miracle we've not yet had need to call on the veterinarian, and Jack says the same. More than one farmer hereabouts ain't been so lucky. Mind you, some fetch troubles on theirselves,' he added with a shake of his head. 'All right, they're exhausted; aye, I get it – we all are. That don't mean you can afford to let standards slip.'

Jimmy thrust his thumb in the direction of the byre, continuing, 'You take Jack in there. He'll have that place spotless before he's through, but others just ain't got his diligence. They're a mucky lot, you see, are cows, and won't think nowt of lying in their own filth to keep warm. But their waste freezes over if the temperature drops low enough, leaving them colder still as well as dirty, which don't do them no good at all. So, aye, it's important to keep their bedding clean and dry as much as possible – lactating cows at any rate.'

'Lactating?' Renee asked him, eager to learn more; his enthusiasm for the subject was infectious. 'Why them especially?'

'Frostbitten teats.'

'Oh dear.' She involuntarily folded her arms across her chest. 'Sounds awful.'

'It ain't pleasant, put it that way. Neither is it good when the soreness gets so bad that they refuse to let their calves nurse, which might then lead to mastitis.'

Her gaze drifting to the wall, she bit her lip. 'Happen we should ask Mr Crawley if we can lend a hand . . .?'

'No, he'll be reet. Besides, the next lot of cows will

need milking in a minute, and someone's got to do it.'

'I'd best get back in case Mrs Crawley wakens and needs me,' Renee told Jimmy an hour and a half later as they left the shed for the clear and biting air of the farmyard. She hugged herself and peered up at him. 'I'll come and find you in the day if I have the time, shall I, see if there's owt I can help with?'

'Aye. Ta, Renee.' He smiled and gave her a soft push. 'Now go on inside and thaw yourself out. I'll see you later.'

Over the next hours, between caring for the livestock and mending fences brought down in the drifts, the men dropped into the house several times for a few minutes to grab a quick sandwich and cup of tea, and Renee made sure she kept the fire burning merrily in the old black-leaded range to chase the chill from their bones. For her part, Maisie and the household duties ensured she was too busy to leave, and before she knew it the sky had darkened and she was taking the lamb out of the small oven. She'd just finished laying the table when the door opened, and Jack and Jimmy entered, bringing a flurry of fresh-falling flakes with them.

'It's never snowing again?' she remarked with a groan.

Jimmy cast her a weary nod. Then his eyes lighted on the table and his face brightened. 'I'm that hungry I could eat a horse between two bread vans. By, this smells gradely.'

'Cooked to a turn, aye,' the farmer agreed, removing his overcoat and hanging it up.

'Looks good enough to eat,' the younger man added, throwing Renee a wink – she shook her head and laughed.

'I should hope so, else we'll all be going to bed with empty bellies. Sit yourselves down whilst I dish up.'

After taking up to the bedroom a plate for Maisie and helping her to eat, Renee returned to the kitchen and sat down to her own meal gratefully. Jack had by this time finished and retired to the next room and his chair by the open fire. Jimmy remained at the table, and she smiled at him through the soft gaslight. 'You're still here – I thought I might have missed you.'

'I *had* better be off home . . . But I don't suppose a few more minutes will matter.'

Secretly pleased with this, she smiled again. 'Course they won't.'

They sat in companionable silence for a while until Jimmy said, 'My older brother got his call-up this morning.'

Her food forgotten, she gasped. 'Oh, lad.'

'I'm worried for him, Renee. What if . . . what if he don't make it?'

'Jimmy.' Throwing caution to the wind, she inched her hand across the tablecloth and laid it on top of his. 'He'll come home, I'm sure. You must think positive.'

143

His fingers curled around hers and he squeezed gently. Eyes locked, they gazed at one another, the quiet hiss and crackle of the fire the only sounds. When he reached out his other hand and cupped her cheek, a feathery sigh left Renee. She closed her eyes.

'Renee . . . Renee, I . . .'

'Jimmy . . .' she responded, knowing that what was in his heart matched her own, had sensed it happening with the weeks. *She* had felt it from the start, possibly from the first time they met on that dark December night when she'd been dragging the makeshift tree from the field. But it could never be, thanks to Ivan. What her father had taken from her . . . She couldn't get her purity back. This lad sitting before her here deserved better. 'Jimmy . . .'

'Renee, I think I might be falling in love with you.'

Now it was too late. The words were out. She dipped her head in despair.

'If I'm one day called up—'

'What?' Her head snapped back on her neck and pure terror gripped her heart. 'But they can't – farming is a reserved occupation!'

'Aye, for now. But if this war drags on for as long as the last one did, they're going to need all the fellas they can get their mitts on. The Women's Land Army are already taking over the roles of farmhands what have volunteered to join up. Mebbe the government might decide to free up *all* young male farmworkers for the armed forces and replace them with women soon. Who can say what might happen?'

Renee was breathing heavily, and her head was

swimming. They couldn't have him. Not Jimmy. She couldn't lose him, wouldn't bear it. 'No, you're wrong. You are, I know it.'

His voice was soft. 'You *don't*, lass. None of us do. Our John receiving his papers today, it's made me realise how real this all is, what little time we all might have. And that's why . . .' Dropping his head, he ran his tongue over his lips.

'Why what, Jimmy?' she whispered.

'Why I had to tell you how I felt. And to ask you if . . . if you'll agree to be my wife.'

It was like a lightning bolt had passed through her. Yet the momentary euphoria that burst through her body was immediately swamped by the crushing reality. *She couldn't.* 'Jimmy, I can't—'

'Not now,' he hastened to tell her. 'Not yet. It would have to be in a few years when we're both older, I real-ise that. But Renee . . .' He leaned across the table until his face was just inches from hers and pressed her hand to his heart. 'Just knowing you're my girl, that you're promised to me and that one day in the future we'll be wed . . . It's enough. It's enough, lass. Say you will.'

Staring into his beautiful jade eyes, she thought her very soul would break from the pain of it. His mouth moved forward to meet hers and she received his kiss with an agonised moan.

'Say you will,' he repeated on a whisper.

The strength it took for her to force out her response defied comprehension.

'I'm sorry, Jimmy. The answer's no.'

*

'Morning, Renee.'

'Morning . . . Jimmy, can we—?'

'Sorry, but I've got work to do.'

'But we need to talk about—'

Again, and in that same blank tone, he cut her off. 'I don't think there's owt left to say, do you?' Face empty, he turned away and carried on walking.

Renee watched him go through a blur of tears. All night she'd lain awake in her bed going over and over in her mind their last conversation. There was no single other thing in this world she'd have wished for more than to be his wife. But what about when the time came for them to . . . *Surely* he'd know, would discover she hadn't come to him intact. What would he think of her then? He'd never forgive her. And she could never reveal the truth, the reality that she was and would always remain Ivan Rushmore's slut. Good God, she'd sooner die than utter the horrific truth of things. Jimmy Wallace must never learn of her father's abuse.

Nonetheless, the damage that her refusal looked to have wreaked on their friendship was like a blade in her breast; she was desperate to make it right, to go back to how things had been, couldn't stand his aloofness, his pain. Throughout the remainder of the morning, she tailed Jimmy like a kicked puppy, desperate for one kind word or the hint of a smile – neither came. Though not openly hostile, his attitude towards her was one he might use with a stranger: sufficiently polite but hollow in its distance.

By the evening, Renee was nearing the end of her

tether. When Mr Crawley left them as he usually did for his fireside chair in the next room, she held her breath in blessed hope. Yet to her dismay, Jimmy rose almost immediately.

'You're going so soon?' she almost cried.

He nodded. 'Ta for the meal, it was nice. Good-night, Renee.'

'Jimmy, wait.' This couldn't continue any longer; she'd had enough. 'Please, sit down.'

'But I said—'

'Aye, and *I* said sit down!'

Who was more surprised by her harsh demand, herself or Jimmy, she was unable to say. For a long moment, they stared at one another in stubborn silence.

Renee was first to submit. Breaking eye contact, she let out a shuddering sigh. 'Please. Please hear me out.'

She thought he'd refuse her, but to her sheer relief he didn't. Avoiding her gaze, he resumed his seat and folded his arms.

'You left last night before giving me a chance to explain,' she began, wondering just what in the world she was going to say to make this right whilst uphold-ing her secret. 'Jimmy, I love you, too.'

His head came up slowly. He opened and closed his mouth. 'You . . .? Then why—?'

'Because I'm no good, and you deserve better.'

The lad was out of his chair and at her side in a heartbeat. He dropped to sit on his heels so that their eyes were on a level and took hold of her shoul-ders. 'Eeh, Renee.'

'It's true, Jimmy. Us . . . it can't be. I'll only end up hurting you, believe me I will. I won't do that to you.'

'There ain't . . . someone else . . .?'

'What? No! No. No, Jimmy, there ain't no other lad. There never could be.'

His eyes showed he believed her. The tension seemed to rise from him, and he smiled. 'I'll change your mind, Renee. One day, I will.'

Her tears spilling, she shook her head.

'Every single day I'm going to show you what you mean to me. I'm going to prove to you you're wrong what you say about yourself. I have to, for you'll never love me proper until you can love yourself. I understand that now. Eeh, Renee, if only you saw what I see. If you only knew how wonderful you are.'

'Oh, Jimmy.'

She sagged into his waiting arms. And, as he tried in vain to hug her turmoil away, she pictured but one man in her mind and cursed him to all the horrors that hell had to offer.

Later, when the house lay slumbering, Renee slipped from her bed and padded across the room. She knew there would be no release in sleep for herself this night, not until she'd got some of her woes off her chest.

Putting on her coat over her nightdress and pulling on her wellingtons, she listened for movement from the Crawleys above, and, when none came, she did what she'd done a hundred times before: she slipped from the house to seek out Ruby and spill to her her troubles.

She found her oldest friend dozing in her crate and lifted her out. It amazed Renee still that the bird hadn't returned to Monks Lane. Ruby had the freedom to come and go as she pleased and yet she always came back to Oak Valley Farm and the barn.

'It were only you what made being there bearable for me, girl,' Renee told her, holding her close and brushing her cheek across the soft feathers. 'Happen it were the same for you, eh, now I think of it? Well, we're together still, ain't we, and in a much nicer place. Eeh, I do love you, Ruby.'

The bird blinked up at her, as though digesting every word, and Renee kissed the top of her head.

'I needed someone to talk to, love, and knew you'd listen. You see, I'm in a terrible, terrible fix and I don't know what to do. Jimmy – you know Jimmy, don't you? You ought to. I've spoke of him to you often enough. Well, can you believe it, girl, he feels the same for me as what I do for him. It's true – he loves me, Ruby. He wants me to be his wife.' A single tear followed its course down Renee's face and dripped from her chin on to Ruby's wing. 'But that can't happen, can it? You and me both know why.

'Other lasses what go to their husbands on their wedding night do so with their innocence in place – they're normal. I'm not, am I? Dad stripped from me the one thing a father never ever should and what's more, Ruby, it's gone for good. Jimmy would hate me if he found out I hadn't come to him whole. He'd assume I'd been free with my fancies to other lads, would think he'd been tricked into marriage and respectability by a common whore. I won't have him think that of me, I can't!

'Why did Dad do it, eh?' The tears ran freely down her cheeks. 'I didn't want him to, girl; not one single time did I want him to do that – never! His violation of my body like that . . . how *could* he, his own flesh and blood? It makes me want to be sick for a week to think on it. He ought to rot in Lucifer's lair for what he's done – aye, for all eternity. He's ruined my life. I hate him, Ruby. I *hate* him.'

When Renee had finally finished pouring out her heart, though her friend hadn't been able to offer her advice she nonetheless felt the better for getting it out of her system.

'Ta, love,' she told her, giving her a last stroke and stooping to put her back in the box. 'Goodnight, God bless.'

As Renee was about to turn to leave, however, something made her freeze to the spot and her blood ran cold: a noise had sounded from beyond the barn doors. *God Almighty, no.*

'Hello?' she croaked, and was greeted with only silence. Tentatively, she made her way across the straw-strewn floor.

Again, she murmured a plea for acknowledgement. Once more, none was forthcoming. She sucked in a deep breath. Plucking up what courage she could muster, she grasped the handles and opened the doors wide.

Deserted.

Peering about the darkness, Renee frowned. Then a movement by the cowshed snared her attention and, squinting harder, she picked out two illuminated orbs that she slowly realised were eyes – and glory be, a wagging tail. The farmer's dog! Relief coursed through her like a tidal wave. *Thank the Lord!*

She clicked her tongue against her teeth and the collie trotted across to her, nudging at her hand for a stroke. Renee chuckled softly.

'Come on, you, you scallywag,' she told it, taking it by the collar and leading the way back to the house.

Sure enough, when she reached it, she discovered the front door ajar and admonished herself inwardly for failing to secure it properly when she'd left. Still, one important fact remained: her secret was safely intact. Animals never repeated anything you said, no matter how shocking – her dear Ruby was proof of that.

'In you go,' she said, shepherding the dog inside and closing the door with an easy smile.

Chapter 12

TRUE TO HIS word, Jimmy had made it his mission to make Renee know her worth. He showered her with compliments at any opportunity, praised her work at each turn, hung on her every word and for the first time in her short life made her feel that what she had to say mattered.

He told her continually how special she was to him, what being her husband would mean to him, and laid out plans for their future together and all the tantalising riches – namely a family of their own making, one day – it might bring. And, though it seared when reality brought Renee crashing back to earth with a bump, still she oftentimes found herself fantasising along with him over the possibilities.

Unused to such positive outpourings, she was unsure still how to react to them, although they did leave her with a warm feeling deep inside. One thing she could be certain of was that Jimmy was bent on bringing her around. Come hell or high water, he was intent on winning his girl, no matter what it took or how long.

As March approached, the end of the long, bleak winter and all it had entailed was at last in sight. The snows were abating and a blithe sun was slowly beginning to stretch its legs and replenish the punished earth with its long-awaited rays. And it was with this first turning of the seasons that Renee began hankering for home and those she'd left behind.

'You mean you're missing your dad?' Jimmy asked her when Top o'th' Brow cropped up in conversation one bright spring day and she made mention of how her past had been on her mind of late. 'But I thought the whole point of coming out here was to be shot of him?'

'Oh, it was – it still is! Missing Dad? God no. No, Jimmy, you couldn't be further from the truth. It's Mrs Flynn I miss most, and even the estate itself to some degree.' She shrugged. 'Happen I'm being daft, ought to just put it all behind me for good and proper.'

'If it's your friend you're wanting to see, then do it, lass. Now the weather's improving, there's nowt to stop youse.'

Renee nodded thoughtfully. 'Mebbe you're right, aye.'

'I could get word to Iris if you'd like me to? Happen she could come and visit you here at the farm one Sunday. Jack and Maisie won't mind.'

'Eeh ta, Jimmy.' She bestowed upon him a grateful smile. Just what would she do without him?

'Owt for you, you know that. Now,' he went on, inclining his head to the field, 'I'd best get on. See you later, lass.'

'You will, Jimmy. Bye for now.'

Bar one or two having developed chapped udders – it happened, however careful you were to keep the skin dry and moisturised, it was simply one of those things, which a home-made lavender oil and beeswax balm was addressing – the Crawleys' cattle remained in good health. Nonetheless, Jimmy was dogged in his checks to their wellbeing, would leave nothing to chance. He really was an excellent and committed hand. Given the opportunity of his own smallholding, he'd have made the finest farmer in the north-west of England and beyond, Renee was sure of it.

Generally, so long as they were able to move around freely, snow on the ground didn't prove a hindrance to cows and, with conditions improved, they had been returned to the pasture. All that remained, now the thaws had set in and the mud was returning, was for the men to up their watch on foot maintenance. Renee, too, had been keeping a keen eye out, ready to report any sightings of limping brought on by bruising or cracking, warts and rot. However, she wasn't overly worried, knew the animals were in capable hands.

The following day, Jimmy sought her out to inform her he'd passed on the message to Mrs Flynn that Renee wanted to see her, and that the older woman would be tickled pink to pay Oak Valley a visit. Renee was giddy with delight.

On the appointed day, she was up with the larks and barely moved from her post by the window, where she was keeping lookout for a glimpse of the familiar figure. Then, towards mid-afternoon, there Iris was. With a squeal of excitement, Renee dashed out across the farmyard to greet her.

'Eeh, lass, you're a sight for sore eyes.' Her former neighbour nodded her approval. 'Some meat looks to have stuck to your bones since last I saw you. You look well on it.'

Hugging her, Renee laughed. 'I feel it, an' all. You're not looking too bad yourself, Mrs Flynn.'

'So, how're you liking it here?' the woman asked when they were sitting at the kitchen table with a cup of tea.

'Oh, it's gradely. Mr and Mrs Crawley have been so very good to me. I couldn't wish for kinder employers, aye.'

'Well, it's glad I am to hear it. I ain't half missed you, lass. Top o'th' Brow just don't feel the same without you, you know.'

'I do miss it, Mrs Flynn. And you, of course.' Renee bit her lip in contrition. 'You mean so much to me, and I would have been in touch sooner, but what with the awful winter and being so busy with the house and farm . . .'

'Tsk, don't be daft, I understand,' Iris was quick to reassure her. 'Besides, it's a fresh start you've gone and got yourself here; you don't want to keep looking back on what's passed, love.'

Renee smiled in relief, yet it proved short-lived as another resident of the estate flitted into her mind. 'How's Lynn Ball?' she asked tentatively.

'Oh, well and good, well and good. I had a word

with her like I said I would after you'd gone, explained the situation.'

'What did you tell her, Mrs Flynn? Was she angry?'

'I thought it best not to mention your true whereabouts, so said you'd upped and left to join the Women's Land Army.' She spread her hands wide and glanced about. 'It weren't an out-and-out fib, really, I don't suppose. Lynn weren't angry, lass, no. Surprised, aye, but not mad. Her next-door neighbour minds the twins for her now, so no harm done.'

'Thank God. I still feel rotten, you know, leaving her in the lurch as I did.'

'Well, you can put your worries to bed, for it all turned out well in t' end.'

'I'm glad.'

The elephant in the room refused to abate and eventually Iris said, 'Ivan Rushmore . . .'

Renee raised her head slowly. 'Aye,' she murmured, relieved somewhat that it had been voiced.

'He's norra well man, lass.'

She frowned but didn't speak.

'Gone right downhill, he has, since you've gone. It's the drink,' she explained when Renee folded her arms and looked away. 'He's at the bottle every day without fail, comes staggering home each night shouting and swearing in the lane loud enough to waken the dead from their coffins. How he manages to go out to work each morning and has kept hold of his job this long, I'll never know.'

Renee's tone was low. 'I won't feel sorry for him, Mrs Flynn.'

'Ay, and nor should you! Friggin' 'ell, no – he don't deserve that. I just thought you ought to know how matters stood.'

'Aye, I know. I understand. Ta for telling me.'

'At least the swine ain't got the faintest idea still where you are. Nor is he likely to find out, no.'

'Was he bad, Mrs Flynn? In t' beginning, like?'

'When you first left? Aye, he were,' she revealed at Renee's nod. 'Searched the streets like a man possessed, he did, banging on doors and causing a nuisance. Course, no one knew where you were so he learned nowt.'

'And what of you? Did he suspect you'd helped me get away?'

'I can't rightly answer that, lass. Either way, he couldn't prove owt.'

'I'd never have broke free but for you, couldn't have managed it alone. Just how *did* you draw him from the house that day, Mrs Flynn?'

A smile lifted the corners of the woman's mouth. 'I told him one of his pigeons had got stuck down my chimney.'

'You never did!' Renee couldn't contain a grin.

'Oh aye. I said I'd seen it hanging about the roof beforehand and knew it was one of his by the silver ring round its leg. He was in my house poking around that fireplace for a good twenty minutes. Black as the hobs of hell, he were, by the time he left.'

Holding on to each other, they laughed until their ribs ached.

'I'm glad you came, Mrs Flynn,' Renee told her

157

with feeling later. 'You will keep in touch, won't yer?'

'Hey now,' the woman chided, clicking her tongue, 'we're friends, ain't we?'

'The best.'

'There you are, then. Just you try and stop me.'

'Happy?' Jimmy asked Renee the next day as they walked the fields together on their mid-afternoon break.

Linking his arm, she sighed in contentment. 'Aye. It was lovely nattering with Mrs Flynn. I hadn't realised how much I missed her 'til I saw her again.'

'Renee, what you told me she'd said about your dad—'

'I don't want to talk about that any more, Jimmy,' she interjected quietly. 'I don't want to think of him at all.'

'I'm sorry, it's just I've been thinking . . .'

'What about?'

'Well, I'd already suspected it'd be no good hoping he'd give permission for you to wed. Now, it looks even more unlikely, don't it? Which means we definitely don't have a choice but to wait 'til you're twenty-one.'

'Jimmy . . .'

'Hear me out, lass,' he insisted, bringing her to a standstill and taking the tops of her arms in his large hands. He rubbed his thumbs up and down them in a soft caress. 'I told you from the off, didn't I, that I don't mind waiting for as long as it takes. So long as

I get to call you my wife at some point, I'll be satisfied.'

'And I told you, Jimmy, that it can never be.' It crucified her to do it, but she must. 'My mind hasn't changed. I can never marry you.'

'Never is a long time, Renee.' It was evident that he was still convinced he'd eventually sway her decision, which tore her heart in two at its futility. 'Who knows what might happen in t' meantime?'

'What are you saying?'

'How's about we get engaged for now? If you do decide in t' future that you really can't bear the thought of becoming my wife, then, well, we'll break it off and call it a day with no harm done. Go on, Renee, say you will.' He lifted her chin with his forefinger and gazed down into her stunned face. 'Knowing you're promised to me, until you've made up your mind for certain at least, would mean the whole world to me, lass.'

She was near to tears – and dangerously close to submitting. Then Ivan's hateful face smashed through her brain, the memory of his grubby, sweaty hands violating her flesh and the feel of the weight of his body on top of her own, and the decision was made for her. She must remain resolute.

'Sorry, Jimmy, but it's still a no.'

Rather than be hurt by her rejection, he wasn't put off. He shrugged, smiled. 'I'll get your consent one day, Renee, you'll see. I'll not rest until you agree to be mine.'

Oh, lad. I don't deserve you. Her heart called to him

159

miserably, but her head, she knew, must always take precedence.

Just how would this pan out for them? Where would it end?

Surprisingly to Renee, it wasn't thoughts of Jimmy that predominated her mind throughout the remainder of the day and into the long, sleepless night that followed. Instead, it was her father who had taken root and refused to leave her in peace, much to her confusion and irritation.

She owed him nothing, *nothing* – and certainly not a single ounce of her pity. And yet it was there all the same, blast it.

If he continued to drink and was unable to work, he'd lose his position at the train station. Then where would he be? How would he live, pay his rent? What would become of him? Moreover, why was she bothering contemplating this?

Renee hadn't the answers to any of the questions that assaulted her without let-up – and in particular that last one. However, she could be sure of one thing and tried her damnedest to remember the fact. Whatever occurred, whatever befell the man who had terrorised her every waking moment for more years than she cared to dwell upon, it would be his own doing.

It would, all of it, every time. She hadn't asked for any of the things he'd made her suffer, had she? He'd done as he pleased, acted out whatever warped desires had brought him pleasure off his own bat, and always had.

Nobody on this green earth was to blame but him. She must never forget that.

When the following week Mrs Flynn paid Oak Valley Farm another visit, it was to deliver news that, despite everything, left Renee reeling.

As of yesterday morning, number forty-six Monks Lane was vacant.

The place she'd called home for half her life, the place which did hold some good memories as well as the bad, had been cleared out and shut up, its occupant vanished.

Where Ivan had gone to, no one could say. Nor should it matter, surely?

The whole terrible chapter was over with. All that remained for Renee to do now was to keep reminding herself that she didn't care.

Chapter 13

Mid-August 1941

'A VERY HAPPY birthday to you, Renee lass.'

Offering her cheeks to receive Jack and Maisie's kisses, a smiling Renee gulped back emotion. 'Ta, thanks, Mr and Mrs Crawley.'

The small birthday tea of cold meats, dainty fairy cakes and sandwiches that she'd prepared was laid out in readiness on the large, square pine table. She'd covered the plates holding the latter with damp tea cloths, to prevent the crusts from curling, and just hoped they would still be edible by the time the other two guests had arrived.

Throwing a glance to the clock, a small frown tugged at her brows. Mrs Flynn had been told three o'clock, and that was still over half an hour away, so Renee wasn't expecting her just yet. Jimmy, on the other hand, was another matter. He'd promised yesterday to be here early, but as yet there was no sign of him.

'This all looks lovely. You've done well, lass, considering,' said Maisie in her soft way. She'd been

162

carried downstairs by her husband to enjoy the jollities and was reclining on the horsehair sofa, which Jack had drawn nearer to the fire. Her speech was slurred and somewhat distorted owing to the last and more severe stroke she'd suffered, but not so much that those closest to her were unable to understand.

Pulled from her thoughts and bringing her mind back to the present, Renee smiled. Restrictions had over time intensified, and things that were by now 'on t' ration' could have filled a list as long as her arm. Tea and margarine as well as all meats had been added the previous year and had recently been followed by jam, cheese and eggs. Not only that but the nation had seen restrictions extended to other items, too, besides foodstuffs: clothing in particular, and as of last month, coal, as more and more miners answered the call to fight.

The issue of food was eased considerably by Mrs Flynn's 'spoils'. Once a week, she would arrive at Oak Valley Farm with her wicker basket groaning under the weight of staples that were becoming increasingly hard to come by. Where she acquired these extras, neither Renee nor the Crawleys were wont to probe; they were simply grateful to get their hands on them. Renee reckoned her cousin Maureen or Linda must have something to do with it but hadn't put her suspicions to her friend. Least said, the better, and all that. Dealing in black-market goods was a criminal offence, after all – the last thing she wanted was the police getting wind of it and anyone landing up in trouble.

Although the coal shortage could prove a trial at times, Renee had never been in a position to be fashion-conscious and so the clothing ration didn't unduly bother her. Today she'd chosen to wear her mother's outfit of white nylon blouse and granite-coloured, calf-length skirt, finished off by the pale green voile scarf, and she looked good, even if she did say so herself. And, despite herself, she was anxious for Jimmy to see her all dolled up.

Usually, he only knew her to be dressed in her plain house dress and pinny, or the muddied men's clothing she would don when helping to work the fields. Though it was true she didn't want to feed further his ever-growing want of her, she still, like most young women of her age, craved to be viewed as attractive, couldn't help it, and she was unable to suppress the hope that, today, he would think her prettier still than he normally did.

'That'll be your aunty, Renee,' Jack announced as a knock sounded suddenly at the farmhouse door, and though she hid it well, Renee couldn't stem the cringe she always experienced whenever he or Maisie made reference to Iris as such.

Keen not to evoke awkward questions regarding her background and circumstances, she'd told the Crawleys right at the start that her parents were long dead and Mrs Flynn was her sole living relative. They hadn't queried this – why would they? – and they welcomed Iris into their home on her visits to her 'niece' freely, for which Renee was both thankful and filled with guilt at her deceit in equal measure.

'Happy Birthday, lass!' Mrs Flynn bustled inside with smiles all round. 'The table looks nice. And by, you yourself don't half look bonny.'

Renee preened. 'Ta, thanks. And how are you? All right?'

'Oh, well and good, lass, well and good.'

'Sit yourself down, Iris.' The farmer's wife nodded to a chair. 'Renee's not long since brewed a fresh pot.'

'I'll not say no, could murder a sup of tea. And how are you bearing up, Maisie? All right?'

'Oh, you know. Can't complain, love.'

As the women settled down for a natter, Renee found herself wandering once again to the window to peer out across the cobbled yard. And, spotting this and guessing who she was keeping a lookout for, Jack lowered his head and escaped to the other room.

Renee watched the farmer go with a bite of her lip. It wasn't her imagination – like Jimmy, Jack was definitely hiding something from her.

She'd noticed a shift in their behaviour several weeks past. She'd frequently catch the older man, when she was in Jimmy's company, watching on with an expression of pity. Though she'd mentioned this to Jimmy, he'd shrugged his shoulders and stated he hadn't seen it himself, before swiftly changing the subject. Renee was left feeling flummoxed, and not only by this issue. Jimmy's own behaviour was also becoming a cause for concern.

His easy smile and normally laid-back way had

been in short supply of late. These days, he appeared decidedly on edge, as though he had the worries of the world on his mind. Again, when she'd pressed him, he'd brushed aside her questioning with little to no real explanation. However, she knew she wasn't dreaming all of this, was certain something was going on. How to find out what, though, and attempt to help if he was unwilling to open up?

At last, Jimmy appeared around the bend and her heart gave a little flutter as it always did at the sight of him. She patted her hair and smoothed down her clothing, then hurried to meet him at the door.

'Hello.'

'Hello,' he responded, giving her a smile. He dipped his head and dropped a kiss to the corner of her mouth, setting her pulse racing.

She tried not to be too disappointed that he hadn't made mention of her appearance. Nor did he, as she'd secretly been dreading, pass comment on her coming of age now being one step closer, the way he had last August on her eighteenth. Back then, he'd held her close and whispered in her ear, 'Just three more years, Renee, and then you'll be your own woman and be free to make your own decisions. And from now 'til then, I'll be praying every day that you make the right one.'

'Happy Birthday, Renee,' he finally offered her now, as though he'd just remembered the occasion. And though it both stung and confused her, she told herself not to be childish and make a song and dance of it. Today was, after all, for making merry and having fun, not causing a ruckus over something so petty.

'Ta, thanks, Jimmy. Come on in.'

Jack had set up the old gramophone earlier in the day, and as they tucked into the spread, they tapped their feet to the music. Talk and laughter soon filled the warm and welcoming room, and Renee was really beginning to enjoy herself. Then she turned to say something to Jimmy, who hadn't expected it and hadn't time to check himself – the expression on his face wiped the pleasure from her own. He looked thoroughly and undeniably miserable. She touched his arm in concern.

'Won't you talk to me? Just what is wrong at all? Please, lad.'

He opened his mouth as if he meant to pooh-pooh her question. Then it was as though the strength he needed to uphold the pretence deserted him – he bowed his head and let out a long, ragged sigh. Inclining his head, he left the house. Leaving the oblivious others to their chatter, she slipped out after him.

When they reached the barn, Jimmy lowered himself on to a straw bale and motioned that she should join him. Resting his elbows on his knees, he raked his fingers through his hair. Finally, he brought his stare around to meet hers. Regret screamed from his eyes. 'I'm sorry . . .'

'Sorry for what?' Dread now knotted Renee's stomach and her breathing had quickened. She licked her dry lips. 'Jimmy, what's going on?'

'I've had my call-up papers, lass.'

No. Her head swam for a moment and she thought she might be sick. 'Tell me it ain't, it ain't true, Jimmy—'

'I can't. It is.'

'When . . .?'

'Weeks ago.'

'*Weeks?*' She was flabbergasted. 'Why on earth are you only mentioning this now?'

'Renee, I didn't know how to tell you.'

She slumped, trembling, and dropped her head in her hands. 'They can't do this,' she rasped. 'You're needed here. Surely they can see that? *Surely* they see how important your job is on the farm?'

His voice was hollow. 'They won't budge, lass. We have tried everything.'

'We? Who's we?'

'Well, Jack, he—'

'I knew it!' Renee's eyes had pooled with tears. 'You two *have* been acting shifty, you have, I saw it. You told me I were imagining things, when all the time . . .'

'I didn't want to worry you unless it were necessary. Jack, he put in an employer's request asking that I might be granted deferment from being conscripted as my position here is vital to the country, but for whatever reason he was turned down. It's come as an almighty shock. We just weren't expecting it, Renee, and I honestly thought there wouldn't come a time when I'd need to tell you. But well, there has, and here we are.'

'You're sure . . . there's nowt that can be done, nowt at all . . .?'

'No, love.'

She closed her eyes in despair.

Bar the rationing and sporadic air raid warnings, it was oftentimes hard to remember they were at war. As suspected, there wasn't much the enemy would want to destroy and so the town had been spared the horrific bombing suffered by larger and more prominent cities.

She'd upheld her habit of not reading the newspapers or listening in to the reports on the wireless and did her best to close her ears to discussions on the farm of developments both here and abroad, talk of the Blitz and battles in far-flung places and invasions of other countries; she found it too depressing and upsetting. Nor had it thus far proved too difficult to bury her head in the sand.

Cosseted here on their deserted farm, it was as if they were in their own private bubble, cut off from the rest of the world and its troubles. Now, though, hearing his news, the illusion was shattered into a million pieces.

This was all too personal and oh so very real. Jimmy was one of them, and he was going away to war. He'd soon be dragged into the deadly madness and there was nothing any one of them could do to stop it. *Nothing*.

'I won't bear it,' she whispered up into his face. 'I'll die without you here.'

Jimmy enveloped her in his strong arms and

dropped butterfly kisses on to her hair. 'I don't want to hear you talk like that.'

'I mean it.' There were no hysterics. She spoke quietly, her admissions dull with truth. 'I don't know what I'll do without you, Jimmy. Not now.'

'I mean that much to you, Renee?'

'You know you do!'

'Do I?' He pulled back to look at her. 'Do I?' he repeated, and there was a note of pain within the tone.

Renee gazed at him through a film of tears as a maelstrom of questions whizzed dizzyingly through her head. Should she . . .? *Let's get engaged.* Just three little words and she knew without a doubt she'd be sending him off the happiest man alive. It would be something to see him through, keep him going. He was the single most precious thing in her life. And yet . . .

Should he survive – which she fervently hoped he would more than anything else in the whole of this world – he'd rightly expect her to uphold her word. She couldn't do that, could she? Jimmy *couldn't* know . . . So just what the hell was she to do? *What?*

'Well, lass?'

'Well, what?' she murmured, knowing exactly what he meant. At least she thought she did – what he said next completely threw her.

'Will you now be honest with me?' he asked her quietly.

'Will I . . .?' She shook her head. 'Jimmy, I don't understand. I am honest with you, always have been.'

'Not quite, Renee.'

Something in the way he'd said it caused the hairs on the back of her neck to spring to attention. *He knew. But how?* her mind cried in the next nanosecond; it was impossible! No one on this earth had any idea bar the two people involved: herself and Ivan Rushmore. And she couldn't very well see her father divulging the news, even if Jimmy did know where he was, which he didn't. She scrutinised his face for a long moment, hoping to spot some mode of clue, but there was nothing. He peered right back at her, not giving anything away.

'Jimmy?'

His voice was as calm as a summer breeze and every bit as gentle. 'I know, Renee. I know what your dad used to do to you.'

A whooshing sound crashed through her ears, then the blood drained away at great speed making her feel light-headed. She lurched, bending double as though she might vomit.

'But *how* . . .'

'Jack.'

'Mr Crawley?' The torturous unambiguity was overwhelming. 'How in the name of God . . .?'

'He overheard you last year – here, in this very barn. You were telling your troubles to Ruby.'

She'd believed it to be the dog skulking about outside in the pitch black, when all the time . . . 'But . . . it was the dead of night—'

'You must have set the dog loose when you left the house,' Jimmy explained, 'and Jack was alerted by the

171

noise. He didn't want to upset you by letting on what he'd discovered. Nor would he have uttered any of it to a living soul, I'm sure, if I hadn't got my call-up. I told him, you see, how I feel about you, but that you wouldn't commit yourself to me. I think he felt sorry for me – that's when he revealed what he did.'

'Christ Almighty.'

'Don't be angry with him, Renee. He only did it because he thought it was the right thing to do.'

'I just can't . . .' She could barely form coherent speech. 'You *know*.'

'Aye. What's more, Renee, I don't care.'

On a gasp, she snapped her head back to gawp at him.

'Nowt could change how I feel about you, lass. Besides, you're not at fault, never. It weren't your doing. It was his, and his alone. I'd like to kill the foul bastard if truth be told.'

'Oh, Jimmy.'

'Renee, my love.'

On a simultaneous cry, they embraced one another tightly.

'I believed you'd hate me if you ever knew . . .!'

'No, no!'

Wrapped in each other's arms, for a full minute they were silent in their shared grief and need for comfort. When finally Jimmy straightened up, intending to speak, Renee was ready for it.

'So, lass, now we've got everything out in the open, will you—?'

'Sshhh.' Stopping him with a finger to his lips, she

bestowed upon him a watery smile. Then she rose and held out her hand. 'Come on, let's get back to the house. We have an announcement to make.'

The fields and hillsides, lanes and streets, basked beneath glorious sunshine the following morning as the newly betrothed couple travelled by tram to the centre of town. It was as if even the weather itself had sensed the importance of the occasion and decided to come out in force to wish them well. The young, besotted pair had never been happier.

'Now, remember what I said,' Jimmy reminded Renee when they had ground to a halt at their stop and were stepping down from the platform. 'The cost is not to put you off. I've a good few pounds saved, so you just choose whichever one takes your fancy. All right?'

Gazing up into his eyes, Renee reckoned her heart might explode with love. 'Aye, lad. Eeh, I'm that excited I'm afraid my legs will give out on me any minute!'

Taking her elbow and guiding her across the bustling high street towards the large Prestons jewellery store on the junction of Deansgate and Bank Street, he chuckled. 'Don't worry, love. If they do, I'll be ready to catch you. Any excuse to hold you in my arms,' he finished with a wink.

Before entering, Renee glanced in the direction of Trinity Street and the train station, but just the once; that's all she would allow herself. That her father might still be employed there – after all, no one knew for sure that losing his position was what was behind him upping sticks and leaving Monks Lane – and might somehow spot her in town didn't worry her, not now. Ivan didn't matter any more. Nor did he wield power to hurt her. Those days were far behind her. She had Jimmy to protect her now. Allowing herself a smile, she lifted her chin with confidence and followed the lad inside.

An assistant greeted them at the counter warmly and put Renee at her ease right away: 'Good morning, madam, sir. How can I be of help today? Are you looking to buy something in particular?'

Renee and Jimmy shared a grin, with the latter offering, 'Aye, an engagement ring.'

'Congratulations. You, my dear,' she added to Renee with a nod, 'will make a most beautiful bride.'

Renee blushed to the roots of her hair but was delighted all the same. 'Ta, thanks.'

'If you'd like to follow me, I'll show you the selection we have in. This way.' She led the couple to a few trays of gold rings sitting inside a glass cabinet. 'Here we are. I'll leave you to peruse them in peace, take your time. Just shout should you need me.'

Alone, as giddy as schoolchildren, they moved in for a closer inspection.

'Oh, look at that one.' Pointing to a ring at the back that held three oval-shaped stones in deep red, Renee sighed dreamily. 'Oh, it's stunning.'

'You like that one, aye?' Jimmy asked her.

'Oh aye. But lad, I'll not choose it, for it's bound to cost a fortune—'

'Now, what did I say? Don't fret over the price.' He scanned the shop in search of the assistant and, locating her, he caught her eye and beckoned her across.

Renee was wishing she'd kept her thoughts to herself. 'Jimmy, don't be wasting her time getting the ring out! I told you, it'll cost the earth – I'll not let you fritter your hard-earned brass. I could find summat equally as lovely for a fraction of the price.'

But Jimmy had stopped listening. He pointed out the ring to the woman and she duly obliged him, disappearing around the cabinet to fulfil his request.

'Well?' he asked Renee when she'd reluctantly slipped the ring on to her finger.

'It's a perfect fit,' she whispered. Twisting her hand this way and that, she watched, mesmerised, as it caught the light from the rays streaming in through the large shop window. 'But—'

'But nowt.' Jimmy's tone brooked no argument. 'If that's the one you've fallen in love with, then that's the one you shall have.'

'Eeh, lad . . .'

Watching on, the assistant smiled, and her eyes told Renee what she already knew and then some: the man before her adored his intended and would make her a fine husband. She was one very lucky woman.

'Will sir and madam be purchasing the three-stone garnet?'

Jimmy's nod was firm. 'Aye, that's right.'

Her face lit up; it was quite clear she worked on commission. 'Very good. A very wise choice. The cost of that particular ring is four pounds six shillings.'

Oh my . . . Renee gazed from her to Jimmy in astonishment. He couldn't afford to part with such a sum, surely!

'Will you be paying the full amount today?' the assistant went on, eager for the sale. 'Or you could, of course, put down half the amount as deposit and pay the rest at a later date?'

'I'll pay the full amount now, thank you.'

'Very good, sir. If you'll give me one moment, I'll put the ring in a box for you, then write out a receipt.'

'Lad!' Renee hissed when they were once again left on their own. 'Eeh, let me choose another. That one's much too expensive!'

He was resolute. 'It's the one you want, and as so, it's the one I want you to have.'

'But—'

'Renee, it's a done deal now, so no more talk of swapping it, all right? The ring is yours, and what's more, I couldn't be more pleased.'

Throwing caution to the wind, with tears swimming in her eyes, she threw her arms around his neck and hugged him tightly. 'I love you, Jimmy Wallace.'

'And I you,' he whispered back, holding her closer. 'Eeh, lass, I'll not make you ever regret marrying me. I'll make you glad yer did every day, I swear it.'

Outside, with the black velvet box holding the beautiful ring sitting securely in the inside pocket of Jimmy's jacket, they stopped to smile at one another.

'Happy?'

'Happy,' Renee murmured, squeezing his hand.

'What say we round the day off with a pot of tea and a toasted teacake at that cafe over there? My treat.' It was the least she could do.

'Sounds good to me. We'll have to make it a flying visit, mind you. I know Jack and Maisie gave us the morning off, but I wouldn't like to be too late getting back and have them thinking we're taking liberties.'

She nodded. 'Come on, then. My nerves are shot – I could murder a brew!'

They emerged from the eating house half an hour later feeling replenished and relaxed. A tram was approaching the stop in the distance, and they set off on a run to catch it.

When they had found a seat and paid their fare to the conductor, Jimmy patted his breast pocket. 'I'll be counting down the hours until I get to slip this on your finger, love. It's going to go down as the best day of my life.'

'And mine, lad. Don't worry, Sunday will be here before we know it.'

They had decided to mark the momentous occasion properly and had asked that their employers, Iris Flynn and Jimmy's father Gordon join them in the official announcement at the farm the next week. Each had been delighted to accept, and Renee planned to put on a small spread again – not without a little help from Mrs Flynn and her food contacts. It looked set to be a brilliant day and both Renee and Jimmy could hardly wait.

Staring out of the window, although barely taking in the passing landscape – her mind was far too preoccupied with her thoughts – Renee cast her mind back to the day before and all that had happened so far in between. It was almost impossible to believe that so much had changed in just twenty-four hours. *Me and Jimmy, soon to be wed.* Her, Renee Rushmore, set to become a married woman! And to think she'd ever harboured notions that the man she loved would turn from her if he learned her secret. She should have given him more credit, should have known better. By, but she'd never feel happiness like this if she lived to be a hundred, she just knew it.

The farmer, his wife and Iris had been more than generous in their cries of congratulations and outpouring of well wishes upon hearing the couple's news on their return from the barn. Their joy had been evident, though all had admitted this hadn't come as a great shock. As Iris had pointed out, anyone with half an eye could see they were made for each other. The only real surprise was that it hadn't occurred sooner.

They had almost reached Breightmet when Renee's mind was brought back to the present with a bump. Two women occupying the seats behind them were talking – and it was painfully obvious that their mock whispers were intended for the whole tram to hear.

'Just look at him, there, in front. A healthy, strapping lad like that sitting pretty at home, eh, I ask you!'

'You're right there,' chipped in her companion. 'A friggin' disgrace, it is, and he ought to be ashamed. Why ain't he out there fighting this war for us, that's

178

what I'd like to know? Nay, but he's content to let *our* men risk life and limb fighting for him.'

'It's just a pity I ain't got a white feather on me, that's all I can say.'

'Aye – hear, hear!'

Renee felt Jimmy stiffen beside her, and anger flooded through her. She was about to turn to give the viper-tongued pair a piece of her mind, but he stopped her.

'Ignore them. It's not worth it.'

'But, lad—!'

'Please, Renee.'

It was then she understood, she saw it in his eyes: this wasn't the first time he'd received such abuse from narrow-minded idiots. How dare they – they didn't know this fine, upstanding man here, didn't know him at all! Never mind that he'd been working his fingers to the bone this past two years of the conflict to keep his fellow man, woman and child fed; no, that seemed to escape their comprehension. All some folk saw before them when they looked at Jimmy and others of his ilk was a coward. *Brainless, unthinking ruddy fools* . . . Renee could have wept for him.

Suddenly, the magical past few days seemed tainted. Not by the inaccurate assumptions of those sods – no, she refused to take any notice of what people like that had to say. It was the reminder of war that had sullied things.

Consumed by her plans for the future, she'd naively shoved the truth that Jimmy would soon be leaving her for the horrors of the battlefields to the back of her mind. She hadn't wanted to dwell on it, to remember . . . But the stark fact of the matter was she had no choice, really, did she? None of them did. Shortly, he would be gone, and she would cease to fully exist.

Biting the inside of her cheek to stop herself from crying, Renee closed her eyes.

Just how was she meant to cope? *How*, damn it?

Chapter 14

THE GET-TOGETHER THE following Sunday went without a hitch and was enjoyed by all. Determined to make it an occasion to remember, Renee and Jimmy did their utmost to put thoughts of the impending separation to the back of their minds, as far as they were able, and the company did likewise.

However, there was no escaping the reality when, three days later, the day dawned for him to leave Bolton for twelve weeks' basic training in Chester. Renee was inconsolable. Even the cows seemed to be mourning his leaving when he went to walk the fields and stroke each in turn in farewell.

'I'll be back before you even get a chance to miss me,' he told Renee, taking her in his arms as they said a last goodbye in the cobbled yard.

His tone had been upbeat; he was putting a brave face on things, but she could tell that inside he was as upset as the rest of them. 'I miss you already, Jimmy, don't you understand?' she sobbed into his shoulder. 'Them in power, I could wring their necks with my bare hands forcing you to go like this!'

'We'll not be parted long, lass. The time will fly by, you'll see.'

And then the proper heartache begins, her mind screamed out to him. *You'll be off to the real thing, in the thick of it, and I'll be out of my head with worry for you every second of every day.*

'Oh lad, I'd sell my soul to the Devil hisself for you not to have to leave me.'

'Come on, now. Wipe them lovely eyes of yours and send me on my way with a smile. Can you do that for me, Renee? Please?'

With great effort, knowing he needed her strength, she sucked in a deep breath to compose herself. Then she plastered in place what he wanted to see and inclined her chin towards the gate. 'Go on, you'd better be off. See you soon.'

'I'll be counting down the days, my love. Ta-ra.'

Renee managed to hold it together until Jimmy had disappeared from sight, then, wrapping her arms around herself, she bent double and sobbed her broken heart out.

They hadn't been apart for more than a single day in what now seemed like forever, and the sear of losing him was like nothing she'd experienced before. Three whole months without him. She'd go mad, she would!

Jack and Maisie, having said their goodbyes to their farmhand earlier, before tactfully leaving the couple alone, were awaiting her return in the house. They were armed ready with sympathetic smiles and murmured condolences as she entered – their kindness undid Renee's resolve again and she wept anew for her absent love.

'I know what you're feeling,' Maisie told her after beckoning her across and taking her hand. 'I went through this same thing during the last war with my Jack. Glory be to God, he came back to me in one piece, and so will your Jimmy to you. You must hold on to hope, lass. You must, it's all we have. All will turn out well in t' end, you'll see.'

And though Renee nodded, she had a very strong feeling without yet understanding why that there were further tribulations to overcome before that day ever arrived.

Time seemed to have ground to a halt the second she'd waved Jimmy off that fateful afternoon. The days and weeks crawled by at a snail's pace – Renee could have screamed to the heavens, so acute was her frustration.

Mr and Mrs Crawley, and even Iris, tried their best to bolster her spirits and prevent her drowning in melancholia, which Renee recognised, and she was appreciative of their efforts, but it just wasn't enough. She pined for her man something chronic and nothing, *nothing* would rectify it until he was once more returned to his rightful place by her side.

They were approaching the first month into his absence when, one crisp cold morning, Jack sought out Renee in the kitchen and asked to speak with her. He looked decidedly ill at ease, and, having grown accustomed now to expect the worst, her guts instantly twisted in dread. She slipped into the seat facing his at the table with bated breath.

'There's no easy way to say this, so I'll just come right out with it – we're selling up.'

'Sorry, Mr Crawley, I don't . . .?'

'The farm, lass. We've found a buyer for it. We leave in a fortnight's time.'

She blinked back in stunned stupor. 'What? Mr Crawley . . . it can't be true!'

'I'm afraid it is.' On a deep sigh, Jack spread his worn hands wide. 'We just can't manage without Jimmy being here, and that's the truth of it. And aye, I could advertise for a new farmhand, but who's to say *he* won't be called up one day as well? We'd have to start the process all over again, God knows how many times, and meanwhile the business suffers for it. No, it just wouldn't work.'

'But . . . what about land girls?' Desperate, she nodded wildly. 'Aye. You could get a few lasses in to help—'

'No, I don't think so. I'll not deny I ain't give that option some thought, but the truth of the matter is, deep down, I just don't have the heart for farming no more, lass. I'm not getting any younger, and what with the way Maisie is . . . My wife could suffer another turn at any time and the next could prove a lot worse – she'll need me to be there for her. Besides, I reckon we're getting out at just the right moment. What with these last winters we've had and another one on the way . . . we'd never cope this time around.'

Renee did understand his reasoning. Nonetheless, her devastation was absolute. 'Jimmy will be crushed; he loves this place.'

'Aye. And don't think I ain't wracked with guilt that he'll have no job to come home to when peacetime comes, because believe me, I am. That lad will be a hero and deserving of better, I know. But it is what it is. Nowt can alter things, it's out of my hands.'

'Eeh, Mr Crawley,' she said on a sigh. It was all she had – what more could she say, after all?

'You yourself will be all right, lass, won't you? Your aunty will take you in?'

It was only then that Renee realised: *she* would be out of a job *and* a home. *Lord, no.* She'd been so preoccupied with Jimmy, she hadn't given a thought to herself.

She could return to Top o'th' Brow now Ivan was gone, it was true, but would she find there Mrs Flynn willing to put her up? It was one thing supporting her in her escape, but to offer her a roof over her head? It was a big decision for anyone. Would her friend be agreeable to the idea?

And if she wasn't? The terror-inducing prospect stabbed at Renee's brain. What then?

There was no one else, was there? She hadn't another single soul to call her own.

Should Iris turn her down . . .

God above, what would become of her?

'Lass? By! To what do I owe this pleasure?'

Leaning forward across the step, Renee kissed the

lined cheek. 'I needed to see you, Mrs Flynn. Can I come in?'

'Has summat occurred?'

'Well . . .'

A small frown of concern knitted Iris's brows. She swung the door wide. 'Come on, fetch yourself inside, love. I'll put the kettle on.'

Minutes later, sitting drinking tea in the familiar and homely surroundings after so long brought a lump of emotion to Renee's throat. Praying for all she was worth, she began. 'I couldn't wait until Sunday and your visit to the farm, had to see you sooner . . . Mr Crawley's sold Oak Valley, Mrs Flynn. The new owners take possession of the place in two weeks' time.'

Her friend's mouth was hanging wide. 'Eeh, what a shame!'

'Aye.' Renee chewed her lips, trying desperately to find the courage to ask the all-important question. 'And well . . . the thing is . . .'

'You'll be jobless and homeless,' Iris blurted, relieving Renee of the pressure, for which she was more than a little grateful. 'Oh, lass, I'm sorry. I know how much you like it there.'

'Aye, I do. I'm really upset, if I'm honest.'

'Well of course, you'll come here to dwell with me.'

The relief at the golden words was overwhelming; Renee sagged in her chair. *Thank God.* 'Oh, Mrs Flynn. You're sure?'

'Tsk! Like you should even have to ask. You'll stop on here with me, I insist.'

Wiping her nose on the back of her hand, she flashed her a wobbly smile. 'You've come to my rescue more times than I can count. Just what would I ever do without you, eh, Mrs Flynn?'

'Hopefully, lass, I've a good few years in me yet before you get to find that out. I'm not due for the knackers yard just yet, you know!'

Feeling lighter of mind than she had in a good long while, Renee allowed herself to relax and enjoy Iris's company. Right now, the going was good, and she intended on holding on to the moment for all she was worth.

In contrast to preceding weeks, those that followed seemed to pass in the blink of an eye. Before she knew it, Renee found herself on a blustery early October morning standing in the rutted lane leading from Oak Valley Farm, waving the van containing the Crawleys and their worldly possessions goodbye. It disappeared around the turn in the road, and she lowered her arm with a deflated sigh.

This was the end of what had been one of the best chapters in her life so far, and she'd regret its passing for a long time to come. However, thanks to her wonderful friend, a brand-new phase awaited her and she mustn't lose sight of that. The past must remain the past. It was the future to which she should look now.

With her small case swinging in her hand and Ruby tucked inside her coat, she passed through Top o'th' Brow at a leisurely pace. Eeh, but it felt good to be coming back, despite everything. Bad memories of life at home aside, the estate held a special place in her heart and always would. Moreover, Ivan wasn't here this time around to mar the experience. Things were going to be just fine from hereon in, she was certain of it.

As she pushed open the wooden gate, Renee saw that the dark brown curtains at Mrs Flynn's front window were drawn, and she frowned. Surely her friend wasn't still abed? She was normally up with the larks. Unless she was poorly and had decided to sleep in a while . . .? Concerned now, Renee hurried for the door.

Upon reaching it, she noticed that the front step was grubby, and her worry intensified. This hadn't been scrubbed and donkey-stoned to a high shine, as was Iris's usual morning habit, in what looked like days. Something was definitely amiss.

Her heartbeat quickening, Renee knocked sharply at the door.

Nothing.

She rapped once more, louder this time, and waited for the sound of carpet slippers shuffling through the hallway, heralding Iris's approach, with her fingers tightly crossed.

Again, it never came.

After shouting her name several times through the letter box to no avail, Renee was beginning to grow frantic and was contemplating attempting to kick open the door when next door's window creaked open and a voice called, 'Renee Rushmore? Is that you?'

Though never a word had passed between them until this day, she recognised the woman who had been her former neighbour. She nodded. 'That's right. I'm looking for Mrs Flynn.'

'Oh, you'll not find her there, lass.'

'What? Why not?'

'Iris has gone away.'

'Gone . . . gone away?' Renee was stunned. 'But where? Why?'

'She took a nasty fall in the back garden whilst pegging summat out on the washing line. Bashed her head bad, she did, and broke one of her legs. It were me what found her, alerted by her shouts.'

Renee slapped a hand to her mouth. 'Oh no! Oh, is she all right? Where is she?'

'Gone stopping with her cousin to recuperate.'

'Maureen.'

'Aye, that's the one. Maureen gorra message to me early this morning to say Iris is doing well and will in time make a full recovery.'

'Thank God!'

'Maureen asked me to keep an eye to the house here in Iris's absence. You were to lodge with her as of today, weren't you, lass?'

Renee gave a distracted nod. But one thing was dominating her mind; nothing else mattered to her in this moment but Mrs Flynn. Oh, that poor, dear woman and what she'd suffered!

'Aye, Maureen said as much,' the neighbour went on. 'I promised to watch out for you to let you know what had happened. Maureen said I was to tell you that you're to go to her house. You'll be welcome there for as long as need be.'

'Oh. Aye. Ta, thanks, I'll do that.'

'You have the address, then, do you, lass?'

She shook her head. 'I have been there before, though. I'm sure I'll be able to find it.'

Minutes later, Renee was climbing aboard a tram on her way to Daubhill.

She alighted at the same stop she and Iris had done the day they visited, when hoping that Linda could help her secure a job, and looked about.

The buildings were vaguely recognisable; however, the further on she walked, she quickly became aware that nothing looked even remotely familiar any more – halting, she scanned her surroundings with a frown. She was totally and utterly lost.

At first, she wasn't unduly worried. She had a tongue in her head, after all – there were houses to knock at and folk to ask. Surely someone would be able to help her. Yet as time went on, she realised she'd been too swift in her assumption. For one thing, she didn't know Maureen's surname. Nor did she have even an inkling as to which road she lived in.

As she'd noted the last time she'd been to the area, these streets and dwellings all looked the same. And asking people something as basic as whether they knew of a woman called Maureen produced more than one snort of amusement – the name was a common one, and all Renee received for her efforts was growing embarrassment.

The temperature had dropped, and evening

shadows were drawing in when she was finally forced to admit defeat. To add to her woes, just then the clouds decided to part and a harsh, icy rain pelted down, enveloping all in its wake – Renee was drenched within seconds.

Taking shelter in a shop doorway, she found herself biting back tears. Just this morning, everything had seemed so promising, and now look at the fresh mess she'd found herself in. Why did nothing seem to run smoothly in her life? What on earth was she going to do?

Tootal, Broadhurst and Lee.

The name struck suddenly inside her head like a thunderbolt. She gasped. The textile place – of course! She could wait for Linda to come out of work and walk back with her to the house. Oh, thank you, Lord, thank you!

Hitching up Ruby with murmured assurances that they would soon be all right, Renee headed back into the street to seek directions to the mill from the first passer-by.

'Aye, I know the place,' confirmed an elderly man who had been hurrying past when Renee stopped him. He turned and pointed to the corner. 'Go down there and it'll lead you to St. Helens Road. Continue on, right the way up until you come to Adelaide Street, and there you'll find Sunnyside Mills. You can't miss it. It's only about a ten-minute walk, lass.'

'Oh, ta, mister.' Renee felt weak with relief. 'Ta very much.'

Sure enough, she found the premises without a

hitch. Taking up position by the gateposts leading to the entrance, she rested her case by her feet and kept an eagle eye on the doors.

Some thirty minutes later the mill workers, some singular or in pairs, others in groups, began streaming out into the dark evening. With her heart racing and everything crossed, Renee hurried forward.

Having never met Linda and possessing no clue as to what she looked like – she wouldn't have known the woman if she'd fallen over her – Renee had but one option open to her, and she put the same question to every female who passed:

'Hello, sorry to bother you, but is your name Linda?'

Time and again, her efforts failed to reap results.

On the odd occasion that someone said yes, her spirits would leap, but when she followed the query up by asking whether their mother was named Maureen, every time the answer was a firm 'no'.

Soon, the crowd slowed to a trickle, and panic began to set in. She'd pinned all her hopes on this idea, couldn't fail. It was her last chance. If this didn't work, she'd be done for!

'Excuse me.'

Feeling a tap on her shoulder, Renee spun around and found herself looking at a fresh-faced young woman wrapped up snugly against the elements in a thick woollen shawl. 'Aye?'

'I couldn't help overhearing – you're searching for someone called Linda?'

She nodded eagerly. 'That's right. You're not . . .?'

'No, my name's Jean. Jean Mayhew.'

'Oh.' The disappointment was crushing.

'Thing is though, I reckon I might know who you're after.'

'You do?' she squeaked.

'A Linda was tasked with showing me the ropes here when I first got the job. And aye, she did mention in passing once that her mam's name was Maureen.'

Euphoria smashed through Renee's breast. 'Oh!'

Then Jean was speaking again, and the new thread of hope shrivelled to nothing.

'Thing is, you'll not find Linda here now. She left the mill at the start of the new year.'

No.

'You don't . . .' Renee was almost too afraid to ask. 'You don't know where she lives by any chance, d'you?'

'Sorry, I don't.' The woman shook her head. Then, clearly unaware of just how important this matter was to Renee, she flashed a bright smile. 'I wish you luck in your search, though, and hope you manage to find her. An owd friend, is she?'

'Summat like that.' Renee's voice was thick with tears. 'Thanks, Jean. Ta-ra.'

Pausing at the end of the street, she leaned her back against the rough brick wall of a pub and dropped her chin to her chest. Then, void of the energy and desire to stem them, she gave her pent-up emotions free rein and wept bitterly.

'Oh, Mrs Flynn. Where are you?'

Naturally, an answer refused to present itself, and nor would it now. She was effectively – utterly – destitute.

'Perhaps Gordon Wallace . . .?' Renee whispered out loud; then, just as quickly, she dismissed the suggestion.

She couldn't go to her fiancé's family for help in this. It would arouse too many awkward questions. The butcher, clueless to the circumstances, had already expressed his puzzlement at the engagement do as to why Ivan Rushmore hadn't shown for such an important event. Mercifully, he'd done so out of earshot of the Crawleys, who believed her father dead, but it had nonetheless caused Renee much alarm. Jimmy had come to her rescue and spun Gordon the line that unfortunately Ivan was too unwell to attend, which had placated him and put a halt to further probing.

However, with an issue such as this . . .? No, there would be no fobbing Gordon off with some cock and bull tale this time. Who, after all, wouldn't turn immediately to their parent in such a dire situation as she found herself? Her future father-in-law would never swallow whatever lies she managed to conjure up, would surely demand to know the truth. That couldn't happen. He and everyone else must never know her dirty secret; the shame would kill her. It was bad enough Jack Crawley and Jimmy had found themselves in knowledge of it – this was two people too many already. Please, God, no one else would ever find out.

Ruined. It was *ruined*, all of it. Totally hopeless. Finished.

She didn't even have the option of sleeping on the streets, not in this weather and with Ruby's welfare at stake. Moreover, without an address, how would she receive correspondence from Jimmy? She'd written to inform him of matters regarding the farm and that she was going to live with Iris, and that was as much as he knew. She needed somewhere, had to send new details to him to continue getting his letters, simply must. They were all that were keeping her going. Besides, how else would he know where to find her upon his return home?

Great Aunt Hannah.

The mere thought of it brought bile to her throat and she was forced to suck in several deep breaths.

Seek out her father's aunt? But what if Ivan was there? He could have been staying with Hannah for all this time, right from the start since leaving Top o'th' Brow. Then again, he might never have gone to her – or if he had, he might have left already, probably found himself a few rooms to rent somewhere, aye. A lot could have happened in the past eighteen months, after all . . .

Could she really take the risk?

But where otherwise? *Where?*

Of course, just as she'd expected, no solution was forthcoming.

There was nothing else for it. She had to try.

Chapter 15

PUNCH STREET WAS one place Renee hadn't forgotten.

Despite only having visited the house and its occupant a handful of times throughout her life – and even those instances had been fleeting – the address was lodged firmly in her mind. Aunty Hannah had possessed a dog named Judy: a great snarling, scruffy and stinking lump of a thing with matted fur and a breath on it like raw sewage, which had the power to tickle your gag reflex from the opposite end of the room. Renee had thought it hilarious that the besotted owner had named her pet what she had, given where they lived, and it had always stuck in her mind. Many years had been and gone since then, however. The hound would be long dead by now, Renee surmised, with not a little guilty relief.

As with Maureen and Linda's home in Daubhill, Hannah's in Deane was of the terraced variety – row upon monotonous row of dull, cramped, two-up two-down dwellings, each identical to its neighbour in every respect. Renee knew a pang of longing for the airy lanes and avenues of Top o'th' Brow as she approached the property but told herself now wasn't the time to be sentimental. Anywhere was preferable to the cold, mean streets after all.

A chink of sickly yellow light showed through the corner of the threadbare curtains, heralding that someone was clearly at home – she licked her dry lips with a mixture of gratefulness and mounting dread. *Should Ivan . . . No,* she told herself resolutely. *I won't think on that possibility. And well, if Dad is here, I'll take to my heels quick-sharp – he'll never catch me, I'm too fast for that.* With a less-than-confident nod to seal the plan of action, she pushed herself forward and knocked.

Shambling steps sounded from within, and moments later a wizened face framed by hair as white as driven snow poked around the partially opened door: 'Aye?'

'Hello, Aunty Hannah. It's me.'

'Colin? Eeh, is it really thee?'

Frowning and shaking her head, Renee stepped closer. 'No, Aunty. It's Renee. You remember little Renee, don't you, your Ivan's daughter?'

Peering harder through rheumy, cornflower-blue eyes, Hannah puckered her toothless mouth in contemplation. Then her face cleared, and she bobbed her head vigorously with a squeak of recognition. 'Ay, aye! Well, I never; so it is. By gum, lass – come in, come in!'

Renee glanced past her towards the living room. Hitching up Ruby and gripping on tighter to her case, she prepared herself for flight. 'My dad . . . he's not stopping here with you, is he, Aunty?'

'Who?'

'My dad, Ivan Rushmore. He's not here?'

'Our Ivan?' The elderly woman shook her head. 'Nay, nay. Not him. I ain't seen or heard sight nor sound from him in donkey's years.'

Thank God. Her body went weak with unparalleled relief. Nevertheless, she had to be certain. 'You're sure?'

'Course I am. I said so, didn't I, and I should know. Come on then if you're for coming inside, you're letting all the heat out.'

Renee nodded. Smiling, she followed on into the house.

The room was just as she remembered it: the large dark sideboard against the far wall festooned with cheap ornaments and trinkets; the tree-coloured sofa set at an angle in the centre of the room facing the fireplace, where brasses hung on the chimney breast; the tiny square table and its two stools set beside the door leading into the kitchen. Though she had to admit that these days everything in the house held a dust veil, was in a most unkempt state – and this included its tenant. Putting down her case and taking stock of her aunt now in the light, Renee couldn't fail to notice the change in her.

Although it was true to say that Hannah had never been what you might call a fastidious homemaker, she'd once upheld a greater standard than these current living conditions – and for herself in particular.

Her thinning locks were lank with grease, her face less than clean, whilst her neck sported a visible tide-mark. What appeared to be congealed droplets of old gravy streaked her whiskery chin, and the flowery wrap-around pinny that she wore was stained and grubby. Renee took it all in discreetly, though inwardly she was dismayed at the sorry picture that was painted.

'Doesn't anyone call in to lend you a helping hand with things, Aunty?' she enquired as matter-of-factly as she could manage. The last thing she desired was to embarrass the woman. 'One of the neighbours, perhaps?'

Easing herself into her sagging chair by the fire-side, she absently stroked the horsehair spilling through the rips in the material and shook her head. 'Nay, lass. I cope here all on my lonesome. Well, I have to, don't I? Ain't got no one, I haven't.'

'Eeh, Aunty Hannah . . .'

Sadness swooped, bringing with it a hot flush of shame to her cheeks. She could have done more. Her father most definitely should have. For whether the truth stung or not, what Hannah spoke was correct: she had no one in this world but her nephew and great-niece. How had their own flesh and blood been left alone and forgotten all of this time to struggle like this? It was unforgivable really.

Renee stooped by her feet and placed a hand gently on her knee. 'I'm sorry, Aunty. So sorry.'

The old woman smiled blithely and patted her on the head. 'Why, lass, what's tha done?'

'It's more what I didn't do,' she murmured. *Only I couldn't get away when living at home, and once I'd gone . . . well. It weren't a risk I could have took, you see. Besides, I didn't have a single clue things were this bad for you, honest I didn't, and if I had . . .* She sighed deeply, heard how futile her inner excuses sounded. 'I'm here now, and I'm going to look after you. Just as well and for as long as I'm able, I will, I swear it.' And Renee meant every word. Hannah needed her.

Her aunt nodded, smiled again. 'You're a good lad, Colin, allus have been.'

Renee's brows drew together in bemusement at being referred to as this mysterious chap again. 'I'm Renee, Aunty, remember? Who's this Colin fella, anyroad?'

The moment the words left her lips, it occurred to Renee who he might be. Ivan had made mention once that his cousin, Hannah's only child, had been killed at the Somme during the Great War – and Renee was certain her dad had said his name was Colin. But why was her aunt mistaking her for him? Tired and dishevelled-looking she must well be after the day she'd had, but she surely didn't appear so rough as to favour a bloke, did she? By God! Chuckling, she shook her head. 'There's a family resemblance between me and your son, is there, Aunty? Is that it – are you teasing me because of how bad I look?'

Though Hannah laughed along, she neither confirmed nor denied it. Instead, she motioned towards the adjoining room. 'Stick yon kettle on, lass, will thee? I'm parched.'

Whilst she brewed tea in the dingy kitchen, Renee found herself wondering over Hannah's circumstances again. For one thing, how was she coping with the war? A quick glance through the grimy window showed a tiny, paved yard barely large enough to swing a kitten never mind hold an Anderson shelter – what did the woman do when the air-raid warning sounded? That would be the first thing on her list to find out, she determined. You never could be sure when the sirens would wail out their call to action and, although the skies had lain silent now for close on three months, who could tell when their luck might change? Renee wasn't taking any chances.

Another thing that occurred to her as she searched for her aunt's paltry ration of sugar, without success, was the issue of money. Just how did Hannah support herself? Did her old age pension stretch far enough? Work in any capacity was out of the question, surely, so if not, then where did she acquire adequate funds to supplement it to keep body and soul together? She'd be sure to tackle that subject, too.

'Here we are, Aunty.' Renee handed the hot tea to her minutes later, then took a sip of her own. 'It's unsweetened, I'm sorry to say – it looks like you're out of sugar.'

'Aye. We're only allowed a bit now, you know, at the shops. Goes right quick, it does.'

'You're right there. But well, the rationing is summat we must endure, eh, and everyone's in the same boat.'

201

'Rationing?' Hannah frowned thoughtfully. 'The war ain't over yet then, nay?'

Renee's own forehead crinkled in response. 'No, Aunty. Course not. Though I wish it *would* hurry up and finish.'

'What were them celebrations for, then, last week? All the country had a big party, do you remember? – I wore my best frock and hat for the occasion, aye.'

'Big party . . .?' She was flummoxed. Perhaps the old woman had dreamt it? 'I don't know, Aunty.'

Hannah clicked her tongue softly and shook her head. 'Ne'er mind. Ignore me. I don't know what's occurring any more these days, lass. It's all one fuzzy blur, in here, you know?' She tapped at her temple. 'I'm tired is all it is, I reckon. Just tired.'

'Aye, mebbe.' Renee's heart went out to her. How cruel old age could be; it was evident that at this point, in the winter of her life, her mind and body were not what they used to be. 'Would you feel better if you had a lie-down, Aunty?' she suggested. 'A kip might do you good. Don't fret over me, I'll be all right here until you rouse.'

Her face split in a grin. 'You'll not disappear then, lass? You're for stopping on here with your Aunty Hannah?'

'If you'll have me.'

'Ay, aye, that'd be gradely! Eeh, you've made an owd woman happy this day, that you have.'

Sighing in relief, Renee gave her a swift hug. 'That's settled then! Now, why don't you go and rest up and in the meantime, I'll make you a nice hot

202

meal. I'll have it all ready for you when you waken. How does that sound?'

'Bloomin' heavenly, lass. You'll find everything you need in yon kitchen.'

When she'd gone and her laboured gait had reached the bedroom, Renee looked around and smiled. They could be happy here, the two of them. She'd have this little house gleaming in no time at all, and her aunt would certainly benefit from some company and care. Yes, fingers crossed, this arrangement could well prove a boon to them both and a blessing in disguise.

Naturally she worried still over Mrs Flynn's state of health and did wish she could see her or even just get word to her, but now she wondered whether fate had played a hand in her failing to find her. If she had located Maureen and Linda's home, she would never have happened upon here, would she, would never have discovered the sorry circumstances she had? And just what would Hannah have done then? How she'd managed alone thus far was a mystery; surely the elderly woman couldn't have gone on like this for very much longer. Now, at least, she had someone to look after her. And Renee was adamant that she would undertake this role from hereon in for as long as was needed. Hannah was family – she refused to shirk what she deemed her natural duty.

The pantry, when she went to investigate, threw up nothing more than a small quantity of flour in a stone jar and a few mouldy potatoes. Shaking her head, she made to close the door again. Then, spying an empty wooden crate on the floor beneath the shelves, which she presumed was for holding vegetables when Hannah had them in, she opened the door fully again and dragged it out.

Ruby had sat untroubled for all this time beneath the shelter of her coat, but Renee knew she couldn't hold on to the feathered creature forever. She was bound to grow restless soon and besides, Renee's arm was beginning to ache. The crate would make an adequate bed for her for the time being. So long as she was comfortable, Ruby wouldn't make a fuss; she never did.

After settling the bird inside and positioning the box in the space between the old wooden larder unit and the wall, where she knew Ruby would feel secluded and secure, she returned to the living room.

Here, she took from her pocket her cracked, faux leather purse and counted its contents. Then she nodded and made for the hall.

Having left the front door on the sneck so she could get back in easily without having to disturb her aunt, Renee exited the house and turned right. Mindful of every step in the thick blackout, she headed at a snail's pace in the direction of the fish and chip shop.

Later, clutching two warm bundles of battered cod and chips wrapped in old newspaper, she'd almost reached Hannah's door when a voice called out to her through the pitch night. 'Hello there. They smell good.'

Renee squinted towards the source of the voice and made out a figure standing in the entranceway of the neighbouring house. 'Hello . . . Aye, they do.'

'You're a friend of Hannah's, then, aye?' the male pressed on, stepping out on to the pavement and halting Renee's attempt at hurrying inside.

Up close, she saw he was the same height as her and, by the tone of his voice, surmised him to be around her own age. A mop of what looked to be light blond curls covered his head, which put her in mind of a poodle she'd once seen, and even in the poor lighting she saw he possessed a nose far too large for his face. Though eager to get indoors, she was nonetheless reluctant to appear unfriendly – she nodded.

'In a manner of speaking, aye,' she told him with a smile. 'I'm Hannah's great-niece, and I'll be staying with her for a bit.'

'Oh, I see.' He sounded pleased at this. 'That's good to hear.'

'I'm Renee.'

'Roy. Roy Westwood.'

They fumbled awkwardly in the darkness, then locating each other they shook hands with a chuckle.

'Pleased to meet you.'

'And you, Roy. Well, I'd best get in and get the grub dished up . . .'

'Course, aye. Ta-ra for now.'

Flashing him another smile, Renee turned and let herself inside the house, securing the door behind her.

After placing her aunt's portion of food by the

hearth to keep warm then feeding a shovel-load of coal to the fire, she settled down at the table and tucked into the tasty feast gratefully. Not a morsel had passed her lips since breakfast; she hadn't realised how ravenous she was.

As she ate, she made a mental note of her tasks tomorrow. The first thing she would do was register at the local shops for her rations. Whilst out, she would purchase paper and envelopes and write to let Jimmy know her new address. She would also buy in supplies to make Aunty Hannah a proper home-cooked meal. Next, she would tackle the house and get everything clean and tidy.

With her plans in place and feeling more contented than she had in a while, Renee hummed softly as she refilled the kettle for tea. Yet the tune soon died, the smile wiped from her lips along with it, by a dull thump from above. *Hannah.*

As she scanned the ceiling through wide eyes, her heart skipped a beat. Then she was rushing from the kitchen and through the hallway and tearing up the stairs two at a time.

'Colin?'

'No, it's Renee . . . Eeh, Aunty Hannah!' Crouching beside the crumpled form on the landing, Renee took her under the oxters and ever so gently eased her into a sitting position. 'What on earth happened?'

'I don't rightly know, lass. My legs gave out from under me.'

'All right, it's all right,' Renee soothed. She

assessed her for possible injury but mercifully saw none. 'Does it hurt, Aunty Hannah? Are you in pain anywhere?'

'Nay, nay.'

'You're sure?'

'Aye, I'm sure. Get me up, will thee, lass, and help me downstairs. I could murder a brew.'

Renee nodded and, taking their time, they made their steady way to the living room. She guided the old woman to her chair by the fire and sat her down.

'All right?'

Hannah nodded. Then, rubbing her hands together, she shivered. 'I'm cowd, lass.'

'Wait there, I'll fetch you a blanket.'

She hurried back upstairs and entered the first room she came to. A salmon-pink, candlewick cotton throw covered the bed beneath the window – this she gathered up and made once more for the stairs.

The door to the spare bedroom facing Hannah's was ajar and, as she passed it, Renee gave a cursory glance inside. Immediately, her eyes alighted on the iron bedpost – and what was hanging there – and the blood in her veins turned to lead. Trance-like, her mouth gaping like a landed fish, she inched her way forward and picked it up.

Her father owned a dark grey trilby just like it.

Wait – dear God no – surely not . . .

In the same instance that the horrifying thought burst through her brain, Renee heard the front door downstairs open and close.

Then the voice. The hateful, terror-inducing, all-too-familiar tones of the man she'd prayed beyond hope to never encounter again floated through the house, wrapping around her like a physical thing and choking the breath from her throat.

'It's me, Aunt Hannah. I'm home . . .'

Chapter 16

THE STREET APPEARED an awfully long distance away, but Renee considered jumping anyway. Perched on the bedroom sill, she opened the window wider and took a long and shaky breath.

Could she make it to the outside and freedom without smashing her skull to bits on the hard flagstones . . .? In this moment in time, she reckoned it was surely worth the try.

A dog barked somewhere in the distance, shattering the silence, and with it her impossible contemplations. If she should break a leg in the fall; what then? She'd be incapacitated, and Ivan would surely hear her cries – she'd be at his mercy completely. The risk was just too great. Furthermore, every possession she owned was downstairs. She couldn't leave without her things, in particular her precious letters from Jimmy – and abandoning Ruby was inconceivable. Besides, just where would she go? This house had been her one and only option, after all. And yet, the prospect of laying eyes on her torturer again, being under the same roof as him and his disgusting ways . . . she'd sooner die, she would! It was all so hopeless, hopeless!

Movement behind her halted her racing thoughts and brought her head around sharply. To her utter horror, she found herself face to face with her father.

'Renee.'

Her tongue was wedged to the roof of her arid mouth. Not for anything could she have uttered a syllable.

'Spotting that suitcase downstairs . . . I barely dared believe it, but it's true. Renee . . .'

'Get away from me.' The warning pierced the air between them like a hot blade through wax. 'I mean it,' she added, icier still as he made to take another step towards her. 'You stay back.'

Ivan dipped his chin to his chest. Then, taking his daughter by complete surprise, he crumpled to the floor, put his head in his hands and began to weep. Renee was powerless to do a thing. She simply gazed back, nonplussed.

'Lass.' His words were punctuated with choking gasps. 'Lass!'

She was at a total loss for how to react. Never in her life had she seen him like this, so exposed and broken down, weak. Gingerly, she inched forward. 'Dad?'

'Don't leave – I'm not going to hurt you, I swear it. Please. Hear me out.'

'What is there possibly left to say?'

Ivan motioned to a chair beside the bed; after a long hesitation and with great reluctance, Renee crossed towards it and perched on its edge.

'Well?'

'Forgive me.'

Her every nerve spiked. She leapt from the chair like a thing possessed. '*Forgive* you? Forgive *you?*'

'Renee—'

'After all you've done, all you've put me through, you have the gall to ask me that?' No fear remained now, only raging fury. She walked towards him, her hands claw-like as those of a wild beast, as though she meant to shred the flesh from his bones – Ivan shrank back. 'For years you violated me. You *raped* your own daughter!'

'No. No, I didn't.'

Something in his tone made Renee pause. Eyes hooded, she surveyed him in silence. Eventually, her mounting curiosity getting the better of her, she murmured, 'What's that meant to mean?'

'It means exactly how it sounds.'

'Tell me.'

He finally lifted his head. Reflected in his gaze was raw and simple truth. 'You weren't begot from my seed. I'm not your true father.'

'How can it be possible?'

'Not here, lass. Come into the next room.'

Having seen to the needs of Hannah, who now sat snoozing by the fire, Renee joined Ivan in the kitchen. Closing the door quietly, she leaned her back against it for a moment and stared at him across the space. Then, willing herself to be strong for the telling to come, she pushed herself on.

Hands clasped tightly in front of them, eyes down-cast, they sat facing one another across the table.

'Sylvia was expecting you when we met. I never did learn who got her in t' family way. All she would say was they had planned to wed but he died, sudden like, before they got the chance. I liked the look of her and offered her marriage instead. She accepted.'

Renee's head was spinning. She didn't know how she felt. 'Why are you revealing all this now?' she eventually managed.

'Because the time's right. I know . . .' He broke off to sigh and run a hand across his chin. 'I know what I've done to you. And I know it were wrong. Wait, let me finish,' he added quickly when she made to blast back a retort. 'Please.'

'Go on.'

'What I put you through were by itself bad enough. But to believe it to be the work of your own father – that you'd known the private touch of your own father . . . well. That has to be harder still for you to think on. Yet now, now you know the way of things, happen you'll bear my mistakes that bit easier, eh? What occurred between us . . . It weren't entirely foul, not if we ain't related. Surely you see it?'

A part of her did, she was unable to deny it. And yet Renee was beyond full rational thought, could hardly process anything, at this moment in time. To learn such a thing, that she wasn't Ivan Rushmore's after all . . . Why, *why* did her mam go and do it? she raged inwardly.

Why chain herself to this man; for reputation's

sake? Security? Surely not love. If only she'd told him where to stick his proposal, both she and her daughter would have been spared so much trauma and heartache.

But I wasn't there, was I? she was forced to remind herself. She couldn't understand what her mother had felt back then; at least not fully, and certainly not enough to make presumptions or pour scorn on her decision. Alone, devastated with grief, undoubtedly terrified to be carrying a bastard child . . . even the man before her now would have seemed like a saviour sent from heaven. In the same circumstances, who was to say that she herself wouldn't have made the same choice? Oh, but it was all such a mess.

'Mam didn't talk about him, my real dad?' Renee put to him after some minutes, involuntarily crossing her fingers and realising she was suddenly hungry for knowledge of this faceless, nameless man she would never get to know. 'She didn't tell you owt about him . . . did she?'

Ivan shook his head. 'Norra peep. Nor did I ask. I reckoned it were best to let sleeping dogs lie, so to speak, and I'm assuming Sylvia were of the same mind. Besides, dredging up the past, living in the shadow of a ghost, it weren't summat I wanted – who would, you know? Wouldn't have done our marriage no favours, that, would it? And so, we never spoke on it. We just got on with things.'

'The fact she abandoned me at all was bad enough.' Hugging herself, Renee's voice was a whisper. 'To think she left me behind with someone she

213

knew full well I have no real blood ties to is unforgivable. How could she do it?'

'I weren't a good husband. It's true – I'm big enough to admit that now. I see I left Sylvia with no choice but to flee.'

'Sounds familiar,' she murmured, staring him square in the eye and was gratified to see him squirm.

'Aye. Like a dog I treated her – worse. Though I came to regret it after she'd gone, it were too late to turn back the hands of time.'

'But *why* couldn't she have took me with her? Why dump me like that, why?'

He let his shoulders rise and fall. 'I don't pretend to have all the answers. Mind, what I do know is this: she loved you. What's more . . . What's more, I'm glad you stayed with me. I am, Renee, more than you could know.'

She watched the tears wobbling on his lashes. She saw the clear tremble of his shoulders as he fought to rein in his emotion, spied the irrefutable regret for all he had done in his gaze. And she felt nothing, not a thing. Nor did she want to. This man had put her through so much and she'd endured it not only through fear but from at times a queer sense of loyalty that even she couldn't begin to pick apart to make sense of. Now, whatever bond she'd thought they shared by nature's hand alone was severed forever. Ivan wasn't anything to her – she owed him nothing. The truth of it lent her wings; she felt utterly free. The realisation was overwhelmingly cathartic.

'Please stay.'

So lost had she been in her wondrous musings, she had to shake her head to fetch her back to the present. 'What?'

'Stay here. Will you?'

A refusal immediately sprang to her lips, but he got in before her.

'Wait, before you say no, hear me out. Will you do that, lass?'

Sitting back, she folded her arms. 'This had better be good.'

'Well, it's like this: despite what's passed between us and what I've revealed to you the night, I still love you. As a daughter, Renee, nowt else,' he hastened to clarify. 'What's more, I'm sorry. And aye, I know that don't sound adequate enough, course it don't. If me tearing out my beating heart would prove to you how much I hate myself for what I've done, I'd do it. I would, right here and now. By, but I've missed you. Near went clean out of my mind, I did, when you vanished. And aye, I'll not deny I were angry at your going, and I'll not say I didn't make some daft decisions afterwards . . .'

'The train station,' she murmured when he broke off to crush a hand to his mouth.

He nodded. 'I drank myself into a stupor night and day, were in no fit state for owt. They gave me the shove and with no means to pay the rent, I lost the house. I'd hit rock bottom, Renee. That's when I came here.'

'I'd been wondering how Aunty Hannah managed alone . . . she hasn't had to, has she? You've been here all the time. She swore to me she'd seen nowt of you. I'd never have stepped foot over the step had I known.'

'The poor owd cock's norra full shilling.' Ivan tapped at his temple. 'And she's only growing worse.'

'I did suspect whether . . . She kept calling me Colin.'

Though he shook his head sadly, the corner of his mouth lifted in amusement – feeling her own lips twitch in response, Renee quashed it quickly and looked away, was resolute to not have him think they had shared a moment, however briefly.

'Colin was her son who perished in the Great War?' she asked.

'That's right. Aye, she's in a world of her own making these days. You know, she'd love nowt more than for you to stop on—'

'Don't.'

'Don't what, lass? All's I'm saying is—'

She cut him off again harshly. 'I know what you're saying, all right. You're trying to guilt me into staying by using a sick old woman as bait. Well, it won't wash. I'm leaving.'

'No, please. *Please*, Renee.'

Glancing down at the fingers that had shot out to desperately pluck at her sleeve, her words came through gritted teeth. 'Get your hand off me.'

Ivan sprang back his arm as though he'd been scorched. 'Sorry. Sorry, lass. I am, honest—'

'You don't ever get to touch me again. D'you understand?'

'I do. I do. But please . . .'

'Please what?'

'Lass, we could make it work. We could this time, I know it. I don't care what's gone before, won't even ask where you've been for all this time if you don't want to tell me. Honest, things have changed. *I've* changed. Surely you must see it?'

She did, recognised nothing in this person here from the volatile and hateful man she'd once known and loathed. Though not for anything would she tell him so.

'I saw the error of my ways right enough and I vowed to do summat about it, to be different. I'll not deny it's been difficult, but I did it. I've toiled so hard on making myself better. I'm not the man you knew, Renee. I'm nowt like him, not any more, and he's never coming back. Norra drop of ale has passed my lips for nigh on a year, you know. Really, it's the truth,' he continued when she lifted her eyebrows in surprise. 'It's the Devil's juice, that stuff, and shan't ever have control over me again, never. I've gorra new job, an' all, aye.'

'Where?'

'The pub up the road.' His eyes danced with laughter; he held up his hands. 'I know, I know – the irony, eh? The place don't tempt me to return to old ways, mind. Not once have I succumbed. Aye, all in all, it's all right. The pay's not bad either, but it's the hours – your Aunty Hannah don't get to see me as much as she should. So, you see, you've no need to fear me or leave this house. Nor would you need to go out to work – my

217

wages cover the running of the household. With you here during the day, Hannah would have someone to keep an eye to her and cook her a hot meal. You and me both, we could look after her proper, like, between us. You must agree she deserves that?'

Recalling her earlier vow to step up to see to the old woman's needs, her eyes flicked to the wall separating them from the living room. She bit her lip. 'Aye, but . . .'

'I promise you, lass, I'm not angry no more that you left, and nor do I blame you for it. Just give me half a chance to prove it, won't you? Please – I'd not bear losing you a second time, I know it.'

Renee was in a quandary. Oddly, she believed every word he was saying. She *did* want to stay and care for Hannah. Besides, just where else would she go should she choose to leave? There was no one else, was there? She'd learned that right enough today. All the same, the idea that she was actually considering this and the prospect of dwelling under the same roof as him again brought her out in a cold sweat. And yet didn't she have Ruby's welfare to think about too, and wouldn't she need an address to give to Jimmy . . .?

As the agonising thoughts rolled on inside her mind, the fingers of her right hand shifted to twiddle the beautiful ring her beloved had placed there weeks before. And, in that moment, she knew the real test had come. She'd tell Ivan about her betrothal – yes, that's what she'd do. And his reaction to the news would reveal to her all she needed to know.

The Ivan of old would have killed her for sure, had seen her as his property, a mere piece of meat whom he possessed to use and abuse at will. He would never have given her up to another man. And the new Ivan, as he purported himself to be . . .? She was soon to find out.

Lifting her head, Renee met his gaze head-on. 'I'm to be wed.'

Ever so slowly, his lips parted. Mouth flapping wide, he gawped at her as though she'd upped and spouted two heads. 'Married?' he rasped after what felt like an age.

'That's right. To Jimmy, Jimmy Wallace.'

'Wallace . . .'

'The son of the butcher at Top o'th' Brow.'

His face smoothed out in remembrance of Gordon. Once, twice, he cleared his throat. Then: 'I see.'

'That's all you have to say?' she pressed.

'Do you love this lad?'

She nodded. 'With all my heart. And Jimmy feels the same for me.'

'You're happy?'

Again, she inclined her head. 'More than I've ever been before in my life.'

'Then I'm pleased for you. For both of you.'

'You are?'

Ivan smiled. 'Aye.'

Renee scrutinised his face thoroughly for even half a hint of deception and saw none. It seemed he actually meant it. 'Well . . . ta, thanks.'

'In t' army, is he?'

'Training, at Chester. He's due home next month.'

'So, in t' meantime . . . you'll stop on here? Will you, aye?'

She so wanted to believe he'd changed, and she did to a large degree. Still, a niggle of doubt refused to abate. But surely he wasn't acting? No way could he have kept this up for all of this time if it were the case; he'd have slipped up by now. The terrible temper he was capable of would have ensured it.

Whilst at Oak Valley Farm, she'd trained herself to shut out all trace of love and feeling for him, had banished him from her heart and her mind and had learned, successfully, not to spare him an ounce of care. Still, some minuscule section of her brain where once he'd lurked was reawakening, and she was aware of it, much to her chagrin and confusion. It reminded her that it hadn't been dreadful all of the time. There had been some pleasant moments between the two of them, however fleeting, over the years. And, despite what she'd discovered tonight, still it was him she saw as her father and possibly always would.

Whatever the reality, he'd provided for her always without a second's hesitation. He'd been the one to put a roof over her head, clothes on her back and food in her belly throughout her life, hadn't he? She was, to all intents and purposes and whether she liked it or not, Ivan Rushmore's daughter. Lord love her, this man was the only father she'd ever known or ever would.

'No matter whose blood it is flows through your veins, you're still my lass, Renee,' he announced brokenly at that precise second, as though he possessed the power to view inside her head.

Though she remained silent, now she didn't deny it.

'Will you stay?'

'I don't know . . .'

'Sleep on it, eh? Say you will.'

The ensuing silence was broken by a sudden call: *doo, doo, doo* – eyes widening in surprise, Ivan turned towards the source. 'The box there . . .?'

'It's Ruby.'

'Ruby? I thought that bird had just got lost on one of her flights or been killed or summat when she didn't come home . . . You mean you've had it with you all along? For all this time?' He was amazed. 'I fetched the pigeon loft here with me – it's out there, in t' backyard. You could stick Ruby in with the others if you'd like?'

She closed her eyes and sighed. In the next moment, she found she was nodding. 'All right.'

'Does that mean . . .? You'll stop here, the night at least?'

'Aye.'

'Eeh, lass. D'you know summat, you've a heart on you as big as the moon, you have really!'

'I'm warning you, though,' she was quick to make clear, 'if you so much as lay a finger on me—'

'I'll not! I swear it. Never again.'

221

'If you do, I'll be gone from this house in half a heartbeat, and you'll not *ever* set eyes on me again. Yes?'

'Yes – a thousand times yes,' he readily agreed.

That night, bedded down on the sofa, Renee slept with the iron poker beside her under the blankets, just in case.

The precaution proved an unnecessary one.

True to his word, Ivan didn't disturb her.

Chapter 17

'COME ON, AUNTY Hannah, let it go.'

'Gerroff, you young bugger, yer.'

'But Aunty Hannah, you can't eat that, it'll make you ill. Give it to me and . . .' Renee thought quickly, trying to remember what foodstuffs they had in, then: 'I'll make you a nice bacon butty instead and a fresh brew, eh?' There was one rasher left and just enough leaves from their rations to make a weak pot of tea, she reckoned, until she went to the shops.

The woman glared at her, her bottom lip protruding in a pout.

'Go on,' she wheedled, slowly easing the filthy cabbage head from the bony yet remarkably strong grip. 'That's it . . . yes!' she breathed in relief as she finally gained possession. She quickly stuffed it into her apron pocket lest Hannah attempt to make another grab for it. 'Eeh, Aunty, what are you like? Where did you even find it?'

'Not telling. Anyroad, you mind your own.'

With a shrug and a sigh, Renee left her mumbling

to the faded flowers on the wallpaper and headed for the kitchen.

She'd been resident in this house for almost a week now and, by God, how she'd had her eyes opened to the strange and sometimes heart-rending world of senile decay. Hannah's moods changed more frequently than the English weather. Be it storm or sunshine or something in between, you just never knew from one hour to the next which of her temperaments you would get.

The situation had given Renee a new-found respect for Ivan. How he'd coped alone with his aunt for all this time was beyond her. Providing care inasmuch as tending to the woman's most basic needs – feeding her and keeping her clean and warm – wasn't too taxing in itself. It was the additional aspects of her condition that left you physically exhausted and mentally drained.

For one thing, Hannah wouldn't stay seated for more than a handful of minutes at a time. She'd either grow restless or forget why she was there and go wandering off into the street. If Renee was busy seeing to her chores in another room at the time and failed to hear her aunt leaving the house, it was left to the neighbours to fetch her back, kindly bodies that they were – in particular the lad Roy next door, whom she'd got to know a little more with the passing days. Renee could only thank them profusely for their efforts, but she suspected that, for most, their understanding was wearing thin – and she felt increasingly embarrassed that they might suspect she was struggling to cope. Not even caring for Maisie Crawley, with all her problems, had been this hard. Something had to be done.

That night, when Ivan had returned from work, she swallowed her pride and put the issue to him. 'We have to talk about Aunty Hannah.'

Lowering his newspaper, he gave her his full attention. 'What's to do, lass?'

'Well to be honest . . . I'm finding things difficult. Really difficult. She can't help the way her mind is, I know that, but . . . It's so exhausting keeping tabs on her all the time. It's like looking after a toddler – I need eyes in the back of my head. I don't know what to do, Dad.'

That she addressed him in the usual fashion came as naturally to her as it always had. She couldn't begin to call him Ivan now, she'd realised, no matter the truth of things; it just didn't sit right on her tongue.

He puckered his brow in thought. 'Is she still slipping out when your back's turned?'

Renee nodded. 'The neighbours have been so good in extending a helping hand and fetching her home, but it can't go on. She's not their responsibility, after all. Nor does locking the front door and keeping the key on me, as you suggested, halt her gallop: she just leaves by the rear door instead on t' pretext of going to the privy. And I can't very well stop her having access to the backyard, can I? It's not humane, that. On the occasions she really does need to go and can't get out, she'll soil herself. Just what's to be done?'

'She's vulnerable in her state of mind, all right. Owt could happen to her out there on her own . . .'

'Aye.'

'Leave it with me,' he said after further rumination. 'I'll try and come up with summat.'

Renee cast him a small yet grateful smile. Still, the obvious change in him had the power to leave her breathless. He really was like a whole other man these days; she'd never have believed it possible.

Attentive, thoughtful, affable to the point of tender: he now boasted all of these pleasing attributes. What was more, he'd remained strictly sober. And, most importantly still, there hadn't been so much as a hint of inappropriateness, not once.

For the first time in her life, she actually enjoyed spending time in his company. Not that she'd voiced the fact to him, mind you. Still, she kept a part of her distant from him, protected; too much had passed between them for her to ever be completely natural in his company. However, she was learning to get to know him, the new Ivan, and she was doing so gladly. What's more, she sensed he was aware of it and that he was thankful for it. It was enough for now.

'So, how's your day been?' he asked with a wave of his hand as indication they should change the subject to something less worrisome. 'You've been hard at work, I see, aye.' He cast the spotless room a satisfied nod. 'It's like a little palace in here nowadays, I must say. Then again, you always were a sound little homemaker, eh?'

She preened at the compliment. 'I've not stopped on the house all week, but it's been worth it. Everything's as it should be, now.'

'I let the place go to rack and ruin, didn't I?'

Renee hastened to reassure him. 'It's no one's fault, you shouldn't blame yourself. You're out at work most days.'

'Well, all the same, I'm grateful, lass. I just hope this Jimmy what you're for marrying knows what a lucky fella he is.'

Nodding, she lowered her head.

'Lass? What is it?'

She opened her mouth to blurt an automatic response that all was well, however the falsehood wouldn't come – sighing, she spread out her hands. 'It's probably nowt, only I ain't had word from Jimmy yet.'

'None?'

'Not a peep.'

'You wrote to him, didn't you, when you first arrived?'

'Aye, the very next day.'

In her letter, she'd explained to him Mrs Flynn's accident and her troubles in locating Maureen's house. She informed him truthfully that she was instead residing with her great-aunt. What she hadn't told him, however, was that Ivan was here.

Why, she couldn't rightly say, other than that it had felt at the time a wise decision. Tactfully omitting this detail was the best thing all round, she was sure of it; Jimmy would only fret should he learn the truth of things. She couldn't adequately explain to him on paper the changes that had taken place, how much Ivan had altered, and so she didn't attempt to. Better that for now Jimmy remained ignorant to the fact, for his own peace of mind. She'd reveal to him the way of things when they met face to face.

'And you gave him this address to write back to you, lass, aye?'

'I did.'

'Only he ain't done?'

A lump had formed in her throat. She swallowed several times. 'No.'

Ivan blew out air slowly. It was clear to her he was trying hard to think of something to say that would reassure her, and it warmed her heart. 'Happen your letter never reached him? You know how the postal service can be, and 'specially so right now with a war on. Or his letter to you might have got lost . . .? I'm sure there's a reasonable explanation for it, Renee.'

The old Ivan would surely have used this to his advantage. That he wasn't grasping this opportunity to plant doubts in her mind as to Jimmy's true feelings for her proved yet again how different he was these days. She nodded, smiled. 'Mebbe I'm just being daft and I'll hear word from him tomorrow.'

'I'm sure you will.'

'Dad?'

'Aye, lass?'

'Ta,' she said quietly, and though her cheeks had pinkened in an awkward blush, her tone was heavy with feeling. 'Your support . . . it means a lot.'

'It took me long enough, though,' he replied just as deeply.

'Better late than never, Dad.'

Contrary to Renee's statement, correspondence from Jimmy didn't arrive the following day, nor the one after that. She penned him another long note asking him to please write back to her. Again, her efforts were met with silence.

Though she knew he wasn't abroad in the thick of things, wasn't risking everything fighting in the real conflict yet, she worried whether he could have suffered an injury whilst training. Their practice exercises must surely involve bayonets and rifles and suchlike – had harm come to Jimmy accidentally?

No way could every single letter that each of them might have sent have become lost – it was impossible. Then what? Nothing would have kept him from getting in touch with her if it was in his power, she knew this, and so something had to have occurred to prevent him doing so. Surely it must have done . . . And on, and on – the what-ifs were relentless. In her more morose moments, whilst crying into Ruby's soft, warm body, she even fantasised about training the pigeon up to be a message carrier, like those they used in the army, so desperate was she to get word to her beloved. A wild and impossible notion for sure, but one she harboured all the same.

The only thing that helped keep the fearful thoughts from becoming all-consuming was Hannah. Her antics showed no sign of let-up, ensuring

Renee was kept on her toes throughout the days and allowing her less time to sit and dwell completely on the man she loved.

This Friday afternoon was proving no different. The old woman had been snoozing in her fireside chair, and a desperate Renee had taken the opportunity to slip out and hurry to the nearby shops for foodstuffs for the evening meal. However, the queues had seen her taking longer than she'd anticipated, and she'd returned home to find the rear door swinging wide on its hinges and her great-aunt gone, nowhere to be seen.

Heaving a mammoth sigh, Renee dumped the shopping in the kitchen. Then, hurrying for the door, she dashed out to scour the cobbled backstreets.

'Renee! Over here!'

She'd just turned another corner when the voice rang out. Whipping around she saw Roy Westwood coming towards her – supporting a belligerent-looking Hannah. *Thank God.*

'Eeh, Roy. Am I glad to see you. Where did you find her?'

He flicked his chin eastwards, setting his yolk-coloured curls swaying. 'Wandering about by the top of the road.' He lowered his voice. 'I think she'd been in the pig bins.'

'What?' Renee was horrified.

In addition to rationing, the government was continually coming up with fresh ideas to ensure that during these trying times the people would have enough to eat. Perhaps hoping to starve them into submission, German U-boat submarines were only too eager to attack ships bringing provisions to British shores, and importing from abroad had become an increasingly dangerous affair. Rather than risk lives unnecessarily, people were pressed to turn more towards staples that their island could produce itself.

As well as encouraging those who had space to keep rabbits and chickens to supplement their diet, the Dig for Victory campaign had been introduced, urging folk to grow their own food. Yet it wasn't only humans who needed sustenance but animals, too, and a further initiative to aid in the country's meat supply had followed: the saving of kitchen waste for pig swill and poultry feed.

Local collection points had sprung up throughout the country's towns and cities, and every household was persuaded to dispose of their food scraps in the large, heavy-duty metal bins provided by the council, who would arrive regularly in their trucks to take the leftovers away to processing plants. This was then sold on to farmers.

Now, taking stock of Hannah's spoiled frock splattered with decaying vegetative juices, picturing her scavenging about in the stinking containers, brought an ache to Renee's chest and tears of both pity and shame to her eyes. 'Oh, Aunty Hannah . . .'

'She were clutching a handful of muddy potato skins when I came across her and refused to chuck them away when I suggested it,' Roy went on. 'Sorry, Renee, but she ate the lot on the walk back.'

'A few times I've found stalks and peelings in her

pockets – even eggshells once, an' all. I caught her with a cabbage head only the other day.'

'I don't know how she manages to lift the lids – they weigh a bit, don't they? Have to, to keep the flies out.'

'I'd wondered where she was getting them from but hadn't thought, never imagined . . .' Renee was flushing scarlet. God alone knew how many of the neighbours had witnessed Hannah doing this – just what must they be gossiping about her family? 'Anyone would think we didn't feed her at home. She gets ample grub, Roy, honest.'

'Course she does.' He gave her a sympathetic smile. 'Your aunt's well taken care of, I know that.'

Though thankful for his kindness, Renee couldn't stem a ripple of distaste as he bestowed upon her another brown-and-broken-toothed grin. Yet it wasn't only his poor hygiene habits that let him down – he was just as unusual in nature as he was in appearance.

His striking mass of girlish hair, wide nose and off-focus, olive-coloured eyes lent him a peculiar enough air on their own. However, his effeminate, almost childlike demeanour and high nasal voice began to set your teeth on edge after a short while in his company. Nonetheless, he was polite and friendly and never without a cheery word. He couldn't help the way he was made no more than any of them could, could he, and besides he was harmless enough.

'D'you need a hand in getting her home, Renee?' Roy was asking now – glancing away guiltily, she nodded.

'Ta, Roy.' Then, on impulse, feeling the urge to atone for her uncharitable thoughts, she added warmly, 'Happen you could join us in a cup of tea, if you've the time to spare?'

'Eeh, aye! I'd like that, I would.'

They each tucked one of Hannah's arms through their own and guided her at a gentle pace back to the house.

'I'll see to the tea, Renee, whilst you tend to your aunty,' announced Roy when they arrived. Without waiting for a reply, he trotted off for the kitchen singing a merry tune, leaving Renee to usher the old woman towards the stairs.

In the bedroom, she undressed Hannah then helped her slip into a clean blouse and skirt. Throughout, the woman put up no resistance. Sitting on the edge of the bed, her hands folded in her lap, she stared into space saying nothing, whilst Renee pulled up the stockings that had ruched down to her stick-thin knees and secured them once more to her garter belt.

'You're all right, now, Aunty Hannah?' she asked eventually, her voice soft.

'Aye.'

'Why did you do it, Aunty?'

Hannah cast her a sidelong look. 'The pig bins, you mean?'

'Aye.'

'Well, it's a waste, in't it, all that grub thrown away for nowt when it can be put to good use.'

Renee shook her head. 'What d'you mean?'

'Hell's bells! You're not reet quick at catching on, you, are yer?' She released a theatrical sigh. 'If you must know, I were looking for some bits for t' dog. Partial to some tasty scraps is our Judy.'

She nodded slowly. It was making sense now, in a nonsensical way of course. 'But Aunty Hannah, Judy's not here no more. She died a long time ago, remember?'

For a moment, a small frown creased her brow. Then: 'Died . . . Oh aye, yeah. She did, you're right.'

'Eeh, Aunty Hannah.' Feeling a rush of love and sorrow for the old girl – by, but the realities of life could be cruel at times – Renee held her close. 'What are we going to do with you, eh?' she murmured.

'Set me free.'

It had been uttered measuredly with no hint of confusion. Pulling back, Renee stared into her face. Hannah locked eyes with her and held them there, captive, and for the first time since Renee arrived here she saw the woman she used to know, the real Hannah, reflected in the lucid gaze.

Her voice was a whisper. 'What d'you mean, Aunty?'

'Set me free.' Again, the tone was level, controlled. 'Do it, go on. Put me from my misery and this life what ain't mine no more.'

'Please, you don't know what you're saying—'

'Aye, I do,' Hannah said sagely with a nod, and Renee knew she spoke the truth. In this instant, her mind had never been clearer. 'Help me, lass. Help me be with our Judy and Colin.'

Her breath catching in snatches, Renee threw her arms around her with a cry.

'Please, lass. Please . . .'

'She's give up, Dad.'

It was late, and Renee and Ivan were sitting opposite one another by the crackling fire. Hannah had been in bed for an hour or so and was sleeping peacefully, leaving them free to discuss the matter openly.

'I just didn't know what to say,' she went on with a shake of her head. 'Aunty knew exactly what she was asking, and she meant every word. What are we going to do?'

Staring into the dancing flames, Ivan took several sips of his tea as though lost in a world of his own.

'Dad?'

'Oh, I don't know,' he muttered. He gave a dismissive flap of his hand. 'Leave her to it.'

She was stunned. 'Leave her . . .? Are you all right? You've not seemed right since you came home from work. Has summat happened?'

'In a manner of speaking.'

Though his tone hadn't been raised, it was undeniably clipped. Renee was stumped. 'What, what is it?'

Ivan raised his gaze to meet hers. In silence, he stared at her for what seemed an age. Then ever so slowly his face relaxed and a smile appeared. He shrugged his shoulders. 'Sorry, lass. I'm reet, honest.'

She wasn't convinced. 'Really? Because if there is something—?'

'It were a taxing shift at the pub, that's all. Just ignore me. Summat and nowt, summat and nowt.'

Renee let the matter drop. Neither did she press him further on the saddening subject of his aunt. It was clear he was in no fit mood right now; happen he'd feel more inclined to discuss things when he'd had a good night's rest? She'd just have to wait.

Though thinking about it, perhaps this latest issue wasn't so shocking to him as it had been to her because he'd heard it all before . . .? Was that it? She nodded to herself thoughtfully.

He'd been resident in this house alongside Hannah far longer than she had, after all; must have seen and heard much more than her. And if the little she'd experienced thus far was anything to go by then it was undeniable that he must have had to cope with a lot since coming here. To all intents and purposes, he looked to have managed admirably. Just look at herself, for goodness' sake: barely a fortnight in and already she was floundering under the pressure. With the realisation, another level of respect for him was born.

Maybe she ought to cease running to him with every little worry and try to figure solutions out by herself? Give him a much-needed and much-earned break from the bother of it all for once. They were in this together now; it was about time she stopped burdening him with everything and began shouldering some of the stress.

Beginning tomorrow, she'd try. Aye, that's what she'd do. Her own problems could take a back seat, must. She had a duty to do, and do it she would. She was more determined than ever.

Both Hannah and Ivan were to be her top priorities. The pair would be all right from now on, she just knew it.

Chapter 18

OVER THE WEEKEND, there were no further issues with Hannah. Though she didn't again make mention of wanting to die, the confession seemed to have brought her a modicum of relief. She came across as calmer, more at peace. Nor was she disappearing from home and having to be fetched back by the neighbours. At last, her state of mind seemed if not improved then at least stabilised.

In contrast, however, and in spite of Renee's best efforts, Ivan's mood had failed to lift. He remained solemn, distant, and nothing she seemed to say or do could bring him out of himself.

By Sunday night, Renee was growing concerned. Was he sickening for something? she wondered. She'd never known him like this before and the uncertainty was becoming unnerving.

After Hannah had gone to bed, she decided to tackle him yet again. And this time, she was determined to get answers. 'Dad, won't you tell me what's troubling you?'

His mouth opened to dismiss her claims once more, but she got back in before he had a chance.

'I just know there's summat, no matter how many times you might say otherwise. Please. Talk to me.'

He remained silent for a full minute, and Renee was about to give up hope that he would open up. Then he sat forward in his seat, elbows on his knees, and steepled his hands.

'Friday,' he said.

'Friday? What about it?'

'When I got in from work.'

'Aye?'

'That lad. What was he doing here?'

She blinked in puzzlement. 'Roy? Roy Westwood, he lives next door—'

'I know who the bugger is and where he dwells; is it an imbecile you think I am or summat?'

The hairs on the back of Renee's neck stood on end. How he'd spoken to her, the snarling mouth and bulging eyes . . . it was like stepping back into the past. She was there all over again, quailing before him in that living room at Monks Lane, her guts twisting in dread of what was to come. *I won't, can't . . .* Never that, not again!

'Well?'

Finally, the real man, the true Ivan, had reared his ugly head. How had she let herself become so complacent? Shouldn't she have guessed that the mask would drop away eventually? She'd been so blind, so stupid. *Stupid. Stupid, stupid . . .*

239

'Answer me, damn it!'

She swallowed hard. 'No, I don't think that. Not you. It's *me* what's been the imbecile, all right!' In a lightning-fast move she dived from her seat and bolted for the door, but before she could reach it Ivan sprang in front of her to block her path. It took every ounce of courage she could muster to face him head-on. Lifting her chin and looking him square in the eye, she murmured, 'You ain't changed really, not a bit. I'm leaving. Get out of my way.'

'Make me.'

'I said—'

His beast-like roar drowned out all other sound and she could but watch, suspended in horror, as he lunged and grabbed hold of her in a bear-like grip. The white-hot fury screaming from his eyes snatched her breath away. He pressed his face close until their noses were touching and growled low in his throat.

'Whore.'

'It was a lie . . . all of it, all the time . . .'

'Aye and I'm done with pretending.'

This can't be happening.

The crippling sear of betrayal was like no other. Tears were spilling down her cheeks. 'You duped me. Why would you do it? *Why?*'

'For fear you'd up and leave me again, why d'you think? I knew that if you reckoned things were different now, you'd stay. And by God did I toil hard to convince you of it.' He laughed harshly. 'Worked though, didn't it? You swallowed every damn word, and more fool you.'

'I believed we were getting on. That maybe we might, just for once in our terrible and twisted relationship, be like other families. Other fathers and daughters, you know? Just average, aye. But no. Not us, not with you. You're not capable, and I was a complete idiot to ever think it.'

In this moment, Renee was experiencing devastation far more than fear, she realised. All this time . . . She had genuinely imagined she'd finally got what she'd always longed for: a normal, decent dad. It had all been a lie. She felt she could have wept herself sick with the pain of it all.

' "Take your time, Ivan, take your time." That's what I kept telling myself. "Let her hear what she wants to hear and she'll come back to you." And you did, you so nearly bloody did . . .' He let out air slowly. 'With that swine you thought to marry giving you the cold shoulder, you came ever closer, were so *near* . . .'

'You're mad,' she whispered.

'I were confident that soon, you'd forget about him altogether and be mine again, proper like,' Ivan went on as though she hadn't spoken. 'But it's never that simple with you, is it? No, not with a whore like you. No sooner were you getting the butcher's son from your system than you moved on to the next thing with a prick: that gormless bastard next door. That's when I finally realised: the nicely-nicely approach don't work with you, no. It's good old-fashioned brute force what Renee Rushmore prefers and always has been.'

'No!' Thrashing wildly as his hand slid beneath her

skirt and up her bare thigh, she fought to free herself with all her might. But her attempts proved as useless as they had ever done: she was no match against his brawn. 'Don't touch me! Don't touch me!'

'Shut it. I'm done with your games, my lass. The time for messing about is over – lie down.'

'Never. *Never*—' The last word died in her throat as in one fell swoop, Ivan put his foot behind her legs and pushed her body backwards, sending her swinging to the cold oilcloth of the floor. 'Please!'

'By God, how much I want this, how long I've waited,' he said between pants, his fumbling fingers at the buttons of her blouse. 'I'll enjoy myself tonight, all right, you see if I don't.'

Renee could barely snatch in a breath; his full frame on top of her own was crushing. She glanced around frantically, desperate for something – anything – to use as a weapon, but there was nothing close to hand. *Dear Lord, please, please help me somehow!* Then just as panic was threatening to consume her, it seemed her creator heard her after all, and a miracle occurred – a voice sliced through the charged air.

'Ivan? Renee? What's afoot down there, what's all the noise for?'

Aunty Hannah! Renee let out a sob of thankfulness. 'Oh, thank God. Aunty, help—!'

'Shut your trap,' Ivan hissed, clamping a hand over her mouth and killing further progress. However, Renee could tell that the interruption had shaken him. His face had paled and his tongue was flicking in and out to wet his lips; he looked decidedly ill at ease. 'Stupid owd cow . . . Ignore her, she'll soon go back to sleep.'

Not on your nelly! Renee's mind screamed, and in the next second she was biting down with all her might on Ivan's thumb. 'Help, Aunty, help!' she bellowed as, with a cry of pain, he removed his hand long enough for her to issue the plea. 'Come quick!'

'Bitch!'

Even though the gag was swiftly back in place, Renee knew only blessed relief at the sound of footsteps coming down the stairs. *Sweet Jesus, thank you!*

'One word out of turn,' Ivan warned, admitting at last defeat and crawling off her to get to his feet. 'Just one, my lass, and you'll regret it. You say nowt. D'you hear?'

But Renee didn't answer. All her attention was on the living room door. And the second that it creaked open, she was off – springing across the floor, she rushed past a bemused Hannah into the hallway. Moments later, she was running full pelt up the cold and deserted road.

'Renee? You come back here!'

She didn't look behind her. Nor did she allow the blackout to get in the way of her escape; tripping and stumbling, her arms thrust out in front of her and feeling the empty air as a blind person might, she pushed on.

'Gotcha.'

She'd just hurtled around another corner when, to her sheer devastation, her waist was encompassed by a pair of strong arms – *no!* How?

'I took the backstreets instead, knew I'd bump into you at the top of the road,' Ivan offered as explanation as though reading her mind. There was smug jubilation in his voice. 'Not as clever as you think you are, are you, eh?'

'Leave *go* of me! I'm not coming back, I'm not!'

'You'll do as you're . . .' However, Ivan didn't get to finish his sentence. A terrible and all-too-familiar sound had snared the night breeze – the air-raid siren.

After such a long interval since the last warning, the sudden wail had the power to shock; the pair froze.

Renee was first to regain her senses. 'Aunty Hannah,' she gasped.

'She'll be reet.'

'But how do you know? I never did get around to asking how she managed during air raids . . . She's no Anderson shelter so where does she go?'

'Under the stairs.'

'Under the . . .? For God's sake, that'll hardly offer much protection should the house suffer a direct hit!'

By now, front doors were opening and residents of all ages, tousle-haired and with coats and jackets thrown over their nightclothes, were emerging into the street. Some recognised friends in the dimmed light of their torches and exchanged murmured greetings, whilst others hurried on in grim silence. Nonetheless, they all shared one thing in common: each was heading purposefully in the same direction. Renee turned back to Ivan searchingly.

'There's a communal shelter at Cannon Street,'

he explained, thrusting a thumb in the general direction. 'Aunt Hannah won't use the thing though, never has done. She reckons if there's a bomb with your name on it then it'll find you no matter what, and that's that.'

'That's daft talk,' Renee snapped. 'You should make her listen, make her go—'

'She'll not do what I tell her. Mind you . . .'

'What?'

Ivan nodded slowly. 'She'd do it if you asked her, I bet.'

Renee knew his game and there was no way on God's green earth she would fall for it. 'You're madder than I thought if you reckon I'd ever step foot back inside that house!'

'And if this don't turn out to be a false alarm—?'

'It will be,' she cut in quickly, needing to convince herself as much as him, 'it almost always is.'

'But what if it ain't?' he pressed. 'What then? You could live with yourself, could you, if summat bad happened to the old bird? Come on, lass, come home,' he wheedled, reaching out to take her hand. 'I'll behave myself from now on, I will—'

'Huh!' Curling her lip in disgust, she snatched back her arm. 'You must think me born yesterday. I'll never return, never. After tonight . . . You're dead to me.' Her words were spoken quietly, icily, without a shred of emotion. 'D'you hear that? Dead. I don't ever want to see your face again for as long as I live.'

'You don't mean that, I know you don't—'

'Oh yes I do.' She raised herself to her full height.

'I'm leaving now, and you won't try to stop me. Do you understand?'

As the warbling siren whined on around them, they stared at one another through the shadows. When Ivan broke their silence, it was with measured laughter – Renee frowned in surprised confusion.

'And just where do you think you'll go, like?' he asked. 'You've nobody but me.'

'That's where you're wrong, see! I have Jimmy, the man I'm to wed. He loves me, and when he's home, he'll take good care of me. He will. He'll know what to do!'

'Course he will, course he will.' Ivan's head bobbed in a nod. Again, he chuckled. 'You keep on telling yourself that if it makes you feel better.'

Renee had had enough of his toxic ploys, refused to be drawn into this, to allow him to try to put into question her and Jimmy's feelings. 'Oh, I'm not listening to this.' She half turned, adding over her shoulder, 'I'm off. You just stop the hell away from me—'

'I wrote to him, you know,' Ivan said, halting her in her tracks.

'Eh?'

'I sent the young buck a letter, aye.'

'No. No, you're lying . . .'

'What's more, I told him *every*thing.'

Something in his tone caused her heartbeat to quicken; she swallowed hard. 'Told him? Told him what?'

'How I'm not your blood father. And that you've always known the truth of it.'

246

'What? But why would you—?'

'How you and me became lovers as you grew older because you seduced me – relentless, you were, in your quest of me. That later, I found the strength to put a stop to it and that's why you ran away.'

'You rotten, disgusting liar—!'

'But well, since living together with Aunt Hannah,' he went on unfazed, 'I came to realise that what we have is a love so deep that we can never be parted. And you feel exactly the same. I explained as how you no longer want to wed him, that he's not to try and find you or contact you again.'

'You didn't say them things to Jimmy. You didn't!'

'Aye, I did. D'you want to know what his reply were?' Ivan murmured.

Renee shook her head.

'He said you're not to worry, he's washed his hands of you.'

'No, he didn't, wouldn't . . .'

'Good riddance to bad rubbish, his exact words were.'

'No. *No.*'

'He said you're a filthy whore, that we're welcome to each other—'

'Stop, stop!' Slapping her hands to her ears to drown out the hateful untruths, she squeezed shut her eyes. 'Jimmy Wallace loves me, would never believe such things.'

'No? Then where are his letters, eh? How come you've heard norra single word from him since you arrived here? Tell me that.'

Though pain struck in her breast in acknowledgement of this, she refused to consider the possibility, that the reason just might be because . . . No, he *was* lying, he was, he had to be!

'So, you see you have nothing, my lass – *no one* but me.'

'No.'

'I'm right and you know it.'

'No! Never. You're nowt but an 'orrible, evil owd bugger and I hate you. I hate you and I wish you were dead!' she screamed.

Ivan's only response was further laughter, and something inside Renee snapped.

Years upon years of remembrance, of pain and terror and unimaginable, unrelenting desolation burst through her brain in a deluge – she hadn't the power to endure it. On a howl she ran at him, arms flailing.

The back of her hand found his nose and even in the darkness she saw the small fountain of blood spurt from it, felt the spray of it across her cheek. Caught off guard, Ivan staggered before losing his footing and toppling sideways. He hit the ground hard, but Renee wasn't done – like a thing possessed she pounced, straddling the stunned man and grabbing fistfuls of his hair.

'Bastard, bastard!' she cried, yanking up his head then slamming it back on to the cobblestones – once, twice, a third time. Again. Again. 'Bastard, *bastard.*'

Eventually – how much longer, she couldn't say – her fury spent, she collapsed, sobbing silently, on to the road beside him.

It was only then she noticed the sounds: the drone of a low-flying plane followed by anti-aircraft fire.

In the same moment that Renee craned her neck skywards, where swept the silver ribbons of search-lights aiming to pick out the raider, another noise took possession of the air. Beginning as a distant whistle, it rapidly progressed into a high-pitched squeal – then: *schoooo!* An enormous bang rocked the world and she was thrown on to her back in the gutter.

Her ears were ringing, her head full of fog; with effort, she rolled on to her front. On legs that felt strangely detached, she pushed herself to her feet.

Disorientated, she stood swaying slightly and gazed about her. The smell of burning reached her nostrils and shouts and screams floated on the mist creeping over the street. Glancing beyond the chimney tops into the near distance, she saw a curtain of scarlet flames rising higher, higher, through the Stygian heavens; it was like a vision straight from Lucifer's imagination. Clapping a hand to her mouth, she shook her head in dumb denial.

A bomb? she asked herself. It surely had to have been. The prospect was petrifying – suppose the German hell-raisers were not finished with them and returned to wreak more carnage? She had to get to safety – must!

Spinning on her heel, she made to skitter for cover – then turned to stone on the spot. There, lying spreadeagled before her, was the one she called her father.

Memories began to trickle back. Of course . . . *Oh, dear God.*

Tentatively, she moved towards him.

A puddle of something black oozed from beneath his head to settle in thin rivulets between the cobbles. Frowning, she squatted down and put her fingers to it. They came back wet, not with black as she'd assumed, but dark red staining. *Blood.*

In a daze, she stood tall once more and peered down at the man whom she knew was dead.

Gone. No more. Finished. Ivan Rushmore would never harm her or anyone else again. In this instance, Renee could feel only gladness at the fact.

By now, the night was ringing with a plethora of sounds: the tinny blare of the air raid warden's whistle and unintelligible yells of the men of the fire guard, a child's confused and terrified cries and the twin barking of bewildered dogs – all pooled together dizzyingly but at the same time barely registered in Renee's brain. Nothing else could penetrate bar the one bare truth: he was dead. Ivan was dead, and she was the cause of it. She was a murderess, a *murderess*. This night would see her life extinguished, too, for she would hang for her crime for certain. And yet, again, right now, she knew not a sliver of regret.

Up ahead, figures appeared around the corner and something inside her jolted, reawakening her senses and galvanising her back to life – she must get away from the scene.

She flicked a last flat and empty look at Ivan. Then

she turned and melted away into the thickness of the night.

She emerged into the next street to a scene of utter chaos. Even in her numbed state she couldn't fail to be affected by what she was met with; mouth falling open, she slowed to a halt.

'Help them! Help my family!' screamed an aged man outside what just minutes before had been his home. He gestured frantically with his flat cap, which he'd been wringing in his turmoil, to the mountain of smouldering rubble, his stare wild. 'They're in there, my daughter and grandkiddies! I were in t' living room, managed to crawl out, but they, they were in their beds and . . .' His eyes swept the open air where the collapsed bedrooms should have been. 'Oh, dear God, please!'

Renee knew as well as he did there would be no survivors. Tearing her gaze away, she stumbled on blindly.

'You evil Jerry scum! You rotten bastards from hell!' bellowed out another voice further up. Standing with legs parted, the overweight woman shook her beefy fists at the sky in unadulterated fury. 'Bombing decent honest folk akip in their beds? Them's your games, is it? Cowards, youse are, that's what. *Cowards*. Just let me get my hands on you – I'll tear you limb from friggin' limb!'

In no doubt that she would indeed have singlehandedly taken on the entire German army given half the chance – and Lord help them – Renee put her head down and pressed on.

More people, shell-shocked and white-faced with shared horror, were gathering; she watched tight-lipped men carrying recovered bodies past her with an air of detachment. *This night wasn't real, it couldn't be . . .* They laid them, one after the other, with care and respect in a neat line in the centre of the road. Then, without a word being spoken, they straightened up and, staring straight ahead in grim focus, returned to the carnage.

Renee was about to move on once more when a hand clamped down on her shoulder and a voice spoke in her ear, ''Ere, just what the devil's your game?'

'Wha—?' Twisting her neck around, she found herself looking into the face of the local air raid warden.

The normally stern and self-assured expression peering out from his woollen helmet against the cold had, this night, deserted him. His voice was hollow with anguish, his stare likewise. He seemed scared stiff. 'You need to take cover, lass, with everyone else. 'Tain't safe.'

'But—'

''Tain't safe,' he repeated, more urgently now, and she noticed tears glistening in his eyes. 'Please, go. For me. And don't budge until the all-clear sounds. All right?'

He believed the enemy would return. Danger hadn't yet passed, and yet more lives may be at stake, it was clear to see. She nodded, and with a small sigh of relief he sent her on her way with a soft shove.

The voices from within the communal shelter reached her as she neared the entranceway – shaky yet loud in fierce defiance, they rang in the charged night: the people were singing.

At any other time, such an affecting display of courage and unity would have brought tears to her eyes. Tonight, however, she could feel nothing, barely acknowledged the act with a passing thought. Shuffling inside the cramped and confined space, she found an empty spot and sat down.

How long she'd been there for, lost in her private, impenetrable bubble, she couldn't say – it could have been weeks for all she knew and cared – but gradually she sensed the mood inside dipping. The singing had become half-hearted as time wore on without news and folk grew more and more anxious. Now, a palpable tenseness was creeping into every corner and showing in the lines of each face.

'Come on, you lot – again!' a teenage girl much wiser than her years called suddenly – sporting an old head on young shoulders is how some would have described her – clapping her hands to bolster further their spirits. 'Follow my lead. One, two, three: *May this fair land we love so well, in dignity and freedom dwell.*'

As though thankful for the interference, the crowd followed the call with gusto. Holding hands in the flickering candlelight, they lifted their voices to the roof, letting them carry to their precious skies and the real-life bogeymen who might lurk within them: '*Red, white and blue. What does it mean to you? Surely you're proud, shout it aloud – Britons, awake.*'

Only Renee remained silent. With a mind full of emptiness, she stared ahead at nothing.

'*There'll always be an England . . .*'

Her father was dead. Her mother was gone. Mrs Flynn was lost to her, as was Jimmy. Jimmy . . . Oh, my love, my dear sweet love . . .

'*And England shall be free . . .*'

She had no one. She needed someone, anyone . . .

'*If England means as much to you as England means to me.*'

But no, she was wrong. She was – how could she forget? For, of course, there was always Ruby . . .

'Ruby!' Then in the next breath: 'Oh my . . . Aunty Hannah!'

Chapter 19

THE LONG SCREAM ripped from her just as the song came to an end and the shelter had fallen quiet. It bounced from the walls and seemed to cling to the stuffy air, bringing sharp intakes of breath from the gathering.

'Eeh, no,' said a woman as Renee made to lunge for the entrance, taking her arm. 'You mustn't leave, not 'til they sound the siren—'

'Let go of me! Let go!'

'But lass—'

'I have to get home, I have to!'

'Renee?'

It was Roy Westwood. She gazed at him in desperation across the sea of heads where he had risen from a bench near the back. 'Tell them, Roy! Tell them I have to go!'

Pushing his way through the swell, he put his arm across her shoulders. 'I hadn't noticed you were here until now, reckoned you'd be taking cover under the stairs with your aunt. Never would come to the shelter, she wouldn't, however much me and Mam tried to persuade her when the sirens sounded . . .' He broke off to gaze at her in concern. 'She's at home then?'

Renee nodded frantically. 'Aye, and I must *go*. I have to check she's all right.'

'What about your dad, is he with her?'

The hairs on the back of her neck stretched to attention. A hush had fallen, and all eyes were on her. The ensuing silence was cloying, all-consuming, and she was convinced that every last person present would surely read her terrible thoughts, see her guilt, as clear as crystal. Perspiration formed on her top lip. She swallowed audibly. 'No. No, he never came home from work at the pub. I went to look for him and whilst I was out, the air-raid warning went off. The warden sent me here. I were scared, scared and confused and I . . . I didn't think about home, about nowt, just came straight to the shelter.'

The lies had dripped from her tongue without her say-so – whence the tall tale had sprung she hadn't the faintest notion. Nonetheless, she was glad of it. But dear God, Aunty Hannah, Ruby . . . She must get out of here, must check if they were safe!

'Roy,' she beseeched him, grasping his hand and squeezing. 'Please, I have to get back to Punch Street—'

'Punch Street, you say?'

She glanced around to see the man who had directed her here shortly before framed in the shelter's entrance. The blackout had clearly obscured his appearance earlier; he looked much worse now in the dim light. His face and hands were thick with grime and his clothing was torn in places. 'That's right. It's my aunty, you see, sir, she—'

'You can't,' he murmured.

'But—!'

'You *can't*, lass. The street, it . . .' The warden broke off to flick his eyes around those assembled, then took a ragged breath. 'I'm sorry to say the majority of Punch Street has been flattened.'

A flurry of gasps and moans went round the shelter. One woman let out a piercing cry then promptly fainted – Renee recognised her as one of her neighbours.

'We can't yet be sure of the full extent of the damage. We'll know more in the morning. In the meantime, an emergency rest centre for those rendered homeless has been set up at—'

Whatever he'd been about to finish with was lost in the sudden, strident note of the all-clear. A collective breath of relief went round the building.

Renee took the signal as her chance – she sprang once more for the doorway.

'Hold your horses, lass!' Having grasped her by the tops of her arms, halting her escape, the warden shook her none too gently. 'Didn't you hear what I just said? It's like a living nightmare out there. Flames and bricks and glass and bodies . . . You can't go galloping off into the night like that, it's too dangerous. And if it's home you're still for thinking of going . . . well. Think again. You'll not get through. The firefighters are on the scene and won't allow it. Best to get some sleep and to think of all that when it's light.'

'Come on, Renee.' Most of the people, faces wreathed in dread of what they might find when they emerged into the frigid air, were leaving the shelter in an orderly fashion by now – Roy ushered her around to join the line with him and his mother. 'Let's get out of here, and don't fret none. Whatever you have to face . . . you're not on your own. Is she, Mam?'

Nora Westwood was a gloomy and rather simple-minded soul in her late fifties. She hardly ever spoke more than two words to anybody – now, true to form, she simply nodded agreement, although Renee wondered whether the woman even knew what was going on.

'Ta, Roy,' Renee told the lad with feeling. 'I don't know what I'll do if . . .' She bit down on her fist. 'Aunty Hannah . . . I must find out.'

When they reached outside, the air raid warden was standing in the road and a small crowd had gathered around him. Renee recognised them as residents of Punch Street and neighbouring Ardwick Street, clearly the worst affected by tonight's tragic attack. With their homes blown to smithereens along with all they possessed in the world bar the clothes they stood up in, they were being advised at last what to do. Renee and the Westwoods moved forward to join them.

'If any of you have friends or relations that can take you in, at least for tonight, go there now,' the warden was saying. 'For those who don't, make your way to Noble Street. The Independent Methodist Church there have opened the doors of their Sunday School to provide temporary shelter.'

People broke off to set forth for the dwellings of others more fortunate. Those who remained – Renee, Roy and Nora included – turned as one in the direction of the church.

'Remember,' was the warden's parting gambit as they were walking away, staring pointedly at Renee, 'please stop away from your houses. Do not attempt to slope off there the minute my back's turned – I'll find out and there'll be hell to pay! It's for your own good, it isn't safe, so please just listen to what you've been told and have patience until tomorrow. Thank you.'

Before continuing with the Westwoods, Renee gave the corner leading off to Punch Street a last lingering look. Then Roy was motioning for her to follow, and with an ache in her chest that threatened to crush her, she picked up her feet and made her reluctant way on.

'Where we going, lad?' asked Nora as they neared Noble Street.

'The church, Mam, to get some kip. Hopefully, we can cadge a brew there, an' all. I'm parched.'

Mrs Westwood seemed satisfied with this and allowed herself to be led without further questions. Renee, on the other hand, had no intention of going to the rest centre. Not yet, at any rate.

'Roy,' she said quietly when they reached the few stone steps leading up to the door, glancing around to be certain that the warden wasn't lurking near by, ready to catch her out, 'I'm going to nip to Punch Street, see if I can find out how our house is.'

'But the warden said—'

'I don't care! I *have* to know how Aunty Hannah is, whether she's alive, or . . .' Tears threatened once more. She bit down on her lip hard to stem them. 'I must, won't rest until I do.'

'Shall I come with you?'

Though grateful of the offer, she shook her head. 'No, Roy. You go on inside with your mam and get her settled. She must be exhausted.'

He wiped his dripping nose on his dirty jacket. Then from the inside pocket he brought out a small torch. 'Here, take this.'

'Ta, Roy,' she said, trying not to openly grimace at the disgusting habit of his – didn't he possess a hanky?

'You'll be careful, Renee?'

'Aye.'

'And you will return here once you've seen how she is?'

'I'll be back, Roy, don't worry.' She had no place else to go to, after all, did she? 'I'll see you soon.'

The short walk seemed the longest of her life. Though desperate to discover Hannah's fate, at the same time the prospect of what might be had her shaking with uncontrollable dread. When finally she turned into what remained of her street and trained on it the thin beam of her handheld light, her worst fears were confirmed. The true horror of what she was met with stripped the strength from her legs; on a whimper, she sank to her haunches.

The row in which Hannah's house had belonged only two hours before was completely obliterated.

'Renee?'

Light filtering through the bare windows shone in prisms across her face; blinking awake, she squinted up at the face hovering close by. 'Roy? What time is it?'

'Gone seven. Here, I've got you some tea.'

She pulled herself into a sitting position and took the piping drink from him. And, as the first few sips chased the sleep fog from her brain, remembrance of the night before smashed through her and she wished with all that she was that she hadn't woken up. With shaking hands, she put the cup down on the floor beside her, drew up her knees and wrapped her arms around them tightly.

'You all right?'

'No, Roy. No, I'm not,' she murmured.

'Sorry about your aunt, Renee. And Ruby. They were gradely owd birds, the pair.'

Oh, the pain . . . 'Aye, they were.'

'There's still no sign of your dad.'

Renee stiffened. Since the realisation in the shelter that it was probable Hannah and Ruby had been caught in the blast, all ideas of Ivan had dulled in her mind. He remained still as but a smudge on her consciousness, but nothing more – certainly not enough to warrant thoughts of any great length.

'I've been watching the door,' the lad went on,

'thought he might have been brought here by now, but no. Where could he be?'

Resuming her cup of tea as a means of something to do, Renee shrugged. 'I don't know.'

'It's a rum do, all right.' There came a pause, then: 'Queerer still, I reckon, him not returning from work.'

She shot Roy a sidelong look. Something in his tone had hinted at . . . was that disbelief? But surely not, she told herself, scanning his face yet finding nothing concrete in his countenance. He had no reason to doubt her version of events, after all. Did he?

She took another sip of her drink before saying, with what she prayed was adequately convincing nonchalance, 'Not really. I'm sure there's good reason for it. He likely had one sup too many last night and bedded down at a pal's house or summat.'

'He's done that before then, aye?'

'Once or twice,' she lied – Ivan, so far as she could recall, had never kept friends.

It was a long moment before Roy responded. Finally, he nodded. Then he turned to her with a smile and patted her arm. 'Happen you're right then. He'll show when he's sobered up. He ain't half in for a shock, mind, when he does, poor bloke.'

Poor bloke . . .? The sympathetic expression, one completely at odds – and totally undeserving – to the demon from hell Ivan Rushmore had been, had her hackles rising. However, she managed to bite back the scathing retort which sprang to her lips. Instead, she made a noise resembling an agreement and drained the remainder of her brew.

The hall was littered with people young and old alike. There were whole families in some cases, along with several couples, and a few elderly singletons sitting with tartan blankets draped around their shoulders looking bewildered and rather lost. Some even had their pets with them; remarkably, cats and dogs seemed to have come to some sort of agreement to put their animalistic instincts to one side and were behaving remarkably. Yet no matter age, sex or even species, one thing bound them now – they each felt it, Renee could sense it – and that was fear of uncertainty.

They were effectively destitute – just what on earth would become of them? In one fell swoop, their lives had been torn asunder, and they could see no hope of changing their circumstances any time soon – at least Renee couldn't, that was for certain. What little family she had were gone, each and every one. Pure and precious Ruby was no more. Iris Flynn, her one true and dearest human friend, was nowhere to be found. Even the kindly Crawleys were gone for good from her life. As for Jimmy . . . She closed her eyes to block out his beloved image. *What of* Jimmy? Had Ivan really spewed only lies last night, or was there a possibility that a grain of truth lurked within the vitriol?

Jimmy hadn't replied to her numerous letters, had he? Just what could the reason be for it if not that he didn't want to hear from her? Had her father truly told him that pack of sickening untruths? More to the point, if he had would Jimmy honestly have believed them?

Pain the like of which she'd never known before seized her faculties. Just what she'd do if she'd lost him . . . She'd die without her man, she surely would. Jimmy Wallace was the single most important being in her life and the only thing that was keeping her going right now; the prospect of their union having been severed, of never seeing him again, was like a knife right through the middle of her heart. *Never* would she bear it.

The Westwoods caught her eye, and she gulped down a ball of panic-fuelled emotion. They – essentially two near strangers – were all she had now, God help her. How had things come to this? She'd been so full of hope and happiness just a few short months ago and now, her life was in tatters. Why did the Lord, the universe, want to conspire against her like this all the time? Just what had she done to deserve it?

Across the room, the door had opened and she watched the air raid warden enter the building and scan its members. His solemn gaze came to rest on her and he removed his tin hat. Renee knew what was to come. Dear God, she did. *But please, I don't want to hear it, to think . . .*

'Morning—'

'I know why you're here,' she cut in quietly. 'The state of the house . . . there could never have been any survivors.'

The man's eyebrows drew together in displeasure, although his tone remained kindly, soft. 'You went back there? Even when I warned you not to?'

264

'Aye,' she admitted, 'I had to. I saw the damage with my own eyes – Aunty Hannah's dead, ain't she?'

'We recovered a body of who we believe to be the occupant of the property, yes.'

'I knew it.'

'I'm afraid that's not all,' he went on, lowering his voice further. 'Emergency workers came across the body of a man at dawn in James Street. It seemed that when the two bombs dropped, he was thrown into the road with the impact and suffered catastrophic head injuries. The identity card found on his person states he is a Mr Ivan Rushmore of the same address. I'm very sorry, lass.'

She closed her eyes. She knew no relief at the assumption, felt nothing.

She wasn't to think of him, she reminded herself. He mattered not, none of it did any more. His reign of terror over her had found a conclusion and that was that. Ivan and what she'd done wasn't important – hadn't she told herself so throughout the hours since?

Yet as the long seconds wore on, having heard the matter spoken aloud by another, she couldn't fail to realise her shock was waning, the numbness that had been her companion throughout melting away, and an overwhelming surge of regret and bone-shaking terror was beginning to take hold.

She was a murderess! By God, she was a monster – what had she *done*?

'Are there any other family members . . .?'

'No,' she croaked.

'Then I'm afraid I have to ask you to come with me to Clive Street Mortuary, to where the fatalities of last night's attack were removed, to formally identify the deceased.'

By now, Roy had left his mother to sidle over to Renee, and she groped for his arm and gripped it for strength.

'Perhaps you could accompany the lass?' the warden began saying to Roy, but Renee stopped him:

'No. It's all right. I'll be all right.'

'You're sure . . .?'

'I am,' she insisted. This was something she must face alone.

'I'd like to come, Renee, honest,' the lad pressed. However, as before, there was a hint of something she couldn't fail to notice – in his gaze this time – that instantly made her wary. Again, it was almost akin to a sense that all wasn't as it seemed, though for the life of her she couldn't fathom why or how – nonetheless, she wasn't taking any chances.

'No, you stay here and look after your mam, Roy,' she said as disarmingly as she could muster. 'I'll be back soon.'

Roy stared deep into her eyes. Then something that very much resembled a smirk lifted the corner of his mouth. 'Aye, all right. I'll be waiting, Renee.'

With no time now to wonder at his behaviour – the warden was leading the way outside – she pushed Roy to the back of her mind and set forth into the chilled morning.

Some twenty minutes later, Renee watched as the

mortuary assistant carefully lifted out an arm from beneath the white sheet covering the victim. She'd been informed that the corpse was in too bad a condition to see the face and that she must identify them by the only other feature discovered that was palatable to view – she knew what it would be, all right, didn't need to ask. Sure enough, glancing down, she saw it: the port wine birthmark staining the back of the right hand. *Hannah.*

'You got what you wanted, eh, Aunty? You found peace at last. Fly high now and be with your Colin and Judy,' Renee told her, stroking the icy fingers. Then, screwing up her eyes, she laid her head on the still chest and sobbed herself hoarse.

The next body appeared exactly as she remembered it. Not a mark marred this face; he looked rested, serene almost, which didn't seem right to her somehow. Why must Ivan be afforded the gift of eternal peace after all he inflicted when she was forced to go on suffering this way? It made not a jot of sense to her, this didn't, none of it did. And yet, much to her chagrin, something was creeping in, a stirring within her breast ... *No.* Renee banked it down fiercely.

'Well, Miss?' asked the uniformed officer present.

Her response was flat: 'Aye, it's him. That's Ivan Rushmore. Can I go now?'

The walk to Punch Street was one she took without conscious thought – somehow, her feet had made the decision for her.

267

The surrounding streets which she passed through on the journey hadn't survived the onslaught entirely unscathed. The blast from this, the most destructive raid they had seen in their town, had spread its tentacles of destruction wide. Few residents and business owners had been spared the effects. Windows had been blown out, and in some instances flying masonry from the bombed sites had travelled impressive distances to smash into other properties, damaging roofs and brickwork. Internally they had fared little better. Chimneys shaken by the vibrations had released avalanches of soot into living rooms, and all the power had been cut off.

At least, however, these buildings remained standing, Renee thought to herself as she skirted past pinny- and turban-wearing housewives and shop owners out in force sweeping the piles of glass, roof tiles and general debris from the pavements. At least they still had a place to call home and their kith and kin were alive and well – unlike herself and others. Insides could be cleaned and repaired, and panes could be replaced. There was no bringing back loved ones, though, was there?

When she turned into her street and took in the true horror up close in the cold light of day, an agonised cry escaped her. The devastation was breathtaking.

Sections of some of the houses still stood, resembling grey skeletons with all the flesh blown from their bones. Others had had one end cleanly ripped away, leaving the interiors exposed to view like giant doll's houses. Then there were the others: the ones that had completely collapsed – like Hannah's. They retained no features whatever, resembled nothing at all. They could have been anything before this travesty: a house, a shop, a pub . . . No one without ties to the place could have possibly guessed what had once stood here from the colossal mound of brick and dust and wood they were reduced to.

Be it novelty – Bolton hadn't yet known a bombardment on this scale during this fresh conflict, had it? – or mere morbid curiosity, the area was teeming with people.

Children predominated – clearly, owing to the circumstances, they had been given the day off school – but adults milled around, too, surveying the carnage. Renee would like to have screamed at them to go away, back to their safe dwellings and families and think themselves lucky – *there but for the grace of God go I* . . . However, she didn't. Instead, she continued on, past the huge crater in the centre of the road, in which lay what looked like a section of a boiler – probably from the engine room of the nearby factory – and sat down on the cold ground before what had been Hannah's home.

'Cor, look at the size of this one!' announced a young lad triumphantly, waving a large piece of shrapnel he'd uncovered, and cutting through Renee's tumult. His friends gathered around to see and marvel over its thickness and weight. 'Ha! Johnny, you've only managed to find a diddy bit – mine's massive!' he boasted to another boy.

'Aye, well, so what. At least my dad's a hero!'

returned Johnny, green-eyed in more ways than one. '*He* was here helping the injured and dying last night whilst *yours* was snoring in the shelter! Rescued a baby trapped in its crib, he did, and saved its life – so there!'

'My dad weren't snoring nowhere!' his opponent bellowed back, furious, clenching his fists.

'He was! He was! My mam said so—'

'Stop, you lot,' Renee called across, halting their row. Being back here and imagining it all, her poor aunt dying alone and scared beneath those rotten stairs, her sweet and defenceless Ruby . . . it was difficult enough without this, and she was dangerously close to tears. 'Please, go and play somewhere else.'

'You heard her,' another voice said in the next breath – craning her neck, she saw Roy walking towards them. He pointed to the corner. 'Go on, get back to your own streets – and take the rest of the ghouls with you,' he added, loud enough for the adults up ahead to hear. 'You ain't wanted here.'

'*You* ain't wanted anywhere, you ugly git!' said the boy with the shrapnel before taking off, his pals hot on his heels.

When the children's peals of laughter had died away down the road, Renee hastened a glance at Roy. Shoulders slumped, he had his hands in his pockets and his head was down to hide his blush – pity for him struck her.

'Take no notice, lad. They're only kiddies and don't know what they're saying.'

'Aye, they do.' Sighing, he lowered himself beside her. 'And they're right, an' all: I am an ugly git.'

'No, you're not,' she fibbed. 'Just ignore them.'

They sat in silence for a few minutes until, with a nod at their shattered abodes, Roy said, 'Eeh, what a to-do.'

'Aye.'

'I'd go and fight the enemy if I could, Renee.' He leapt to his feet and, raising both fists, proceeded to shadow-box complete with sound effects. 'They'll not have me, though: I've got hammer toes, wouldn't be able to march. D'you want to see?' he asked, bending down to untie his bootlaces.

'No!' Then doing her utmost to mask her horror at the notion: 'No, you're all right, ta, Roy.'

'We know now how folk in other places must feel, eh?' he said, resuming his seat. 'Manchester and Liverpool and London and that – just imagine this every night like what they get.'

It was a terrible prospect – Renee shuddered. Up until now, their war on the home front had been but a burdensome one, it was true. Besides the fear for their menfolk away fighting, the nuisance of food shortages and the like had been the worst that Boltonians had had to contend with – yet now look. Please God they had had their lot and that this death and destruction meted out on their town wouldn't become a regular thing.

'This is the second time Mam's escaped summat like this, you know,' Roy went on. 'Aye, during the first lot: a German Zeppelin flew over Deane and

271

dropped incendiary bombs – she lived on Kirk Street then, not far from here. September 1916, it were. She walked away from that without a scratch and the same this time around – jammy or what?'

Renee murmured an agreement. 'Aye, that is lucky.'

'They reckon the Jerries were going for the gas-works on Spa Road last night.'

'Oh.'

'Aye, but we copped it instead.'

She swallowed hard. 'Yes. Yes, we did.'

'The number killed in this raid is about a dozen, I heard. And nearly seventy maimed and injured. All ages, babies even—'

'Roy, please. Can't we talk about summat else?' she whispered, a tear escaping to run down her cheek.

'Like what?'

'I don't know – anything. All this . . . it's getting on my wick.'

He thought for a moment, then asked, 'So, how was it, at the mortuary?'

Renee gazed at him in amazement. Just when she thought he couldn't possibly be any dafter . . . 'Horrible, Roy; what d'you think?'

'Was it them, then, Hannah and your dad?' And at her nod: 'I thought I'd find you here, knew you'd come instead of going straight back to the church. Well, it stands to reason, don't it, that you'd want to feel closer to them, and you must do here.' He glanced about, then shrugged. 'Don't think there will be owt left worth salvaging, will there?'

'No, I don't think so.'

'All our things, everything we own, gone.'

Her mother's possessions, the final link to her, finished forever . . . 'Aye.'

'The backyards are buried under a ton of bricks; I noticed on the way here. Poor Ruby and the others, eh? They'd have been squashed to buggery.'

Didn't he possess even an ounce of tact? He was really beginning to get on her nerves. 'Don't say that.'

'But it's true,' he pressed on regardless. 'Them being trapped in their loft like that, they wouldn't have stood a chance—'

'I *know*, Roy. Don't you think I know? Now please, enough.'

'Sorry,' he mumbled after a long pause. He flashed her that terrible smile of his that she disliked so much. 'I never did know when to shut up, that's my trouble.'

'It's all right, really.' He couldn't help it, could he, after all, the way he was? 'I don't mean to snap at you; I'm just upset.'

'About your aunt?'

She nodded. 'And my dear Ruby.'

'What about Ivan?'

The unexpected question threw her for a moment; she glanced away. 'Aye. Course.'

'Ooh, look!' he said suddenly, pointing ahead. A Ford emergency food van, blackout covers attached to its headlights, was pulling up in the road. 'Gradely – fancy summat?'

Renee shook her head. 'No ta, I'm all right.'

'Oh, go on; it'll do you good. You went out earlier with nowt but a brew inside you and I'll bet nothing's passed your lips since. Wait here, I'll fetch you a bite.'

She hadn't the energy for further protest; with a shrug, she let him go. He took his turn in the queue that had formed at the back of the van, where a hatch built into the rear door had been thrown wide to distribute food and drink to those in need, and was soon returning with two white plates balanced precariously in one hand and two brown mugs in the other.

'Tea and porridge,' he informed her with the toothy grin. 'Get it down you.'

'Ta.'

'That's all right, Renee.' Again, that grin of his. ''Ere, I wonder what we'll get later at the Sunday school? Sausage, mash and beans, I'm hoping, with sponge pudding and custard for afters – that's my favourite. I've heard there's another emergency canteen been set up to feed the bombing victims without homes or power to cook for theirselfs in Flash Street – we should nip down there an' all, cadge another hot dinner. What d'you reckon?'

Renee frowned. 'No, Roy. You shouldn't do that neither.'

'Why not?'

'Because it's taking more grub than you're entitled to. Besides, them extra meals could go to someone else in need. Greedy is what it is. Greedy and dishonest.'

274

'Oh aye?' he retorted in high dudgeon, surprising her; he'd never taken this tone with her before. 'You're a fine one to talk about being dishonest, that you are!'

'Roy? What d'you mean by that?'

Devilment danced in his gaze. 'I know what you did, Renee.'

'What I did . . .?'

'You lied – to me, and to everyone else. Your dad did arrive home from his shift at the pub because I saw him with my own two eyes.'

Her heart was drumming painfully, and a bead of sweat travelled the length of her spine. She licked her lips. 'No, Roy, you're wrong—'

'Renee, I spoke to the bloke!'

'What? When?'

'Last night. I were standing at my door, you see, and he was just going into Hannah's house, and I said, "Goodnight, God bless, Mr Rushmore." "Go to bleedin' hell," he says back to me, then he stomped off inside. So, you see, you lied.'

Head spinning, she blinked about her in desperation for an adequate response – anything that might placate him – but could think of nothing. She had nothing! *Dear Lord, help me* . . . 'Why didn't you tell me all this before?' she finally managed.

He shrugged. Then: 'I don't think your dad had his head bashed in by the blast at all.'

'Roy—'

'I think summat else – *someone* else – is to blame for it, aye. But don't worry, Renee,' he finished with a

275

wink, 'your secret's safe with me. You're my very best friend, ain't you, after all?'

And you're not nearly as daft as you like to make out, she thought to herself, going cold all over. *Oh no, not by a long chalk.*

As if reading her mind, Roy smiled.

Chapter 20

SHE'D SWAPPED ONE nightmare for another, that was the top and bottom of it.

Three days had been and gone since Roy had called her out on her crime and in that short space of time, her fate had been sealed.

He'd made known his hold over her immediately. Not with aggression; no, he was much too clever for that, she'd come to learn. Instead, he would make subtle comments on the sanctity of friendship and what he expected from their own – along with hinted consequences of what going against him might mean for her. In the main, prison. And without another soul to turn to, no funds and nowhere to go, a way out of this fresh hell had begun to seem an impossible one.

On the Friday, he came rushing into the rest centre to announce with a whoop that he'd found them a new house no great distance away. He was to pick up the keys and rent book from the landlord at six o'clock that evening. His mother Nora was as pleased as pie. Renee was altogether too numb with disillusionment and hopelessness by now to feel much of anything.

'Well, Renee?' Roy asked, wiggling his eyebrows, chest out in pumped up pride. 'Did I do good, or did I do good?'

She forced a weak smile. 'Aye. Well done, Roy.'

'You'll like it, aye; it's a sound little place.'

Her brows drew together slowly in a frown. 'But what does it matter if I like it or not?'

'Why d'you think?' He laughed loudly like a braying donkey. 'You'll be coming to live with us, of course!'

'No, Roy, I couldn't . . . couldn't do that I—'

'Why not?'

'Well because . . .' *God above, this just gets worse and worse. Dwell beneath the same roof as this strange and conniving man-child and his mother . . .?* She couldn't – wouldn't! 'Because it wouldn't be proper,' she gabbled out.

'Don't be daft! Loads of folk take in lodgers – and that's what you'd be, our lodger. Ain't that right, Mam?' he added, turning to bestow on the older woman a sickly smile. 'Renee will move in with us, won't she?'

'If it's reet with my son then it's reet with me,' Nora affirmed. 'You're more than welcome.'

'Anyroad,' Roy continued, and his gaze took on a spiteful edge, 'it's not like you've anywhere else to go. Is it?'

Tears were threatening. She shook her head. 'You know I don't.'

'That's settled, then. Eeh, Renee, it'll be gradely. You'll see.'

Later, as the three of them passed through the streets to their new home having collected the particulars on the way, Renee asked herself for the dozenth time how things had come to this. She should have insisted to Roy that he was barking up the wrong tree when he first insinuated she'd played a hand in Ivan's death. Yet her shock at the time had left her unable to deny it with adequate conviction, and the fact that she hadn't had only strengthened his belief. Now look where this had got her. Moving in with him . . .? Just how had things escalated so quickly? What on earth was she to do?

Maybe she could give them the slip, hotfoot it away from here and him and his thinly veiled threats as fast as her legs could carry her? But to *where*? From the sound of the extent of Mrs Flynn's injuries, she would be under her cousin's care for a good while yet and so there would be no point in attempting to seek her out at Top o'th' Brow. And, as she'd already exhausted every avenue in tracking down Maureen and Linda's address, the hope of finding her friend another way was completely lost to her.

The single other option she had was to visit Gordon Wallace. Surely there was a chance he'd be willing to put up his future daughter-in-law . . .? Is that what she still was, though? Had Ivan really sent those lies to her betrothed? Did Jimmy even want her still? She couldn't be sure of anything any more.

Just what did Roy Westwood plan to gain from this

279

game of his – and to her, that's what this was beginning to feel like. He wasn't mature or intelligent enough to fully appreciate the seriousness of the situation – nor understand the true gravity of what informing on her would mean – she was sure of this. Did he really have it in him to go to the police with his suspicions, or was this merely a ploy to keep her in his favour? More importantly, could she really risk putting him to the test?

Surely if she played him on his own level then, in time, she could convince him he was wrong, that she hadn't attacked Ivan? It had to be worth trying; what other choice did she have? Moreover, right now he was her only means of dragging herself out of destitution – any roof over her head had to be better than none. And besides, as the old adage said: keep your friends close and your enemies closer. At least she'd know the next move, if any, he was planning if she was in close company with him.

'You're glad you're here, ain't you, Renee?' Roy whispered across to her that night as they lay on the hard living room floor beneath a few thin blankets he'd begged from the church, his mother snoring between them.

Grateful for the darkness, she pulled a face. Then as genuinely as she could muster: 'Aye,' she said. 'Ta for taking me in. You're a good friend, Roy.'

He settled down to sleep with a sigh of contentment, leaving Renee in peace to try to come up with a scheme to get herself out of this.

*

'But *why* won't you? Just give me one good reason, go on.'

Doing her utmost not to lose her temper, Renee met his stare head-on. 'Because, Roy, I don't want to.'

He flounced to the orange box that was acting as a chair by the fire and threw himself on to it to stare sulking into the flames. 'You're just boring, that's what.'

'Aye, mebbe I am,' she responded mildly. 'But the answer's still no.'

It was Saturday night, and for the past half an hour he'd been trying to cajole her into going to the cinema with him. It was the last thing she desired. Besides, she was still yet to visit such a place – and she certainly didn't want her first time to be with this lad. She wanted to be in Jimmy's company when that day came, was resolute on this, and Roy's childish moans and pleas wouldn't persuade her otherwise.

'It's good, you know, at the Regent. And it's only on Deane Road – we could walk it, wouldn't even need to get the tramcar.'

'Even so, we can't go frittering away money we don't have,' she pressed on, as a means of shutting him up.

'We deserve to enjoy ourselves, don't we?'

'Not when we should be saving up for this place. We don't have a single scrap of furniture, do we, and we can't live like that. Then there's your mam: we can't leave her here alone whilst we go swanning off to the pictures.'

'Oh, don't worry about me, I'll make do,' Nora butted in.

'See,' said Roy jubilantly. 'She don't mind. Go on, Renee, what d'you say?'

'I've said it already: no.' Whilst mother and son were out today – Nora at her cleaning jobs and Roy to a nearby building site where he'd secured a few hours' work – Renee had spent the morning and afternoon making the house liveable. She'd scrubbed and swept until she was exhausted and her hands were raw, and all she wanted now was to have an early night.

'I'll tell on you if you don't come.'

The whispered warning stopped her dead in her tracks. She lowered the blanket she'd been unfolding and gazed at him open-mouthed. 'What?'

'I said I'll tell on you, to the law, if you don't come to the Regent with me.'

'You don't mean that, Roy. For God's sake—!'

'Aye, I do.' He rose to stand in front of her and, lifting his chin high, stared down his nose at her. 'So, unless you want to be carted off to the cells, you'd best get your coat on, hadn't yer?'

A rumble of anger was growing in the pit of her gut and her hands had begun to shake – for two pins she'd have run at him and clawed his eyes from his head for him if she'd been able to. But she wasn't, she mustn't, and he knew it. His reckless streak was a dangerous one and could result in no end of trouble for her should he choose to act upon his threat. *Damn him!* For how long would he keep this up? Would it

282

ever know an end? Just how much more of this living nightmare would she endure?

'Well?'

Her reply came through gritted teeth. 'All right, Roy. I'll come.'

'Can we sit on the back row, Renee?' he asked when they arrived and were queuing by the booth to pay for their tickets.

'What on earth for?'

'*You* know.'

Oh, she did, all right. Well, if he thought to manipulate her into anything like *that*, he had another thing coming! 'No, we can't. We're friends, nowt more.'

He pouted for a moment, then asked, 'Well can I at least tell people that you're my girl? Please? They don't have to know the truth.'

Hell's teeth . . . 'Roy, I'd rather you didn't.'

'But can I though, eh? Oh, go on, don't be so rotten.'

'But why?'

'Because I've not had a girlfriend before, and folk round our way reckon I'll never have one neither. It'll be one in the eye to them if they see me with you on my arm; oh, it will that!'

With a mammoth sigh, she relented – anything for a bit of peace. 'All right, Roy. If you see anyone you know, and they ask, then aye: you can tell them I'm your girlfriend.' By, but he was pathetic really. However, she couldn't see the harm in letting him have his little pretence. 'But definitely no back row,' she hastened once more to make it crystal clear. 'Will that do you?'

He nodded excitedly and flashed his horrible smile. 'Ta, Renee.'

Despite herself, when they stepped inside the hall and she saw the large screen, a feeling of magic overtook her; a smile lit up her face and she turned with a look of wonder to the smartly dressed usherette standing at the ready to guide them to their seats by torchlight. So, this was what the cinema was like – by, she'd wondered on it for so long she could barely believe it was happening. Oh, but how she wished Jimmy . . . *Stop. Don't think of that*, she was forced to tell herself quickly as sudden tears stung. *Just for one single night put him from your mind.*

'Excuse me, could you shift your legs a bit so me and my girlfriend can get through?' Roy announced loudly to a young couple they were passing along the row.

The emphasis he'd put on their apparent relationship was cringingly obvious – Renee rolled her eyes. 'Roy . . .'

However, he ignored her, saying instead to the next person then the next: 'Me and the lass here – she's my girlfriend – we'd like to get past if you don't mind.'

Folk were beginning to snigger; she felt embarrassed for him. Couldn't he see how foolish he was making himself – and her – look: 'Roy, for God's sake, sit down,' she hissed. She pulled him into a seat. 'Look, the film's about to start . . .'

Afterwards, Renee felt she could have floated home – she'd enjoyed each and every second of it. Even Roy had eventually behaved himself. Next time she visited the cinema, it definitely would be with Jimmy, she determined. *Oh, please God.*

'I need to go.'

Dragged back to the present, Renee frowned at Roy in confusion. 'Sorry, what?'

'I said I need to go. *Now.*'

Noticing he was clutching his private parts and hopping from foot to foot, she clicked her tongue. Did he really have to make it so obvious? It was like being in the company of an infant: 'Well go then. You don't need my permission.'

'You'll be here when I get back?'

'Course I will.'

'You mean it? Promise me,' he whined.

For the love of . . . 'I promise. Now, will you hurry up before you have an accident?'

He did, and she was watching him go with a shake of her head when a hand tapped her on the shoulder. Renee turned in surprise – then did a double take at who was standing before her. It *was* her: 'It's Jean, ain't it? Jean Mayhew?'

'You remembered! I weren't sure you would but thought I'd come and say hello when I spotted you.'

Renee smiled at the woman she'd got talking to weeks before outside Sunnyside Mills. 'I never forget a face.'

'Only addresses, eh?' said Jean, winking.

'Aye!'

'Well, at least you found your friend in the end, eh, so no harm done. So, lass, how've you been?'

Renee blinked in confusion. 'I'm fine, ta . . .' she answered distractedly, then: 'Sorry, Jean – I found my friend? What d'you mean?'

'Linda.' Jean motioned towards a dark-haired young woman standing just feet away.

'That's Linda?' Renee's heart threatened to smash through her chest. 'Jean, you're sure?'

'Course I am. You mean the two of you ain't here together—?'

'Sorry, I have to go,' Renee told her. 'And thank you!' Seconds later she was rushing across to the elusive Linda. 'Hello.'

The young woman smiled. 'Do I know you?'

'No, you don't, but by *God* am I glad to meet you!' The tears were running freely down her face. 'I've been looking for you, you see, and, and I didn't know where, where I might—'

'Don't take on so, lass.' Cutting off Renee's garbled chatter, Linda spoke kindly, soothingly. 'Slow down and start again. Now, why have you been looking for me? Who are you?'

'Mrs Flynn. Mrs *Flynn*.'

'Our Iris? What about her?'

'I'm her friend, her very best friend from Top o'th' Brow, and—'

''Ere, hang about.' Her lips parted in pleasant surprise. 'You're not Renee, are you?'

'Yes!'

Linda laughed. 'So, you're the lass I've heard so

much about. Well, I never. Iris never stopped going on about you . . . We were expecting you, yer know. We couldn't understand it when you never showed.'

'I couldn't remember the address. Then I got talking to someone at the mill where I knew you worked, had hoped to find you there, but she said you'd left and . . . Oh, Linda; I'm so happy I could dance!'

'Steady on; you won't half get some funny looks doing that,' she responded, with a grin.

Renee matched it – her glee at the prospect of seeing her friend again was at fever pitch. 'Please,' she asked, 'if you're on your way home now, could I come with you?'

A look of mild puzzlement crossed Linda's face. Nonetheless, she nodded: 'Aye, lass, if you'd like.'

'Oh, thank you, I would. I couldn't wait another minute to set eyes on Mrs Flynn again; I've not seen her in what feels like forever . . . What?' she added when Linda's face fell. 'What is it?'

'Lass, Iris ain't at our house.'

'Eh? But—'

'She was, it's true, but she's not there now. She returned to her own home weeks ago.'

The revelation was like a blow to her stomach – she staggered. 'But her neighbour on the estate, she told me that Mrs Flynn had bashed her head bad and broke her leg. She made out that she'd need looking after for a good long while.'

'Well, she must have a fondness for exaggerating, that's all I can say. Iris suffered a sprained ankle, that's all – it soon mended. She were only with us for three days.'

Renee was light-headed with shock. All this time . . . 'All this *time*?' she rasped out loud. 'Dear God!'

These past weeks – it had been for nothing. Had she known Mrs Flynn had returned to Top o'th' Brow so swiftly, she'd have gone to her like a shot. Everything she'd suffered, everything that had happened . . . It could have all been so very easily avoided. She felt sick to her soul with grief.

'Who's this?'

It was Roy, back from answering the call of nature. Renee closed her eyes in despair.

Linda smiled. 'Hello, I'm—'

'Renee's my girlfriend,' he butted in almost defensively, as though he expected the young woman to spirit her away from him. 'Ain't that right, lass?'

Her patience snapped: 'Oh, shut up, Roy! Sorry,' she added to a bemused-looking Linda, 'we have to go. It was nice meeting you.'

'Oh. All right. Well, it was nice meeting you, too, Renee. And you, Roy!' she added with definite amusement. 'Ta-ra.'

'Come on, you,' Renee growled, practically dragging the lad outside.

'What's up?'

'You, that's what. You've done nowt but embarrass me tonight with your stupid talk and daft ways. Why do you have to be so . . . so . . .'

'Thick as a brick? Is that what you were going to say?'

Her anger only mounted at his woebegone

expression. *Yes!* she wanted to scream into his face. *Yes, it was, because it's true. You're also a spiteful, manipulative young devil and I rue the day I ever met you . . .! Calm yourself,* she warned. *God willing, all this will soon be over now. Don't ruin it for yourself.*

'Well, Renee? Was it?'

She sighed. 'No, Roy. I'm sorry, ignore me. I've just had a bit of bad news, that's all, and my mind's all of a tumble.'

'What bad news?'

'It don't matter. Come on, let's get home.'

That had to be by far the biggest lie told yet in the history of mankind, she was certain. Oh, it mattered, all right. But by Christ would she put it right.

Chapter 21

'HELLO, MRS FLYNN.'

'Renee?'

'Aye, it's me.'

'Eeh, lass. Lass!'

On a sob, she threw herself into the woman's arms. 'Oh God, how I've missed you!'

'Come on inside, come on now.'

Once in the living room, they stood staring at one another for a long moment. Then they were laughing and embracing again, their shared joy at being reconciled evident to them both.

'I've been worried out of my mind . . . where in the name of all that's holy have you been, lass?'

Renee's smile slipped slowly from her face. She inclined her head to the table. 'I think we'd better sit down.'

'I've been hoping and praying you'd turn up at my door,' said Iris when they were seated, reaching across to pat Renee's hand. 'The good Lord heard me for sure, aye.'

'I just can't believe . . . I never dreamed you'd have

been back home all this time, Mrs Flynn. I'd have returned in a heartbeat had I known; couldn't believe it when Linda told me.'

'You've seen our Linda? But when? She never said!'

'I only met her last night and that were by pure fluke. You see, I couldn't remember your Maureen's address; it had gone clear from my mind since my first visit there with you. I tried to track down her daughter at her place of work but was told she'd left. I was out of options, hadn't an idea what to do, and so—'

'You sought out Ivan's aunt,' Iris finished for her.

She gazed back in stunned stupor. 'Aye, but how did you know?'

'Eeh, lass, I've a lot to tell you . . .' Sighing, the older woman shook her head. 'I'm buggered though if I know where to start.'

'Mrs Flynn? What is it, what's going on?'

'Let me open from the beginning, lass, else I'll only get myself all muddled up.' Iris nodded, then began. 'First things first, I reckon you'll be wanting to know about young Jimmy.'

Her heart banged painfully in response to hearing his name. 'You've heard from him? If so, it's more than I have.'

'Aye, and you know why, don't you? You didn't give him the right ruddy house number – that, or he was reading it wrong from your first letter telling him of the Punch Street address. You were dwelling at number twenty-eight, am I right?' And at Renee's astonished nod: 'Well, it seems Jimmy had been sending his replies to twenty-six next door!'

'Twenty-six?' That was the Westwoods' house. 'But the neighbours never mentioned . . .'

Roy.

He had a hand in this; she just knew it. She'd been going out of her mind with whys and what-ifs, feared Jimmy had given up on her. She'd even begun to wonder whether Ivan might have actually infiltrated her post. However, clearly not. No, for all the time it had been . . . *The wicked, wicked swine!*

'Jimmy got in touch with me asking if I'd heard from you,' Iris went on. 'According to him, he'd written to you every day, but you always wrote back saying you'd had nowt from him and begging him to respond. He was at a loss what to do, was beside himself with the thought of you believing he'd abandoned you.'

Tears blinded her; she could barely speak past the huge lump of emotion clogging her throat. 'So, Jimmy . . . he ain't given up on me? He does still love me?'

'What! He's daft about you, lass – nowt's changed there, you can be certain of that.'

'Thank *God.*' The relief was insurmountable – for a full minute, she wept joyous tears. Eventually, she asked, 'How did you work out the mistake with the house numbers, though, Mrs Flynn?'

'Well, when I learned from Jimmy where you were, I'd planned to visit you to check you were well. Only before I had the chance . . .'

'The bombing,' Renee said, nodding.

'Aye. Eeh, lass, what you must have gone through . . .

I hotfooted it up to Deane the next day and learned from the residents that a lass named Renee had dwelled not at twenty-six but number twenty-eight before it was hit, but that mercifully, unlike your poor great-aunt, you'd survived. They said the homeless had been offered shelter at the nearby church. Off I went to try and find you, but it wasn't to be. A woman told me no one was stopping there with your name, and so I had no choice but to go home and pray you'd get in touch with me.'

'I must have been at the mortuary identifying . . . when you arrived. Oh, I can't believe I missed you.'

'You mean you *were* staying at that church all along?'

Nodding, Renee was nonplussed. 'But why would that woman say I weren't? Who was she, Mrs Flynn, did you catch her name?'

'I didn't, no.'

'Well, what did she look like?'

'Oh, she were a reet scruffy mare; a bit simple, I think. And the gnashers on her . . . could eat an apple through a letterbox with them things, she could!'

Someone matching the description exactly instantly sprang to mind and her fists tightened in anger: Nora Westwood. Roy's handiwork again, no doubt. He'd have been with Renee at Punch Street by that time, she realised, so didn't get the opportunity to speak to Mrs Flynn himself – had he instead briefed his mother to lie in his place should anyone call asking about her? Must have done. The slippery young . . . Of all the diabolical things to do! Just what the hell was wrong with him at all?

'The one with choppers like a racehorse . . . You know who it was, don't you?'

'Aye,' Renee admitted through clenched teeth. 'Oh, Mrs Flynn, I ain't half had a terrible time of it . . . I kept summat back from Jimmy,' she blurted, flushing crimson. 'I told him it was just Aunty Hannah I'd gone to dwell with, but it was a lie. Ivan was there, an' all.'

'Oh, dear Lord, no.' Iris was horrified.

'I know, I know . . . It was stupid of me. He tricked me, Mrs Flynn, had me believe he'd changed. Only it was one big ruse to get me to stay. He . . . He . . .'

'Tell me, lass.'

'He tried to rape me.'

'Wha—!'

'Again.'

'*Again*?' The woman's mouth was flapping in sheer disbelief. 'You, you mean to say . . .?'

'It had been going on for years,' she confirmed. 'I told no one, couldn't. Now . . . I reckon you of all people have a right to know.'

Shoulders heaving with emotion, Iris rounded the table to clasp Renee to her breast. 'A nasty sod I had him down for, aye . . . but not that. Never that! If only I'd known. If only I'd *known*. You poor lass. Eeh, you poor sweet lass!'

Renee clung to her. 'Don't ever berate yourself – you couldn't have known.' By, but it felt good to tell her at long last. Never would Renee have believed it, but it did.

'Lass. Lass, there's summat . . . summat I need to tell you, I—'

'Please, Mrs Flynn,' she insisted before her nerve went, 'I have summat I must tell you first.'

'But—'

'I must get this off my chest. It's about Ivan.'

'You mean there's more?'

Oh, there was that. 'Aye,' she whispered.

'What is it, lass?'

'I killed him.' She nodded. 'I bashed his head in on the cobblestones – the authorities suspect nowt, believe he was caught in the bomb blast.'

The ensuing silence, interrupted only by the ticking of the clock, was deafening.

'Say summat,' Renee begged when she could bear it no longer. 'Please.'

'Good.'

'Good?'

'That's right.' Iris's voice was thick with conviction. 'I'm glad. What's more, I hope that filthy evil bastard is burning in the scorching pits of hell, now and for eternity.'

'But—'

'No buts.' Feeling her way back to her seat, the woman dropped into it. Face void of colour, she ran a shaky hand across her mouth. 'The law think it an accident, you say?' she murmured.

'They do, but Mrs Flynn . . .'

'That's all right, then. Let them go on believing it, aye. The important thing is that Ivan Rushmore's gone at last – and what's more, you're in the clear. It's over, lass. No one, no one ever has to know—'

'But someone already does. That's what I've been trying to say. And let me tell you, they shan't have any qualms about informing on me should I go against them. So, you see, it's far from finished with. I'm done for.'

'Just you leave the devil to me.'

'Mrs Flynn, I don't know about this . . .'

Having filled the woman in on what had transpired regarding Roy and his dogged attempts to keep her where he wanted her, Iris was ready to wage war of her own. She'd donned her coat and was in the process of securing the flower-patterned headscarf beneath her chin, however, so up was her temper and so thin her patience that the fiddly knot was proving too much for her, and she was growing more irate by the second – Renee intervened before her friend blew her top completely.

'Here, let me.'

'Hard-faced, snidy young swine; I'll do for him, I will! Threatening you as he has been, just who does he think he is, eh? Aye well, I'll show him threatening, all right. He'll ruddy well think so when I've finished with him.'

'What will you do?'

'I don't rightly know in this moment, but I'll think of summat, you can be sure of that!'

'Please, you won't make matters worse for me, will you, Mrs Flynn?'

'And how could they be that, lass? Just look at the sorry state you're in – nowt can be worse than this. Fret not, Renee. I'll sort the bugger out, you wait and see.'

Though undeniably fearful of what the confrontation could mean, she knew a wave of unequivocal relief to know she wasn't alone in this any more. Furthermore, there was no one else she'd have chosen to have in her corner than the woman before her. But would it work? Would Iris really make a difference, help to resolve this horrible situation? With no other hope left, she had simply to trust that she could.

They arrived at the Westwoods' house shortly before mother and son were due home for the day. In silence, they made themselves comfortable on the wooden crates by the dead fire to await Roy's return.

'So, where's the odd fellow at?' Mrs Flynn asked at length. 'He work, does he?'

'He's not in a permanent position, no. Roy just seems to flit from job to job – a few days here, a week or so there, you know? He does what he can get. Mind you, he don't look to do too badly off it, always appears to have brass in his pocket.'

Iris sniffed. 'He would. His type always land on their feet somehow or other.'

The minutes ticked on. Finally, the front door opening sounded; the women braced themselves for the battle to come.

'All right, Renee?' Roy's greeting melted at the sight of the newcomer seated beside her. Eyes widening, mouth gaping, he pointed a finger. 'What in the hell . . .? What's *she* doing here?'

Surprised at the reaction, Renee turned to Mrs Flynn – and her confusion grew as she saw her friend was staring right back at Roy with equal stupefaction.

'You?' Iris managed at last. She laughed mirthlessly. 'Well, I never. You young dog, yer.'

'I don't know what's . . . I don't, don't understand . . .' Roy was gulping for air like a fish out of water. 'What's happening?' he whined.

Renee was just as desperate for answers: 'Will someone please tell me what's going on? You two know each other?'

'That we do.' Iris nodded sharply.

'But how?'

'How do *you* know Mrs Flynn?' Roy cut in to cry accusingly at Renee. 'You'd better tell me, now!'

'Oi, gobshite.' Iris was across the room and had gripped him by the front of his jacket before he had time to blink. 'If anyone's for answering some questions here, then it's you.' She pushed him unceremoniously towards the makeshift chair she'd vacated. 'Sit, you swine.'

He obeyed with all the docility of a child. 'Why, though? What have I done?'

'Me laddo here,' said the older woman, addressing Renee, 'is a spiv. Ain't that right?' she added to Roy and was obviously gratified to see him cringe. 'And to think you've been frightening the lass here with your wild claims when, all the time, the only criminal around here is you!'

'Spiv?' asked Renee, shaking her head.

'Aye – he deals in the black market. Well known for it, he is, around Deane – Daubhill, too. Scraping by on a few hours' honest work, my eye. He's nobbut a common thief.'

'Aye, and so are you!' he shot back. 'It's how we know each other. You and that cousin of yours; the pair of you are just as bad as me!'

'Oh, stop your bloviating,' Iris replied as cool as a cucumber. 'The thing is, lad, we're careful, unlike you. Nowt can come back on us. *You* on t' other hand . . .'

'What d'you mean?' He'd paled to the colour of tripe. 'The law are on to me?'

She gave a sombre nod. 'I'm afraid so. They were asking our Maureen questions about you only the other day.'

Renee was watching the scene unfolding in tense silence. Might this actually work? Would Roy really swallow her friend's lies?

For his part, he looked as though he might cry. He licked his dry lips. 'She didn't tell them owt, did she, your cousin?'

'No . . .'

'And she won't, will she?'

'Who's to say?' Iris shrugged. Then her mouth stiffened and she jutted her face into his. 'Me, though – well. I'm a different kettle of fish altogether, my lad.'

He began to whimper. 'But I don't want to go to prison—!'

'Prison?' she interjected. 'Oh no – it's the noose for you should the police get wind of your activities.'

'The noose!'

'Oh aye. They take a very grim stance on this sort of thing. It's a hangable offence is black-market dealing during a war.'

'No. No! I don't want to die, Mrs Flynn. Don't tell on me. Don't!'

She made a pretence of considering his pleas. Then slowly, concisely, she said, 'I suppose it'll depend on you.'

'How so?'

'Will you get it into your head that, whatever you reckon the lass here did, you're wrong?'

He glanced at Renee then back to Iris. 'But she ain't denied it.'

'She's not admitted it neither,' the woman pointed out. 'Anyroad, even if she had sworn she'd done nowt wrong, you'd not have took a blind bit of notice, would you? So where was the point?'

He thought for a while, then sighed. 'I wouldn't have gone to the police really, you know. I just wanted to make her stay with me. Now she'll leave, won't she, and I'll be on my own again.'

'You've got your mam,' Iris told him. Then, just to be certain she'd made him see sense: 'At least for now. One word out of turn about Renee and I'll have you locked up quicker than that.' She snapped her fingers. 'Then where will you be, eh? As for your

300

mam, well, with nobody to look after her she'll finish up in the workhouse. Is that what you want?'

Roy shook his head wildly.

'So, we'll have no more daft talk about Renee doing Ivan harm?'

'No, Mrs Flynn.'

'I'll find out, you know, if you ever say owt to anyone—'

'I'll not. Honest. You can trust me!'

'I hope so, lad. For your sake, I hope so.'

Minutes later, Renee was standing on the pavement with her saviour, facing a sorry-looking Roy at the front door. She nodded once and he returned it.

'Goodbye, Roy.'

'Bye, Renee.'

'Look after yourself,' she murmured. That they had basically been forced to scare a simpleton clear out of what few wits he possessed didn't sit lightly with her. However, what choice had they had? Despite everything, she was regretful that things had come to this.

'I swiped your post,' he said suddenly, and his bottom lip wobbled.

'I know.'

'I never read 'em, honest. I can't read.'

'It's all right, Roy.' And it was, had to be. Where would be the point in continuing with it now?

'They were lost in the bombing else I'd give them you back. I would.'

'It don't matter.'

'Ta. Ta, Renee.'

'Look after yourself, eh?'

'I will – and the same to you.'

The women were halfway down the street when suddenly Roy called out behind them tearfully: 'I just want a girlfriend, that's all! Is that too much to ask? Is it?'

'No, lad,' Renee called back. 'It's not too much to ask at all. But it can't be me. You'll find someone, one day. You will.'

'You promise?'

'I promise. There's someone for everyone, Roy.'

He wiped his nose on his jacket. Then, nodding, he smiled. 'Ta-ra,' he said, waving. 'Ta-ra, Renee.'

She waved back. Then, linking Iris's arm, she released a colossal sigh of relief and led the way to the tram stop for home.

It was late and the familiar living room was bathed in cosy gold light. Looking around through half-closed eyes, Renee experienced a rush of pure contentment. Then her gaze came to rest on the other woman sitting facing her, sewing, and a soft sob caught in her throat. Alerted by the noise, Iris glanced up.

'All right, lass?'

'I am now, Mrs Flynn. I can't tell you how happy I am to be here.'

In this moment, for the first time in a long time, all was well in her world. If she could have held on to this feeling forever and never let it go, she would have done.

'And the same goes for me, an' all,' Iris told her with a smile.

'I still can't believe it worked, you know,' Renee murmured. 'Roy, he will keep his word, won't he?'

'Huh, that one shan't say nowt, you can be sure of that. And 'ere,' she added when Renee bit her lip in remembrance of the scene earlier, 'don't you be feeling guilty for what we had to do. Needs must, lass. The swine was prepared to go on blackmailing you to keep you prisoner there – that ain't on; he had to be stopped.'

She nodded. 'I know.'

'You've suffered enough of that throughout your life, don't you think?' Iris added softly.

'Oh, you're right there.'

'Well, there you are then. Time to put it all from your mind now and look to the future—' She broke off suddenly and looked away. 'Renee . . .'

'Mrs Flynn?'

'Eeh, lass . . .'

Watching the older woman drop the material she held into her lap to cover her face with her hands, Renee was at her side in an instant. 'What's wrong?'

'I don't know how to say it, I . . .'

'Mrs Flynn.' A sense of dread was creeping over her. 'You're starting to scare me. What is it?'

'It ain't only Jimmy I've heard from just recently – I had a letter from Jack Crawley, too.'

'Oh?'

'Maisie: she died, lass. Her husband said it were quick, she didn't suffer none.'

Renee shook her head sadly. 'Was it another stroke?'

'Aye. It happened in her sleep by all accounts, and Jack found her next morning. But that's not . . . it's not the main thing I need to tell you. There's summat, summat else, and . . .' Closing her eyes, the woman let out air slowly. 'I was all for telling you earlier – do you remember? But you got in first about what you did to Ivan, and I didn't get the chance to . . . Then when I learned about that Roy, I figured it needed dealing with right away and what I had to say to you could wait. And when we got back from Deane, I figured you'd had enough drama for one day and that I'd tell you what I knew in t' morning instead. Now – well. The longer I've left it for, the harder it feels to get it off my chest . . .'

'Just say it, Mrs Flynn. Please.'

'Jack Crawley asked in his letter if I'd attend Maisie's funeral if I could – we'd grown friendly, hadn't we, whilst you were at Oak Valley. Course, I couldn't have missed saying goodbye to her, so I went. After the service, we all trooped back to his brother's farm – a smallholding, it is, just outside Preston. The Crawleys had been staying with him whilst they looked for a little cottage near by. And well, it was at this here farm that . . . that . . .'

'That what?'

'I saw her.' Iris grasped Renee's hands and squeezed. 'Sylvia.'

A whoosh of blood coursed through her ears; she shook her head slowly. 'My mam?'

Iris nodded. 'Jack's brother had three land girls working for him, and she was one of them.'

What?

'And to think it's the lie I spun to Lynn Ball all that time ago about you, upping and joining the Land Army, when all the time Sylvia had actually gone and done it for real, and we hadn't a clue. What are the chances, eh?'

'I don't . . . don't believe I'm hearing this . . .'

'Me and Sylvia were fair shocked as well, lass, and no mistake. Renee?' she added gently.

'I just, I can't . . .'

'Renee?' Iris pressed.

'What, Mrs Flynn?'

'She wants to see you, your mam.'

Renee's eyes widened. She blinked.

'Desperate to, she is.'

Mam . . .

'Well, lass? Will you do it? Will you meet her?'

Epilogue

THE DINNER WAS a triumph of ingenuity; they had all agreed. Renee was very proud of herself.

'Three cheers for the chef,' announced Iris Flynn when the last morsel had been consumed and they were sitting back with full stomachs and smiles. 'Hip, hip . . .'

'Hooray!' the Christmas guests joined in with delectation.

'Hip, hip . . .'

'Hooray!'

'Hip, hip . . .'

'*Hooray!*'

'Ta, thanks,' Renee told them with a pleased blush.

Owing to food restrictions, it hadn't been an easy task. However, she was glad she'd put her foot down and insisted they get by, as the majority of the population were forced to – and that meant no black-market goods. The notion didn't sit as easy with her any more since the confrontation with Roy West-wood regarding his nefarious dealings – a first-rate hypocrite is how she'd have felt – and though Iris had initially hummed and hawed, she'd agreed to Renee's decision.

Instead, they had used their initiative, had hoarded their rations for weeks in advance and augmented the main meal with plenty of vegetables. Even the scarcity of dried fruit for the festive pudding hadn't posed too much of a problem. Bulked out with grated carrot and breadcrumbs, it had hardly tasted any different. The sense of accomplishment was reward enough for all the hard work.

'I still say we should have had a proper bird, mind,' Gordon Wallace grumbled good-naturedly. His elder son John was abroad fighting and, to save him being alone, they had extended Jimmy's invite to spend the day at Monks Lane to include his father, which he'd been happy to accept. Shaking her head at the comment, Renee chuckled. Turkeys were difficult to come by, but, given his profession, the butcher had promised them with a wink and a tap of the side of his nose that he knew how to get his hands on one – until Renee had quietly but firmly put him in his place. If the rest of the nation must be satisfied with alternatives, then they would be, too – a plump goose had been delivered to Iris's house instead.

'Well, I liked it; never have been much fond of turkey, if I'm honest,' her beloved was quick to defend her; reaching beneath the table, Renee felt for his hand and squeezed. He returned the pressure, and they shared a soft and besotted smile.

'Pair of soppy buggers,' Iris muttered, but there

was no mistaking the joy shining in her eyes for the couple she loved as her own kin.

'Eeh, love's young dream,' Gordon agreed with a roll of his eyes before throwing back his head and filling the room with his hearty guffaws. 'By, they don't know what they're letting themselves in for!'

'Shurrup, you – don't be putting the poor devils off before they've even got going,' Iris told him with a dig to his ribs. However, there was laughter in her tone. 'Mind you, you are bloody right!'

'I think I'll make a start on the washing-up.' Renee rose and began to stack the dirty dishes. 'Don't youse be turning my man's thinking whilst I'm gone, though,' she told Iris and Gordon with a wag of her finger. 'If I get back and he tells me he's changed his mind and that marriage ain't for him no more, I'll have your guts for garters, so be warned!'

'Bossy little madam, ain't she, Gordon?' Iris cried to the butcher, yet it was clear by both their expressions that they were glad of just how much she'd come out of her shell these days and that the cripplingly awkward girl they had once known was a thing of the past.

'Don't be long,' Jimmy murmured, reaching up to caress her cheek.

'I'll not,' Renee promised. Then, turning to the fifth member of their party who, with a soft smile, had been watching the proceedings on the sidelines, she asked tentatively, 'Maybe you could dry whilst I wash, Mam?'

Sylvia's pleasure at the suggestion was plain. She was on her feet like a shot. 'I'd like nowt better, lass.'

They had been at their chore in awkward silence for a few minutes when Sylvia said with feeling, 'Ta for asking me along today. It means more to me than you could ever know.'

Feeling tears prick, Renee kept her head down. 'Ta for coming. I'm . . . I'm glad you did.'

'Lass?'

'Aye?'

Sylvia eased the plate from her daughter's hands and turned her gently by the shoulders to face her. 'Look at me,' she whispered thickly. 'Please.'

It took Renee a long moment to muster the courage to meet her eye. The love coursing back in the desperate gaze was her undoing; on a choked sob, she walked into her mother's ready embrace.

'I'm sorry, Renee. Eeh, I'm so very, very sorry.'

'I know, it's all right, you've said—'

'And now I'm saying it again. And I'll go on saying it, lass, until my dying day, for what I did to you . . . it was unthinkable. Unfor*giv*able—'

'No, Mam. I forgive you,' she insisted. And this she meant, wholeheartedly. 'It's just going to take some time, getting to know one another again, that's all. We'll get there, in time.'

'I don't deserve you, my precious girl.'

'Aye, you do. We've both earned it, this happiness.' She nodded to reaffirm the fact. 'It's only Ivan Rushmore that we didn't deserve.' Her mother had confirmed the man's statement already: he really hadn't been Renee's birth father after all. For once in his miserable life, on that at least he'd been telling the truth. 'But he's gone, now,' she went on, 'and all that's done with. All right?'

Sylvia flashed a watery smile, nodded. 'All right.'

Iris's revelation all those weeks ago had completely knocked Renee for six. The pain of her abandonment had resurfaced as strongly as if it had happened only yesterday, attacking her in wave after wave, until she worried she might not endure it. Yet with the passing of the days, her anger, pain and resentment had slowly but surely diminished, and she'd been left with but one emotion that rapidly grew to inhabit every corner of her mind: a fierce and consuming longing. At last, she'd been ready to give her answer.

With the arrival of the first frosts, in early November the funerals of Hannah and Ivan had taken place in a joint service. It had been a quiet affair with only Renee and Iris in attendance; never had the former been more grateful of anything when it was over and done with and she and her friend were on the tram heading back for Top o'th' Brow and the fresh beginning she seemed to have been craving for what felt like forever. A fortnight later, Jimmy had returned home. The following day, he'd accompanied Renee to Preston to see Sylvia.

That first meeting with her mother was something of a blur to her now. It had involved tears and laughter, questions and explanations – and, on Sylvia's part at least, plenty of self-recriminations. Renee had spent the train ride home in a fulfilled but numb kind of haze. She'd been under no illusion, knew there and then that their new-found relationship wouldn't be plain sailing. Trust would need to be rebuilt, and that couldn't happen overnight. The whole thing would take some getting used to, for the both of them, for sure. But she was willing to give it a try if her mother was. And Sylvia certainly seemed to want to, which boded only positively for their future.

'So, how's your bottom drawer coming along, Renee?' asked Iris a little later when mother and daughter joined the others in the living room, the pots having been put away and the kitchen spick and span once more. 'Is there much more you need, now, lass?'

Sitting beside Jimmy, she cast him a pink-cheeked smile. 'Not too badly, Mrs Flynn; and no, just towels and a couple of tablecloths I think, and then I'm done.'

'Well, that's good. Eeh, the wedding will be upon us before we know it, eh!'

It can't come soon enough for me, the couple told each other with their eyes.

Sylvia had of course agreed to give her consent to the union, and Renee and Jimmy had decided to set the wheels in motion; why wait? If this war had taught them and plenty of others anything it was to grab with both hands every ounce of happiness that came your way. God alone knew what tomorrow might bring, after all.

'When is it you go back, then, lad?' Iris was asking

311

Jimmy now, and Renee's gaiety slowly diminished. His unit had recently been stationed on the Isle of Wight to undergo extensive training in mine laying and bomb disposal and the like, which Renee knew she must be grateful for – it had enabled him leave home for Christmas, which for men engaged in operations further afield had been an impossibility. However, she didn't want to talk about this, to think about it, not now. Not yet. She tried to close her ears to it, but of course, there could be no escaping the answer. It was inevitable:

'The day after tomorrow.' He sighed. Then, evidently sensing Renee's disconcertion, he added with forced brightness, 'But fingers crossed, the time will pass quick enough, and I'll be back to wed the girl of my dreams. Eh, lass?' he finished to Renee with a soft wink.

Though she nodded, her bottom lip had begun to tremble, and she was thankful when Jimmy stood and held out his hand.

'Come on, love. Let's get a bit of fresh air.'

Understanding, the trio watched them go with nods and gentle smiles. In the garden, Renee breathed in the cold breeze gratefully.

'Better?' he asked her after a while.

'Aye. I'm sorry, Jimmy. It's just . . .'

'I know, lass.' His arms tightened around her. 'I feel it, an' all. But I meant it, what I said in there: we'll be together again before we know it, you'll see.'

'And I'll be Mrs Wallace.' She giggled. 'Sounds funny, that does.'

'A nice funny, I hope,' he teased, tickling her and making her laugh again.

'Oh aye.' Shedding Ivan's surname could never be anything other than a heavenly blessing. 'A lovely funny, in fact.'

'Don't let him in, Renee,' Jimmy said quietly as though following her train of thought, and she held on to him tighter still. 'There's no place for him in your mind no more. We promised, remember?'

'I remember.' He knew all about the circumstances of Ivan's death and he'd reacted when she'd told him in much the same way as Iris had. A monster had been removed from the world and that could never be a bad thing.

'We've a lot to look forward to,' Jimmy went on. 'Mebbe our own little farm one day; just think on that.'

She nodded against his chest. Jack Crawley and his brother had discussed the idea with him enthusiastically and at great length in Preston, had vowed to help him all they could once he was back in civvy street for good. 'You deserve it. I know it's always been your dream.'

'*Our* dream, now, lass. It wouldn't mean owt without you.'

'I love you, lad.'

'I love you, too, with all that I am.'

'The war will be over soon, won't it, Jimmy?'

'I don't know,' he answered truthfully. 'There is one thing I'm sure of, mind.'

'What's that?'

'Whatever happens, however long it takes, I'll come home to you, Renee, I swear it.'

She didn't doubt him for a second.

All of the badness was behind her. Only the good remained now.

If only . . .

'Ruby.'

The whispered name rose above the rooftops. And Renee was certain she heard the call – *doo, doo, doo* – in response.

ABOUT THE AUTHOR

Emma Hornby lives on a tight-knit working-class estate in Bolton and has read sagas all her life. Before pursuing her career as a novelist, she had a variety of jobs, from care assistant for the elderly, to working in a Blackpool rock factory. She was inspired to write after researching her family history; like the characters in her books, many generations of her family eked out life amidst the squalor and poverty of Lancashire's slums.

Turn the page to discover more gritty and gripping sagas from Emma Hornby . . .

**Will Mara find the courage to make
an impossible choice . . .?**

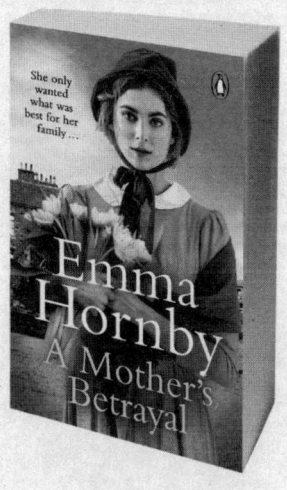

Manchester, 1867

Mara longs for a peaceful life free of violence
and poverty. But she has married into the O'Hara
family, who have a reputation for drunkenness and
quick tempers. Her eldest stepson Conrad is the
worst of them all – a brute and a criminal who
makes Mara's life a misery.

But when Conrad is accused of a crime he didn't
commit, Mara is the only one who can prove his
innocence. Perhaps this is her chance to finally
free her family from his toxic influence . . .

**Will Mara clear Conrad's name, or will she have the
courage to break away from her stepson's villainy?**

With all the odds stacked against her, can Phoebe find the strength to overcome her past . . .?

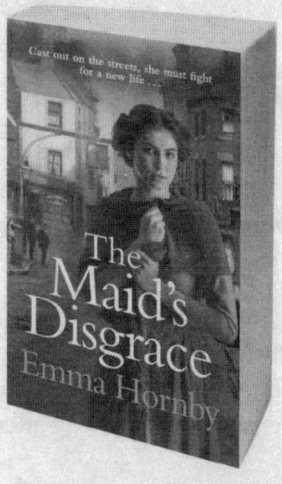

Phoebe Parsons is a liar . . . a shameless harlot with unscrupulous morals . . .

Phoebe Parsons is destitute, disgraced, and alone. After her mistress tragically dies, Phoebe is forced back on to the poverty-ridden streets of Manchester by her unforgiving new master. Desperately searching for work as a domestic maid, Phoebe soon discovers her reputation is in ruins.

Fearing for her future and haunted by the harshness of her abandonment, Phoebe finds herself living with thieves and drunks in the smog and squalor – until she meets Victor Hayes. An officer removed from his duty and shamed by a cruel lie, Mr Hayes is a kind face among the uncertain threats of living in the alleyways. But Phoebe soon realises the sacrifices she must make to rebuild from the ground up . . .

As their two worlds collide, can they make a new life from the wreckage? Or will the judgement of their peers make a pauper of Phoebe?

AVAILABLE NOW